MYSTERY
CON
R92

GONE
TO THE
DOGS

GONE TO THE DOGS

Susan Conant

A Perfect Crime Book
DOUBLEDAY
NEW YORK   LONDON   TORONTO   SYDNEY   AUCKLAND

A PERFECT CRIME BOOK
PUBLISHED BY DOUBLEDAY
a division of Bantam Doubleday Dell Publishing Group, Inc.
666 Fifth Avenue, New York, New York 10103

Doubleday is a trademark of Doubleday, a division of
Bantam Doubleday Dell Publishing Group, Inc.

All of the characters in this book are fictitious,
and any resemblance to actual persons, living or dead,
is purely coincidental.

Book design by Tasha Hall

Library of Congress Cataloging-in-Publication Data
Conant, Susan, 1946–
Gone to the dogs / by Susan Conant.
p.   cm.
"A Perfect Crime book."
I. Title.
PS3553.O4857G6   1992
813'.54—dc20   91-41171
                                        CIP

RCN 0-385-42378-0
ISBN 0-385-42378-0

FIRST EDITION
1   3   5   7   9   10   8   6   4   2

July 1992

Dedication

In August of 1990, Janelle Fowlds and her associates at the all-volunteer Becker County Humane Society participated in a raid on a puppy mill near Detroit Lakes, Minnesota. Their efforts brought an end to the neglect, abuse, and suffering of more than a hundred Alaskan malamutes, golden retrievers, Norwegian elkhounds, Samoyeds, Siberian huskies, and dogs of numerous other breeds. For many months after the raid, Janelle Fowlds continued to work for the well-being of the rescued dogs and puppies. With thanks from the Alaskan Malamute Protection League as well as from the author, this book is dedicated to Janelle.

Acknowledgments

For help with this book, I want to thank Barbara Beckedorff, Laurel Morrissette, Gail and Rick Skoglund, Joel Woolfson, D.V.M., and my beloved companions, Frostfield Arctic Natasha, C.D., T.T. and Frostfield Firestar's Kobuk.

GONE
TO THE
DOGS

1

IF YOUR NAME IS HOLLY WINTER, Yuletide can be a real bitch. When I say *bitch,* I know what I'm talking about. I earn my living in the world of dogs. In the pages of *Dog's Life* magazine, including the pages occupied by my column, *bitch* is a neutral word for "female dog," and when I tell you that I have two Alaskan malamutes, Rowdy and Kimi, a dog and bitch, I'm not swearing. But Holly Winter? In December?

I make the best of it. Take Christmas cards. If your name sounds like an ecumenical version of Merry Christmas, you don't have to wish anyone Season's Greetings, Happy Holidays, or Health and Happiness Now and in the Coming Year. You just sign in the white space below the picture of your spectacular dogs. In this year's picture, the best ever, Rowdy and Kimi are wearing snazzy red harnesses, and they're pulling their sled across a field of snow. The sled is piled with red-blanket stand-ins for bags of toys. The dogs' plumy white tails are waving over their backs, and their big red tongues are hanging out of their eager, grinning faces. Festive and woofy.

In case you wondered, I would like to add that Rowdy and Kimi are certainly not wearing those humiliatingly stupid reindeer-antler headbands you can order from R.C. Steele, New England Serum, J-B, and the other discount pet-supply houses. My picture doesn't reveal the detail, but the dogs have on Velcro-fastened red velvet bow-tie collars that I copied from the ones in the R.C. Steele catalog. The originals cost about twelve dollars apiece, and I whipped up Rowdy and Kimi's for practically nothing. The R.C. Steele version, though, is presumably durable. My homemade collars were starting to fray by mid-December, when the dogs had worn their finery only twice, once for the Christmas card photo and once for pictures with Santa. And, no, I did not drag my dogs to some shopping mall to wait in line with the kiddies. The occasion, it so happens, was a benefit for the Animal Rescue League.

As I was saying, to preserve the velvet collars for Christmas, I was saving them for special occasions, one of which was Rowdy and Kimi's visit to the vet for rabies boosters. The fancy dress wasn't mandatory—you don't really have to get spiffed up for church or temple, either—but I warn you: Ministers, priests, and rabbis may overlook dirty, ragged coats, tartar-encrusted teeth, untrimmed nails, and unswabbed ears, but veterinarians do not. All creatures bright and beautiful?

The late afternoon Boston commuter traffic zooming along in both directions in front of the clinic was so ferocious that I stopped wondering whether my Bronco would get hit before I could make the turn and instead tried to decide whether we'd get front-ended, rear-ended, or side-swiped. I suddenly wished I'd crated the dogs instead of leaving them loose behind the wagon barrier. When a break came, I slammed my foot on the accelerator and roared into the parking lot. Ms. Evel Knievel.

I'd just killed the engine, scooped up the ribbon collars, and opened my door when a bright, educated voice rang out my name. A lot of Cambridge women have those classical-music-station voices. Maybe they're what you get for a big donation to National Public Radio. For a pledge of a hundred dollars or more, you get an NPR voice or a radiotelegraphically correct sweatshirt. My friend and tenant Rita's friend Deborah must've forked up twice: She never left home without the voice, but on that unseasonably warm December day, she also wore one of the sweatshirts. Deborah's skin is either naturally oily or heavily moisturized. Some stylist must've promised her that with a body perm, she could just wash her brown hair and then forget it. Forget it? Whenever Deborah looked in the mirror, she must have noticed that sprouting from her scalp were the crisp liver-colored ringlets of an Irish water spaniel. I mean, how could she *forget* a thing like that? The woman with Deborah had very short, dark, distinctly human hair and wore a red jersey outfit I'd admired when I'd seen it in the window of Pirjo, a tiny place on Huron Avenue where I can't afford to shop. Envy? Of course.

If you live somewhere normal, you probably think that after hailing me, Deborah introduced me to her friend, and you're right, except that in Cambridge, names are incidental. An introduction here consists of telling each person what the other one does for a living. Psychotherapists, though, usually don't even do that; unless stated otherwise, it goes without saying that everyone else is a therapist, too.

"Karla's at the Mount Auburn," Deborah said. I understood what she meant because Rita, who's a psychologist, speaks the same *patois:* Karla, Deborah was informing me, worked as a psychotherapist at the Mount Auburn Hospital. Then Deborah explained me to Karla. "Holly is Rita's landlady," she began, then added, "Holly's a, uh, dog writer." She sneezed, pulled a tissue from her pocket, and wiped her nose. "Is that what you say?"

"Dog writer," I said. Self-explanatory, isn't it? Still, I felt compelled to expand. "I write about dogs."

People usually say, "Oh, isn't that interesting," as if it weren't—it is—or they ask me whether there's some quick,

easy way to get their dogs to come when they're called—
there isn't.

"Really?" Karla said. She paused. An unspoken word
formed on her lips. *Outré?* or maybe *quaint*. "Rita talks about
you," she added ominously, extending a tentative hand for
me to shake.

If she expected me to give my paw, the mistake was
natural. Brush two malamutes, and you end up disguised as
a third. Except for the knees, my jeans were okay, but bits
of pale, fluffy malamute undercoat clung to my old black
lightweight hooded sweatshirt, the one with the kangaroo
pocket. Worse, my hairy, oversize, once-black socks were the
pair my teenage cousin Leah had made me buy. Slouch
socks? Is that what they're called? Out of some misguided
sense of family loyalty, I'd smooshed them around my ankles the way Leah always did. She'd persuaded me that the
socks were definitely not too young for someone just over
thirty. They were.

Anyway, the embarrassing thing wasn't the shirt or the
socks or even the fur. When I pulled my right hand out of
the pocket of the sweatshirt, out tumbled a mess of semi-
powdered freeze-dried liver and some desiccated, long-for-
gotten bits of cheese. I train with food.

"Dog treats," I said feebly, wiping my palm on my
jeans. I nodded toward the Bronco.

Karla withdrew her hand and said, "Huskies." Malamutes aren't, of course.

"Beautiful," Deborah said.

Like most other malamute people, I have a spiel that I
usually deliver when someone mistakes the dogs for Siberi-
ans—malamutes are bigger than Siberian huskies, never
have blue eyes, and all the rest—but today I just said
thanks. Deborah and Karla took off on long, confident
strides. They probably discussed some fashionable topic in
female psychology. Bonding rituals. Women and self-es-
teem.

I inched open the tailgate of the Bronco. I had the

collars looped around my left wrist, and I groped with my right hand until I had a solid grip on the dogs' leashes. Rowdy and Kimi wagged their tails, licked my face, and squirmed to get out of the car. Because Rowdy was a little closer to me than Kimi was, I grabbed his regular rolled-leather collar first and held it tightly while I wrapped the velvet ribbon around his neck and tried to line up the Velcro strips to fasten it neatly. The first time, I got it on too loose, and just as I was ripping the little plastic teeth apart, Kimi spotted something compelling across the street, a dog running loose, a child eating an ice cream cone, or maybe nothing more than freedom itself. I should, of course, have fastened her leash to some solid object in the car or, failing that, locked it in my fist, but as it was, the loop at my end of the leash hung around my wrist. When Kimi barged past Rowdy and shot out of the car, she and her leash flew beyond my reach.

I shoved Rowdy backward into the Bronco, slammed the tailgate, then stepped toward the traffic, as camouflaged in my black jersey and navy jeans as Kimi was in her dark wolf gray. Both of us blended invisibly into the twilight. Some of the cars speeding by had their headlights on. Kimi's full mask—her black cap and goggles and the black bar down her muzzle—absorbed the light and left her nearly invisible as she pranced back and forth along the white line separating the two lanes of dog-crushing metal speeding southward from the two lanes heading north. The cars and vans shot by her like a barrage of bullets from a pair of double barrels aimed at each other. My beautiful dog capered in the cross fire.

Seconds later, no longer playful, she began to watch for a break. Taller and wiser, I saw none, but stood helpless, almost in the street, my heart thudding painfully, the whoosh and roar of the traffic sucking at my clothes. I desperately needed to guide Kimi, but what could I shout to her? *Stay!* And wait to be hit? *Kimi, come!* And be killed instantly? Waving my arms, I screamed to the passing drivers:

7

"Stop!" Then desperately, over and over, "Help me! Stop! Please stop!" A dark van veered toward me. The driver leaned on his horn.

In the two lanes close to me, the traffic was even heavier than on the far side, but slower. A Mercedes doing a good forty or fifty in this thirty-mile zone missed Kimi by inches, and in the lights of a demon-driven Saab, I saw on her pretty, gutsy face an expression I'd almost never seen there before: the flash of raw fear. No longer prancing, she paced slowly, ready to bolt. I knew what would follow: panic, a dash, the squeal of brakes, and the horror of metal on flesh, Kimi in agony, maimed, dead, and all of it my fault, the inevitable result of my vain need to doll up creatures born perfect.

Then a black pickup with a cheery, red-ribboned wreath on the front grille headed straight for Kimi, and I really lost it, shrieking and bellowing. As I was about to hurl myself through the traffic, a stranger appeared on the oppo-site side of the street, dodged between a Volvo wagon and a battered Chevy sedan, raised a fist toward a delivery truck, dashed, leapt, and miraculously ended up in the center of those death rows of traffic with Kimi's leash in one hand and the other wrapped protectively around her hindquar-ters. Light-clothed, towering over the cars, he succeeded where I'd failed, commanding the traffic to a brief halt, leading her safely to me. I grabbed the dense, soft fur around Kimi's neck, rubbed gently, and felt beneath her coat for the unbroken bone of her skull.

Her tail wagged, and her eyes smiled.

I'm no good at sappy speeches. "Jesus," I said to the man. "Who are you?"

Remember how *The Lone Ranger* always ended? That's how I felt, except that Kimi was the one with the black mask, unless a beard counts. This guy's was dark, like his hair, and scissored short, mustache and all, not the usual Cambridge professorial Vincent Price pointed-chin type or a thick, full mass of Santa curls. Also, the Lone Ranger always wore white, and this tall stranger was dressed in light tan pants and a faded beige jacket, but I don't think Clayton Moore ever had the kind with a rib-knit waist and cuffs. To anyone other than me, my lone ranger probably looked like a forty-odd-year-old off-duty photocopier repairman on his way to play candlepins at the local bowling alley. I wanted to kneel and kiss his feet.

"Jesus," I repeated, without waiting for the guy to answer. " 'Thank you' doesn't even say it."

"Forget it," he said, stroking Kimi, then thumping her on the shoulder in the manner of someone who likes big dogs with deep, wide chests that resonate with comforting booms. "The traffic isn't so bad on that side, and, hey, I've got dogs myself."

"Oh," I said brightly. "What kind?"

Suppose that instead of saving Kimi's life, he'd just punched me in the stomach, converted me to Rosicrucianism, or failed to sell me tax-free municipal bonds. Anything. It's a reflex. Tickle me, I giggle. Stick a finger down my throat, I gag. Tell me you have a dog, I ask what kind.

"Mutt, I guess you'd say." He shrugged his shoulders. "Not like this." He jerked a thumb toward Kimi.

"Oh, what kind?" I asked again. *Mutt,* by the way, is not what I'd usually say and not what I'd ever write. The word is banned from the pages of *Dog's Life,* as is *mongrel.* A dog that's half one breed and half another is a cross, like a Lab-golden cross. A something mix means that the dog's part something, like a Dobie mix or a shepherd mix, unless his ancestry is anybody's guess, in which case he's simply a mix or, better yet, an all-American.

"Uh, kind of like a shepherd. I only got one now." Despite the weird sixty-degree weather that had tricked lots of forsythia into mad bloom, the sun was setting promptly on its December schedule. By now, it was so dark out that I couldn't see his face clearly, but he sounded so sad that I didn't ask about the other dog or dogs. I wondered whether he'd had one killed by a car and whether that was why he'd taken the risk of saving Kimi. "Bear, his name is," he added, his voice suddenly unapologetic, his face breaking into a smile.

"I'd like to see him," I said. True. Mention a dog, and I'd practically always like to see him. "Um, my name is Holly Winter. This is Kimi. The one in the car is Rowdy."

Rowdy's nose was plastered to the window, and his eyes were fixed on the dried liver and cheese I'd spilled on the asphalt several mental eons ago. If he'd watched it being deposited there during the early Pleistocene, his gaze wouldn't have wandered since.

"John. John Buckley." Our savior nodded and held out his hand. I shook it. For what it's worth, his clasp was muscular.

"You live around here?" I asked.

"Just, uh, moved here," he said, stepping away. "Hey, I gotta—"

"Well, if you need a good vet for Bear, this one's terrific." I gestured toward the clinic. "He's a friend of mine, so I'm sort of biased, but he really is good. Hey, come in with me. Come and meet him."

"Uh, thanks, but I gotta go."

"And," I added enthusiastically, "if you want to do any dog training, there's a really good club here, Cambridge Dog Training. Every Thursday night, at the armory. On Concord Avenue, right near the Fresh Pond traffic circle. It's not far from here. Beginners' starts at seven."

"Uh, thanks, but like I said, he's—"

"That doesn't matter," I interrupted, eager to give him something. "There are lots of mixed breeds there, and you can show at fun matches. You can get all-American obedience titles, the whole thing." Having already held him up when he wanted to leave, I pressed on. "Or you can just fool around and have fun. And you're new here. You can meet people. We'll see you there, huh?"

He stopped inching away. "You can show a dog that's not, uh, AKC? You sure about that?"

Need a translation? The AKC is the American Kennel Club, the largest dog registry in the United States.

"Yeah, positive," I said. "I'll tell you about it at dog training. I've got friends who do it. I'll introduce you."

As he moved away, I repeated the information about the Cambridge Dog Training Club, thanked him again, and impulsively reached for his hand. He extended it. I took it and squeezed hard, wanting somehow to maintain contact with him. I must have leaned toward him, too. His breath smelled faintly of whiskey. Well, if he drank in the afternoon, so what? Jesus turned water into wine. Rescue my dog, you resurrect me.

2

ONE OF THESE DAYS, Steve Delaney, D.V.M., is going to lift a dog that's an ounce too heavy for him, wreck his back, and have to quit hefting dogs the size of mine onto the metal exam table. It hasn't happened yet.

After he'd run his hands over Kimi's haunches, then mine—*your* vet isn't quite this thorough?—he hoisted her onto the table, where she crouched rather uneasily, but ran her wet red tongue over his smooth forehead and whiskery cheeks. Steve doesn't intend to grow a beard, but he's always getting up in the middle of the night for emergencies, then sleeping too late to have time to shave, or else plain forgetting, so his face usually looks as if it's entering what I'm told is the itchy phase and is definitely the scratchy one.

"So it was my own damn fault," I said, concluding my recitation of Kimi's near miss.

He nodded absently, gently raising Kimi's upper lip and peering at her molars. "You've been brushing?"

"Yes. You aren't listening."

"I'm examining your dog," he said. I was examining him. Steve is tall and lean, with greenish-blue eyes and wavy brown hair, but what do details matter? He has a rumpled look that makes you vow that he won't get enough sleep tonight, either. "She wouldn't have stood a chance, you know," he said, without, I might add, putting all the blame on me. "And you didn't get the guy's address?"

"Yes, I did."

"Cambridge?"

"Cambridge is a place. What was I supposed to do? Ask for complete ID? Maybe he'll show up at dog training."

"How drunk was he?"

"He wasn't drunk; he'd been drinking. All I did was smell whiskey on his breath, and I didn't even notice it until he was leaving. But I probably wasn't paying a lot of attention. Here I am ready to throw myself under a car trying to get to her, and all of a sudden, out of nowhere, he jumps through the traffic and grabs her? If he'd been drunk, he'd be dead now. And he wasn't staggering, and his speech wasn't thick or anything. Anyhow, what do I care? If he wants to freebase cocaine and rescue my dog, I'll hold the spoon."

"I'm seeing some tartar," Steve said.

"She eats the toothpaste, and then when I try to brush, she chomps on my hand," I said. "And if I wrap my finger with gauze, it's worse because her teeth go right through it. Maybe he just started drinking when his dog died. The dog got killed by a car," I added, "and he took to the bottle and started rescuing other dogs from the same fate."

Steve opened the demirefrigerator where he stores perishable medications, vaccines, and milk, which isn't medicinal, but he hates those nondairy powders. The combination is perfectly safe. Steve is a really good veterinarian, and even an incompetent one wouldn't mistake a vial of rabies vaccine for a carton of milk and end up immunizing his coffee.

"Would you hold her?" he said.

I wrapped my arms around Kimi's shoulders and hugged her hard against me, partly to comfort her in case the shots hurt, but mostly to prevent her from suddenly twisting, lunging, and sinking her lupine canines into Steve's arm. Some vets routinely muzzle all big dogs—a few cowards muzzle all dogs—but Steve hardly ever uses a muzzle. Also, he knows how brave Kimi is. In fact, she hardly flinched.

Then I returned Kimi to the waiting room, handed her over to Rhonda, one of Steve's technicians, and returned with Rowdy, who is, if anything, an even more cooperative patient than Kimi. He always yelps and howls when I inflict what he defines as real abuse, namely, a bath, but I'd held him dozens of times while Steve was giving him shots, sticking an otoscope in his ears, or squirting kennel cough vaccine up his nostrils, and I'd never felt him so much as momentarily tighten his muscles.

"So is Miner here yet?" I asked as Steve jabbed a hypodermic into Rowdy's rear. Since Steve had taken over from old Dr. Draper a few years earlier, he'd been running what should have been a two-person practice all by himself. Lee Miner had been hired—on probation—as the second D.V.M. Steve needed.

"Yeah." He parted the fur on Rowdy's underbelly and checked for fleas.

"Don't tell me," I said. "Let me guess. You're thrilled with him. I can hear it in your voice."

"Holly, he's been here all of one day, all right?"

"How bad is he?"

"Lee's got good training, he worked with Patterson, he comes highly recommended, and we've been over it all, okay?" The only veterinarian Steve entirely trusts is himself. I'd been pushing him to get help, but when Lee Miner had called to ask whether Steve was hiring, Lorraine, who really runs things for Steve, had said yes and had told Miner to send his resume. According to Steve, Lorraine was the one who'd hired Miner. "What he is," Steve continued, "is meticulous."

"Really? That's good, isn't it?"

"Yeah, and he's real good with cats, real good. And Patterson said he has good hands." Oscar Patterson, D.V.M., hadn't meant what I mean if I tell you that Steve has good hands. Patterson probably hadn't used the phrase at all. In fact, it seemed to me that in his letter of recommendation, Oscar Patterson had compared Miner to some obscure Greek god who was presumably the patron of fine motor skills. Patterson not only wrote poetry, but got it published. "And," Steve added, "Jackie, Lee's wife, is real, uh, lively."

"What's that supposed to mean?"

"Like I said, lively. Vivacious."

"I know what *lively* means. Anyway, is it going to work out? They're happy with the apartment? They're getting settled in?"

According to Steve, Lorraine had evicted him when she'd hired Miner. The apartment came with the job. It's spacious, light, airy, pet-welcoming, soundproof, and rent-free. The average affordable apartment in Cambridge is a basement room in a no-living-things slum. Furthermore, in a city in which every unoccupied parking space turns out to be located in a tow zone, it offers ample off-street parking. Oh, and it's directly above Steve's clinic. Any normal Cambridge veterinarian would've rented the place to five or six desperately broke graduate students, but Steve had always liked it, and the Miners had evidently been glad to get it. They were young, and I assumed that Lee Miner was still paying off big loans from veterinary school. His wife was starting a master's program at Lesley College in January. His loans and her tuition? Of course they liked the apartment.

"They haven't complained yet," Steve said as he

rubbed the soft fur between Rowdy's ears. At the risk of bragging about my own dog, let me mention that Rowdy has what's considered the ideal malamute head, namely, broad and moderately rounded across the skull. His ears are medium-size triangular wedges set wide apart, and he has a good blocky muzzle, too. Gorgeous dog.

"And," Steve continued, "the house is okay." He'd rented a little white cape on Little Spy Pond in Belmont, just over the line from Cambridge, about ten minutes from my place, where I reserve my first floor exclusively for myself and my dogs, and rent the other two apartments. I like it that way.

"So did you ask him about Patterson?"

"Jesus, Holly. He's probably sick of it."

"Well, Bonnie isn't sick of it," I said. Bonnie's my editor at *Dog's Life*. Oscar Patterson, D.V.M. had vanished from his New Hampshire clinic about ten days ago. The news had taken three days to reach Bonnie, and, since then, she'd been pestering me to do a story about Oscar Patterson and his disappearance, but what can you write about a total mystery? The lack of facts had ignited a firestorm of speculation in both the dog and literary worlds. "She wants anything," I said. "He breeds foxhounds. He believes in pyramids."

"Does he?"

"How would I know? I only saw him once. I got dragged to a reading he did, maybe four years ago. It was incredibly boring." Ever been to a poetry reading? In Cambridge, they're hard to avoid. If you're lucky, they're held at cafés, where you can order coffee. Then you can drink it and fiddle with the silverware instead of having to sit still with nothing to do. "He did have a sort of dramatic manner," I said. "His voice went up and down. Maybe he was too abstract for me."

I didn't say it to Steve, but the idea of a veterinarian-poet or vice versa had originally hit me as ludicrous. Ascariasis? Sarcoptic mange? Is this the stuff of sonnets? But romance isn't fashionable now, anyway. Even so, Oscar Patterson's poems weren't about pets and diseases, and probably I set myself up for disappointment by looking forward to something like a free-verse update of the epitaph Lord Byron wrote for the monument to Boatswain, his Newfoundland, but with a medical explanation of why the dog died, of course. Everything Patterson read when I heard him was pastoral: How I moved to the country and found depth in a shallow pond. . . . Look, I grew up in Owls Head, Maine. Show me a shallow pond, and I see a few bony pickerel, a lot of weeds, and a muddy bottom.

But could I tell you something about Oscar Patterson? His poetry didn't move me, and neither did his dramatic style of reading it, but one detail about Patterson's life really got to me and left me with the sense that I knew the child he'd been. I didn't learn this crucial fact from Oscar Patterson himself but from a thumbnail sketch of his life that appeared on the flyleaf of one his books. The guy who took me to Patterson's reading—this was before Steve—had brought the book along for Patterson to sign. I remember feeling embarrassed about that. To ask Patterson for his autograph hit me as gauche, very un-Cambridge. As I understood it, in Cambridge the point wasn't to fawn over celebrities but to become one yourself or, failing that, to act as if you could be instantly famous if you so desired. In the paraphrased words of a great American poet—not Oscar Patterson—I was a veteran sophisticate in those days; I'm a no-finesse novice now.

Anyway, as I'd sat drinking bitter espresso in the café while waiting for Patterson to appear, I'd glanced at the flyleaf and read about Patterson's life. What got to me was this: Patterson grew up in the Bronx, where he lived just down the street from a veterinarian. From the time Patterson was just a little kid, he worked for the vet as a kind of living incubator. When the vet had to perform a Caesarean on a bitch, he'd call Patterson, who'd stand by to assist. As the vet removed each tiny puppy from the mother's womb, he'd place the newborn in Oscar Patterson's outstretched hands, and Patterson would clean the puppy, warm it, cradle it, and feel it take its first breath right there in the palms of his hands. Although the bio didn't say so, the little boy must have felt as if he'd given life to those puppies, as if he'd whelped them himself.

I could have written my editor an article about the young Patterson and puppies, of course. The episode was nothing he'd confided to me. Even so, my knowledge created what felt like a weirdly personal bond between Patterson and me. Have you ever seen color photographs or, yet worse, a video of the birth of a human baby? Well, if I ever have a baby, there'll be no cameras. That's how I felt about Patterson, too: I didn't want to see his surrogate canine motherhood spread out on the pages of *Dog's Life*.

"Anyway, Steve," I went on, "what Bonnie really wants is something about how Patterson's dog is so heartbroken that he hasn't moved from the door since his master disappeared. Or how the dog's suddenly started baying weirdly, and you can tell that he's hearing his master's voice."

"Does Patterson have a dog?" Steve asked.

"Don't ask me," I said.

"He has Burmese cats," Steve said. "And an iguana."

"Damn. Maybe he has a dog, too."

"You know," Steve said, "considering the circumstances, you sound kind of flip about all this."

He was right, of course. "Do I?" I said. "Yeah, I guess I do." Rita . . . Remember Rita? Let me make a Cambridge introduction. She's a psychologist in private practice. Rita, my friend and tenant, claims that when I sound heartless, I'm actually defending against the "potentially ego-disintegrative affect that is the legacy of your childhood history of repeated unresolved loss." As may or may not be obvious, she means that my parents raised golden retrievers. Loss? One day the pups were there, the next day they'd been sold to strangers. What's more, the one flashy trick that the remaining goldens never mastered was the ultimate show-off stunt of living forever. So I don't like to have anyone just disappear. But who does?

"What circumstances?" I asked Steve.

"For one thing, Geri's pregnant," Steve said.

"I don't even know who she is," I said.

"The woman Patterson lives with. Geri Driscoll. She's pregnant. Lee's wife, Jackie, told me. But don't pass it along, huh?"

"Of course not," I said. "But isn't Patterson a little old to, uh, have to get married? I mean, at his age? He must feel sort of ridiculous."

Steve smiled. "He's all of forty. But it's not like that. I gather he seemed real happy about it."

As Rita would say, may I share a fantasy with you? I imagined that Geri would need a Caesarean and that Oscar Patterson, scrubbed and gowned for surgery, would reach his latex-gloved hands into her uterus to deliver the infant himself.

"So why did he take off?" I asked.

"Don't ask me. I don't know that it was voluntary."

"You probably didn't ask," I said. "You should've asked Lee Miner. Speaking of him, when do I get to meet him?"

Steve lifted Rowdy's eighty-five pounds of what you'd swear is steel-laced concrete off the table and onto the floor. "Would you not do that?" I said.

All he did was laugh. Sometimes I think that Steve sees all dogs as wet and bloody all-but-unborn puppies he's just delivered.

Anyway, when we got to the waiting room, Kimi and Rhonda weren't there, but on one of the plastic-covered benches sat a young woman with short, wiry black hair exactly like the coat of a Scottish terrier. What's more, and I am not making this up, her face was long, her head was large for her body, her legs were really quite short, she wore black tights, and—I swear it's true—her dress was Royal Stewart tartan. Her terrier—you guessed?—promptly flashed a good scissors bite, then let out a prolonged menacing growl, and, head and tail up, black eyes snapping, staunchly hurled himself, all twenty pounds, to the end of his red leash. Yes, this little dog, no more than ten inches at the withers, was joyfully picking a fight with an Alaskan malamute. Totally crazy, right? The little guy was waiting there for a dose of veterinary psychiatry. Wrong. This animal madness is known to Scottie fanciers as "real terrier character."

Rowdy's ears perked up, his hackles rose, and a gleam of delight sparkled in his eyes, but I could tell that he was more interested in enjoying the show than intent on getting into a real scrap. Even so, he jerked forward, but I spoiled the fun by calling him to heel. Probably because we weren't in the obedience ring, he obeyed.

Meanwhile, the woman was hauling in her dog and scolding him in the elated tones that terrier owners use when they chastise displays of what they privately consider the ideal temperament. Her voice was low and throaty: "Willie, that will do! Quiet! *Hush!*" She eventually succeeded in silencing Willie by dragging and shoving him around the corner of the reception desk and thus blocking his view of Rowdy. To Steve and me, she said brightly: "He really means it! He's not kidding!"

"Yes," I said. "I believe you!"

"He'll take on anything! He's a perfect fiend."

"Well, he's awfully cute," I said truthfully.

"Don't let his looks fool you," she corrected me. In case I doubted her word, she added: "I've taken him to everyone! We saw Dickie Brenner once, and then we saw Lila Goldstein!" In case I still wasn't convinced, she pursed her lips and said in a deep, chilling tone: "Twice!" Gazing down happily at Willie and evidently speaking as one with him, she added: "We didn't like Mr. Brenner, did we? We're never going back to him. And Mrs. Goldstein didn't understand us. But that's all right! Because now we're going to the Monks of New Skete!"

I know when I've been effectively demolished. You

know who the Monks are, don't you? Besides breeding German shepherds and writing first-rate dog-rearing books, they train dogs and give workshops. Any dog dreadful enough to have outdone his fellow couch destroyers, ankle nippers, rug soilers, lawn excavators, garbage stealers, and leash lungers to the extent of requiring three local consultations *and* the Monks of New Skete? Well, that dog had singled himself out as a world-class monster. I eyed Willie with respect.

"Holly," Steve said, "I'd like you to meet Jackie Miner. This is Holly Winter." Steve's an immigrant. He grew up in Minneapolis.

Before Jackie and I had had a chance to say that we were happy to meet each other, Lee Miner, her husband and Steve's new assistant veterinarian, appeared from the back of the clinic, and I'll have to admit that my first thought about Lee was that Jackie would never need to take *him* to the Monks. Lee Miner was a tidy, compact, pale man who held his elbows close to his sides and kept blinking his hazel eyes.

"Pleased to meet you," Lee said when Steve had introduced us. Even his enunciation was precise. He immediately sealed his thin beige lips. Then all three Miners—Jackie, Lee, and Willie—performed what I took to be a family ritual: Jackie yanked on Willie's leash. When she'd positioned Willie at her left side, she tightened the leash, leaned down, and rested her weight on his hindquarters until he sat. As soon as she was standing upright again, she gave Lee an almost imperceptible nod. On signal, Lee took small, careful steps forward until he stood directly in front of Jackie and Willie. Bending from the waist, Lee then reached down and tenderly scratched the top of Willie's head. As Lee straightened up, Jackie tilted her head toward him as if inviting him to scratch her head, too. At the last second, though, she puckered her lips and gave Lee's proffered cheek a noisy kiss.

Except for having been raised in only slightly divergent

sects of the same faith—Steve's family had English setters, whereas mine believed in golden retrievers—he and I had very different childhoods, but we both loved Red Rover. Remember? In case you don't, two teams of kids link arms and face each other. To make a solid link, you clamp your hands around the forearms of the kids next to you, who get the same hard grip on your forearms. It hurts already, right? Then the leader of one team calls out the name of a kid on the other team, who has to charge across and try to break through whatever pair of locked arms he wants. Get it? The leader says, "Red Rover, Red Rover, send Sally right over." If Sally decides that you and Jim are little runts who make a weak link, she runs like hell at your locked arms, and while she's trying to break through, you're trying to stop her. A kid with dog-handler's wrists has a big advantage at Red Rover, but what the game really requires is wild ferocity. That's what compensates for the red, aching forearms.

The point is that although Steve is a really gentle guy, he's the first person you'd pick for Red Rover. Lee Miner, though, looked as if his game hadn't been Red Rover at all. I was willing to bet it had been Quaker Meeting.

3

IF YOU'VE EVER TAKEN AN untrained dog to a beginning obedience class, you probably remember the paradox: The dog acts so wild that it's almost impossible to register him for the first lesson. You try to ask whether you've come to the right class at the right time, but your dog begins yelping so loudly that you can't hear the answer. Somebody hands you a pen and a registration form, but you can't fill in the form or write a check because your dog, who has already wrapped his leash around your ankles, suddenly lunges at a beast four times his size, thus jerking the pen from your hand and your feet from under you. As your head cracks the floor, you wish you'd see stars—beautiful and imaginary— but what glows before your eyes is a hideous vision of the future: week after week of this unremitting humiliation at the paws and jaws of man's best friend.

But if you're lucky enough to show up at the Cambridge Dog Training Club, a round, bright-eyed face suddenly looms over you. One small, rather pudgy hand reaches down to pull you up, while another, equally small and pudgy, grips your dog's leash with surprising strength. "It's happened to all of us," a cheery voice assures you. This woman has to be lying. You don't care. You're grateful someone has taken charge. She goes on: "You're all right, aren't you? Of course you are. Here, I'll hold him for you." You have met Hope Wilson.

According to the membership lists distributed yearly by the Cambridge Dog Training Club, Hope has wirehaired pointing griffons. It may well be that she does. For all I know, she may own and train five or ten of them, in other words, a high proportion of the United States population of the breed, which is recognized by the American Kennel Club, but very few individuals. It's a terrific breed, but let's face it: How much demand is there, really, for a dog specifically developed to hunt in Dutch and French swamps? And, membership lists or no membership lists, it's hard to imagine plump, soft-skinned, gentle Hope with gum boots on her feet, mosquito netting on her head, and a rifle slung over her arm, plodding from tussock to tussock in fatal quest of harmless avian marsh-dwellers. Of course, it's probably also hard to imagine some Inuit version of me, mukluk-shod and fur-swathed, vaulting over the leads from floe to floe, but everyone's seen me with my malamutes, and no one's ever seen Hope with any kind of dog at all.

All this is to say that at seven o'clock on Thursday evening, when Hope and I were at the desk at the Cambridge Armory checking in people and dogs for Vince's beginners' class, Rowdy was on the floor behind our chairs, securely tethered to the bleachers that run along that wall of the battered old armory, but Hope didn't happen to have a dog with her and was hence free to concentrate on rescuing new handlers from their subprenovice dogs.

"Big group," Hope said gleefully to me, not only because obedience enthusiasts are as delighted as are any other true believers to witness a high turnout of converts, but also because beginners' classes, inevitably larger than advanced classes, provide the financial backbone of any dog-training club. Our club happens to have a lot of money, but we still like to feel self-sufficient.

A newcomer approached the desk, a pretty, formally dressed dark-haired woman with a lively young Dalmatian bitch bounding around at the end of a leash. The woman's English had a light Spanish accent. "This school is for beginning dogs?" she asked tentatively.

"Yes," I said. "She hasn't had any training before? This is her first time?"

I thought the woman was going to laugh. She shook her head. "Samantha is a very spoiled girl. She has her own chair, only for her. And my husband wants to sit in this chair."

Even though I explained that basic obedience doesn't exactly dwell on the subject of vacating chairs, the newcomer remained interested. While Hope took temporary charge of Samantha, the woman wrote her name and address, as well as Samantha's name and breed, on our registration form, and then wrote a check for fifty dollars, our fee for the entire eight-week beginners' course. After that, Hope and I helped register a German shorthaired pointer, a couple of mixed breeds, and what both Hope and I took to be a puli mix, an outstandingly cute medium-size, brownish-black dog with a long, curly, fluffy coat.

I'm always curious about dogs, of course. "He's, uh, puli and . . . ?" I asked the owners, a pleasant-looking father and son, both of whom, incidentally, had short, straight hair and resembled one another, not the dog. People like Jackie Miner are the exception. The true identicality of most dogs and their owners lies only in their souls.

Hope made a guess: "With some Portuguese water dog?"

The father and son both smiled, and the father said proudly, "Actually, he's a Charlee Bear dog. Supposed to look like a toy bear. It's a new breed."

And, once I knew what a Charlee Bear dog is supposed to look like, this one did: soft, fluffy, and cuddly, a stuffed

animal come to life. And Hope was right: Although we
didn't know it at the time, there is some Portuguese water
dog in the breed.

The father took a seat on the battered bleachers, and
the straight-haired boy led his curly-coated dog to the dirty
rubber mat stretched on the floor along the opposite side of
the big, shabby hall, where the two of them found a place in
the chaotic line of handlers and dogs, all kinds of dogs,
giants, toys, purebreds, mixes, crosses, near-puppies, and
the inevitable, unmistakable adolescent males whose naive,
trusting owners had put off obedience training until pu-
berty surprised them even more than it did their half-grown
pups.

Just when I'd given up on my lone ranger, he poked his
head around one of the swinging doors between the hall and
the front entry, ran his eyes over everything, and caught
mine. I waved, and then, because he looked half ready to
bolt, I got up and went to the doors. Well, never mind about
the man.

In the unflattering light of the unshaded overhead bulb
in the unprepossessing armory entry glowed a dog, God,
what a dog, maybe eighty pounds, with a tawny red-gold
coat, golden-brown eyes, a broad head, a black nose, and a
long-legged, muscular, four-square build. Here I saw a dog
who didn't belong to any particular breed, but who obviously could have served as the standard-defining progenitor
of . . . ? Let's call it the Royal Golden Shepherd.

I held a hand out to the dog, who sniffed it curiously.
Once he'd given me tacit permission, I ran my palms over
the thick ruff around his neck. "Bear, right?" I said.

"Bear," said John with the expression of apologetic
pride you see on the faces of plain, dull parents who've
produced a glittering, beauty-contest-winner baby.

"Hey," I said, "the class is already starting, so you better get registered. You're here for beginners', right? It's fifty
dollars for eight weeks, and then after that, you can join if
you want, and it's only three dollars a lesson, so it's a good

deal. Anyhow, see if you like it. You need to go to the desk over there."

John and Bear headed toward Hope, and I followed, almost afraid to watch Bear. If he had an awkward, clumsy gait or turned out to be cow-hocked, I didn't want to see it, but I needn't have worried. He moved like a prince.

Then, damn it, as I was about to make sure that John felt as welcome with Bear as he'd have been with a national-specialty winner purebred, Hope, obviously thinking of the Charlee Bear dog, glanced at Bear and said pertly to John, "And I'll bet this one only looks like a shepherd mix, right?" I glared at Hope. "But he actually belongs to the rarest breed in the world."

The muscles in John's face tightened. In spite of the presence of lots of dogs of no particular breed, he must have felt taken aback, sure that I'd lied to him about the club welcoming everyone. In lieu of wrapping my hands around Hope's muzzle and clamping her jaws shut, a procedure at which I'm fairly deft, with dogs at least, I did some fast talking: "We just had a Charlee Bear dog, and neither of us knew what it was, because it's a new breed, and we both thought it was a mix, so Hope's just kidding, right? This is John. He's the guy I was telling you about who rescued Kimi the other day, when she ran into the traffic, and this is Bear, and they're starting with Vince, so we better get them signed up. Also, he wants to know about all-American C.D.'s. Do we have a copy of *N.E.O.N.* around somewhere?" I turned to John. *"N.E.O.N.* is *New England Obedience News.* They give mixed-breed titles or whatever. Anyway, never mind, you can register after class."

That ludicrous tactic is occasionally worth a try with dogs, too. John probably didn't even know what a C.D. is— Companion Dog title, grammar school diploma—but, then, I'd probably been jabbering too fast for him to catch anything else, either. Or maybe he never intended to leave. At any rate, he unzipped the same faded khaki jacket he'd worn on the day of Kimi's rescue, tossed it on the bleachers, slipped a metal training collar on Bear, hooked it to a standard six-foot leather lead, and joined the parade of handlers heeling—or, in most cases, failing to heel—their dogs in a big loop around the hall.

"Did I put my foot in it?" said Hope, her gentle face chagrined. "Or did I put my foot in it? Sorry about that. It is a shepherd mix, isn't it?"

"Yeah, I think so. With some Saint Bernard somewhere?" I was guessing aloud, half to myself. "The color's a little like a golden, but I really don't see any golden there. Mastiff? And there's got to be some northern breed. Siberian, maybe? Malamute? His coat's thick."

After that, we sorted through the registration forms and talked about the other new dogs. I had an admiring eye on a golden retriever bitch of about six months, a fabulous obedience prospect, but Hope misinterpreted my stare and said something you hear all the time about perfection, namely, "Look at that! It's totally disgusting!" The yapping of a . . . Well, to avoid hard feelings, let's skip the breed. As I was saying, one high-volume, nonstop pubescent male drowned Vince out, and the new handlers kept looking at one another and stopping to try to catch his commands. A few of the quick ones discovered the trick of watching the two experienced handlers, club members with new dogs, who couldn't hear Vince, either, but who'd taken so many of his classes that they usually knew what came next. The rank beginners with big, rambunctious dogs had all come dressed in wool sweaters and were sweating profusely. What did they expect? Obedience *is* a sport, after all. One dog had an accident, the handler pretended not to notice, and Vince made him clean it up anyway.

Bear distinguished himself from all the other dogs except the super golden and one black Lab by heeling really quite decently and by ignoring what's usually the irresistible provocation of the young, unneutered male dogs. John clearly had the makings of a good handler. For one thing, he didn't do all that shifting around, hand flapping, head tilting, and jiggling you usually see. In fact, he had natural talent. I'd seen it before. My cousin Leah learned to handle like a pro in practically no time. The Bachs and music?

Hope noticed it, too. "Why'd you tell him to come to beginners'? You should've told to him to come at eight."

"I asked, and he said he hadn't trained a dog before, so what was I supposed to tell him? Maybe he's one of those people that, you know, go to the library and get a book on dog training and actually do what it says."

"Anyway, never mind him," Hope said eagerly. "So tell me everything about Oscar Patterson."

"You know as much as I do," I lied. "Probably more. A week ago Sunday, he was there. A week ago Monday, he wasn't."

"You haven't asked what's-his-name? Steve's new vet? It would've been the first thing I asked him."

"I'm going to. I have to. I'm supposed to be doing some kind of story, not about what happened to him, necessarily, but, basically, anything. What he was like, that kind of thing, and something about suspicions of foul play, or did he just decide to take off? And so forth."

"Well, don't believe everything you hear," Hope said. "If you ask me, some of these women just wish they'd been the one he ran off with, and if it can't be them, they at least want it to be someone."

"Well, Patterson did sort of have that reputation," I said. "It was part of his image."

"What's this guy's name? The new vet?"

"Lee Miner." Then I tacked on an assurance that he was a full-fledged human being: "He and his wife have a Scottie."

After we'd both expressed admiration for anyone trying to obedience train a terrier, any kind of terrier, Hope resumed her efforts to pump me about Lee Miner. At first, she insisted that I must know more about Patterson's disappearance than she did. When I'd convinced her that she was wrong, she filled me in. "Somebody brought a dog in to his

clinic, and it didn't make it, and the owner was yelling at Patterson, and probably Patterson was yelling back at him. This vet, Miner, has got to know about it. Maybe he was even there. Ask him. Anyway, look. You have enough dogs, and sooner or later, something happens, some vet does something, some jerk, and you could kill him for it, right?"

She stopped. Steve Delaney had just arrived with his shepherd, India. He was hanging around near the door with the other advanced people, who were waiting for the beginners' class to end. By the way, if you think that golden retrievers are the only disgustingly perfect obedience dogs, you should see India.

"*Some* vets," Hope added, "not all of them."

"Yeah, I know what you mean. You remember when Ron had Vixen spayed?" I said. Ron Coughlin is our club treasurer. "And he knew something was really, really wrong, and his vet kept telling him to quit worrying, it was all normal? And then, sometime in the middle of the night, he took her to Angell, and, of course, he was right. She had a bad infection." Angell Memorial, which is run by the MSPCA, has a twenty-four-hour emergency room. "If she'd died? You know, his vet never even saw her. He just talked to Ron on the phone. Well, if she'd died, Ron wouldn't've killed him, but he'd have felt like it. I mean, obviously, she lived, but that's how he felt anyway."

"Ron didn't do anything, did he?"

"No. He changed vets, but other than that, I think he just wanted to forget it. But that was different. That guy was really a lousy vet, and everybody'd been telling Ron all these horror stories about him, so when it happened, Ron must've felt it was partly his own fault, for not listening to people. But Patterson is supposed to be good. Or was. That's what Steve told me."

"Somebody could blame him anyway. When you lose a dog? God, it's so awful. And if you thought it was the vet's fault? Anybody'd kill for that. It's only human. You're not in your right mind."

Vinnie, my last golden, died gently. Even so, Hope had unintentionally tapped my permanent grief. To avoid thinking about Vinnie, I said, "Let's get these people checked in. I want to get Rowdy warmed up."

"Go ahead. I'll do it," Hope offered as the beginners' class started to break up. "There aren't all that many."

I slipped Rowdy's training collar over his head and snapped on his lead. He rose, shook himself all over, and started singing out a long series of happy *woo-woo*'s. Then he caught sight of Bear dutifully approaching us at John's side. As usual, Rowdy barged forward to initiate a ritual exchange of sniffs. I kept a vigilant watch, because I'll swear that to other male dogs, Rowdy had always smelled exactly ten months old, which is when testosterone levels peak. He could be sitting squarely at my side with his sweet eyes locked on my face, but the other males weren't fooled. All they ever noticed was that hormonal reek.

But Rowdy and Bear performed the ritual peacefully. Bear must've smelled of something besides testosterone, some friendly hormone that blasts the nostrils of other dogs with an odiferous message that says: "Hey! I'm a nice guy." Farfetched? Let's say that Rowdy and Bear liked each other.

While I was answering John's questions about obedience titles for mixed-breed dogs, Steve came over. I introduced him to John. Human males don't have to sniff; they read testosterone levels in each other's eyes. I suspect that they may even see sharp digital printouts invisible to women. Anyway, if they'd had to rely on their noses, Steve's wouldn't have picked up a trace of whiskey on John, and, like Rowdy and Bear, each male seemed to decide that the other was okay. Steve took John to meet Ron Coughlin, who knows all about titles for mixed breeds because Vixen has an all-American U.D. from *N.E.O.N.* Foreigner? A Utility Dog title from *N.E.O.N.* Remember? *New England Obedience News.* You'll be fluent in no time. I could teach for Berlitz.

Rowdy and I did some brisk heeling. He retrieved his dumbbell a couple of times, and then I got out three plain white cotton work gloves to give him a few minutes of practice on the directed retrieve. It's a Utility exercise, of course, and we were working in Open, but he enjoyed it, and the practice helped to build my confidence that we'd eventually make it to Utility. Besides, even if you never leave home, it's handy to have a dog who'll sight along your arm and retrieve whatever you're pointing toward—your keys, your scarf, the book you're too lazy to retrieve yourself. If you fall, break your leg, and can't get to the phone, you can send the dog for it—assuming it's cordless—and don't laugh. That's really happened. In the sacred words of the Good Booklet, the American Kennel Club Obedience Regulations: "The purpose of Obedience Trials is to demonstrate the usefulness of the pure-bred dog as a companion to man." Or any dog as a companion to anyone, including woman, too, of course. Oh, yes, if you don't show, maybe you wonder why Obedience Trials is capitalized. The explanation is the American Kennel Club capitalizes almost all words that have anything to do with Itself or Its Sacred Animal: Obedience Trial, Dog Show, Long Down, Directed Retrieve, Tracking Test, Golden Retriever, Malamute, and thousands of others. My father carries this loyal stylistic practice to an extreme. He always capitalizes the *d* in Dog, of course, and when he's feeling really enthusiastic, he writes the whole word in uppercase letters, usually followed by an exclamation point: DOG! But, then, he's a religious fanatic.

4

"HOPE THINKS PATTERSON WAS MURDERED by one of his clients," I told Steve. "She says all that talk about how he was lured away by a woman is just gossip. She doesn't know about Geri being pregnant, and, naturally, I didn't tell her. So what about the rest of it? Is it really just gossip?"

We were in the house he was renting, seated at the scarred butcher block table by the big kitchen window that overlooks the pond. In front of me were arrayed a fish sandwich, a large chocolate shake, a large order of french fries, and a garden salad with ranch, all picked up at McDonald's after I'd left the armory and dropped Rowdy at home. Steve doesn't exactly cook, either, but the kitchen of the house he was renting had a microwave, and he'd discovered an Indian food shop that sold things like frozen beef *vindaloo*, TV dinner curried prawns, fresh coriander chutney, and bottled lemon pickle.

When I'd arrived at his house, he'd just irradiated four trays. One contained minuscule squares of an okay chickpea concoction you could substitute for corn bread in the event of rationing. I also recognized one that's like creamed spinach with some nonfood ingredient stirred in, say, sandalwood incense. The other two trays had lumps of meat in reddish brown sauces that didn't smell like any of the choices to get with Chicken McNuggets. After offering to share, he'd upended all four trays on a plate and spooned on four or five kinds of chutney and pickles, not dill, either.

"Gossip," he said, forking a lump of meat that would have dermabraded a normal American mouth back to the womb. "You ever met Geri?"

"No," I said. "Have you?"

"Yeah, at a conference. Geraldine, I guess her real name is. She and Patterson have been together for years. They seemed real tight to me, and I didn't notice him looking around. Don't you want some of this? The top of my head's sweating already."

"I eat American. It's patriotic, like cars, okay?" I ripped open the plastic packet of good, wholesome ranch dressing and dribbled it evenly over my salad. "Maybe I'd like a Nissan Pathfinder, but I drive a Ford Bronco."

"All this stuff comes from New Jersey," he said, "at least the frozen stuff."

"So he wasn't looking around? Was there anyone to look at?"

"Oh, yeah, a whole bunch of veterinary students, some other women, but Patterson didn't act that interested. It was more like Geri was running interference for him, that kind of thing. If anyone was looking around, it was her, not him."

"Were the Miners there?"

"No. That's part of the idea of not doing a one-man practice. Ask Lorraine. You've got somebody to cover for you, so you can get away without having to scout around for someone to fill in."

"You want some? I got a large fries," I said. "There are plenty left. So, anyway, is that story true, about the client and the dog that died?"

"Yeah, it seems to be. I get the feeling that Lee doesn't want to talk about it. But Jackie'll tell you all about it." He pointed to my milk shake. "Can I have some of that?"

"Of course," I said. Dog ownership renders you nearly incapable of disgust: You've not only seen it all, but wiped it off the floor afterward. Steve used that chocolate milk shake to wash down lemon pickle piled on sandalwood spinach, then downed a half-bottle of Japanese beer as a chaser. My stomach didn't even lurch. "So what'd Jackie say?"

"This was a week ago Sunday," Steve said. "Lee got a call about a dog that was in bad shape. At night. Late. And so he told the guy to bring the dog to the hospital, and he'd meet him there. This was a regular client, not somebody new. So as soon as Lee got there, the owner left. Then Patterson showed up."

"What?"

"His house is right nearby. It's like a farm, I guess. Maybe it was a farm originally. Whatever, he and Geri live right there. So Patterson must have heard the car or seen lights or something. So the dog's there, and he's real sick, should've been brought in sooner."

"What was wrong with him?"

"Jackie didn't say. Anyway, Patterson showed up and took over. Sounds like him." Steve got up, returned with the lemon pickle, and started eating it right out of the jar. "He's, uh, kind of a dominant individual," he said. That's his phrase for Rowdy and Kimi, too. I like dominant individuals. "He's just that kind of guy. So he told Lee to go home."

"And did he?"

"Yeah, except that when Lee was leaving, the owner showed up again and started yelling. Lee knew the guy, and so I guess Lee thought things might get rough, and he didn't feel like sticking around. Jackie didn't say it that way, but that's what it sounded like to me. You can't take her too seriously. The dog died, and if you listen to her, he'd've lived if Lee'd taken care of him, that kind of thing."

"Is that possible?"

He shrugged his shoulders. "What she says is that the owner showed up and started hollering like a madman, and Patterson was yelling back at him about how he should've brought the dog in sooner."

"Maybe he should have," I said. "So Lee just ran away?"

Steve shrugged again. Then he leaned back, tilted his chair, and kept it balanced on two legs. "Jackie says Patterson told Lee to leave, and when Patterson was in that kind of mood, Lee didn't like to stick around."

"And?"

"And nothing. End of story. It took them a while to work out that Patterson was gone. Next morning, Geri thought he'd got up early and gone to work. And at the hospital, they thought he was home."

"What about the owner?"

"Yeah. After a while, sometime the next day, when Oscar still hadn't shown up, Lee or somebody called the police. Geri didn't want to do it, at least according to Jackie. Jackie says that when Geri really got it that Patterson was gone, she was afraid people'd think he ran out on her."

"So what *did* Geri think?"

"That Patterson was playing some kind of a game. Geri thought it was some kind of bad joke or that he'd taken off and he'd turn up after a while. But everyone at the clinic took it real seriously, and after forty-eight hours or whatever someone called the police. And when the police heard about the circumstances, they started asking the dog's owner some questions. And after that, the owner took off."

"So they're still looking for him?"

"I don't know. It's been over a week. Maybe he's shown up by now."

"Have you ever heard of that?" I asked. "An owner getting that mad?"

"They get mad," Steve said. "But it's more likely to be because, once the animal's dead, they don't want to pay. Or when they thought he was dying, they'd pay anything for you to save him. Then once you do, they decide you're overcharging, or the animal would've been fine if they'd just kept it home."

"But malpractice does happen," I said. "Like when Ron had Vixen spayed? Before he started taking her to Dr. Draper? And some owners must end up suing. I mean, this *is* Massachusetts." If you live somewhere else, you may not realize that this is the personal injury capital of the United States. "They don't usually murder their veterinarians or even get violent, but they do get mad enough to sue, I'll bet."

"This was New Hampshire," Steve said. "Just over the line. I don't know what the law is there, but in most states, you know, it's different from M.D.'s. Most states, the burden is on the veterinarian to prove that the animal didn't die because of malpractice. Or negligence. Guilty until proven innocent."

"I know," I said. "Do you ever worry about that? About getting sued?"

"Not really. That part's like M.D.'s. If you know the people, you're working together, you keep them informed, most people aren't going to sue you."

"And I suppose if they aren't going to sue you, they aren't going to murder you, either. You know, Steve, I didn't exactly know Patterson, but it's sort of hard to believe, uh, not just that he'd leave his practice like that, but that he'd run out on Geri. I mean, they weren't high school kids." Then I told Steve about what I'd read on the flyleaf of Patterson's book. I half expected Steve to say that I was being corny, but he didn't.

In fact, his face broke into a big open smile. "Yeah, it's real special. There's nothing like it. They come to life in your hands."

"And Patterson was just a little boy," I said. "Maybe I'm . . . I don't know. It doesn't jibe. A guy who's had that experience? And it was important to him. It's why he became a veterinarian in the first place. That's what the fly-leaf said. I keep thinking that the last thing a guy like that would do is run away. Anyway, the sad thing is that if Lee Miner hadn't got scared that night, maybe nothing would've happened. No wonder Miner doesn't want to talk about it. I'm surprised Jackie does."

"She'll talk your ear off about anything. I was thinking, if she'd been there instead of Lee—" Steve laughed and made a low Scottie growl. "Not much would scare her off."

"Yeah," I agreed. "She'd probably have dug her teeth into somebody's ankle. That must be hard for Lee to take."

"Christ, Holly." Steve looked directly at me.

"Lee's only on probation," I said. "It doesn't have to be permanent. And the idea of hiring somebody isn't a mistake at all. You're exhausted all the time. Maybe this particular person won't work out, but somebody will."

Steve looked out the window toward the darkness of the pond as if he hoped to see something rise from it, preferably an unemployed veterinarian.

5

THE PROSPECT OF A LIMITED-ENROLLMENT intensive semi-nar on frozen semen might not persuade you (or even me) to abandon your lover and your dogs for a conference in Minneapolis, but, according to Steve, artificial insemination was more complex than I supposed. In ridiculing the confer-ence and in refusing to go with him—he was staying with his mother—I was displaying my ignorance. If I thought that either he or I already knew everything there was to know about thawing methods, for instance, I was only kid-ding myself. I apologized and swore that I took reproductive management very seriously. I practiced it, didn't I? In fact, I assured him, I hated to miss the whole conference, espe-cially the keynote address, titled—and I'm not making this up—"Why Spoil the Fun?"

After I'd dropped Steve at Logan on Friday morning, I returned home. If you know Cambridge, you've probably noticed my house because of its proximity to a local landmark: Mine is the red three-decker right next to the little, narrow spite building on the corner of Appleton and

Concord. And don't ask me why it's called a "spite" building. It was presumably erected during a property dispute involving a former owner of my house. Anyway, one long brick wall of the spite building runs along half of my side yard, the rest of which is securely fenced to enclose what will become a charming city garden if I ever cure Kimi of digging.

Rowdy was a ferocious digger until the memorable day when I dragged him out of an especially deep hole, wrapped one hand around his muzzle, pointed the other toward the depths of his pit, and loudly informed him that if he succeeded in tunnelling straight through to the Orient, he'd emerge in the homeland of a breed known as the Chinese edible dog. If he didn't want to end his days bathed in soy sauce, I yelled, he'd better reform pronto. And he did. Soon afterward, though, I adopted Kimi, who rapidly proved herself a fearless canine backhoe, strong, tireless, and impervious to warnings and threats about cultural differences in attitudes toward her species. If the route of the Iditarod Sled Dog Race led straight down from Anchorage into the bowels of the earth instead of to Nome? Well, with Kimi as my lead dog, I'd be Susan Butcher.

So that's where I live, in the red house beyond the spite building and the earthworks, and when I returned there from Logan, I forced myself to resume work on an article about the Chinese crested, which was about to be promoted from the AKC's Miscellaneous class to full recognition. The Chinese crested is a very small dog, under ten pounds, and I believe that it's either inedible or never eaten. There are two varieties of Chinese crested: the powderpuff and the hairless. The latter has hair on its feet and on the tip of its tail, and a longish tuft on the top of its head, hence the name. The first Chinese crested I ever saw had black and white spotted skin, and—Jesus, never say I said this, because it could cost me my job—I thought that it looked like the shrunken and shaven result of crossing a Dalmatian and a cockatiel. If you own one, well, I'm sorry, but, honestly, the first time you saw one, didn't you think . . . ? Oh, you didn't? Well, now that Chinese crested fanciers have started to put obedience titles on their dogs, the breed doesn't look funny to me, either.

Besides, as I told Rowdy and Kimi late that afternoon, no one who is training two malamutes for brace obedience is in a position to laugh at other dog owners. The whole point of brace competition is that the two dogs work as one, to which the Alaskan malamute replies, "Me first! Me first!"

I'd moved the Bronco to the street, and we were training in my driveway, which ranks somewhere below the Longfellow House and Harvard Yard in walking guides to Cambridge, but on that sunny, blue-skied, sixty-five-degree afternoon, deserved special mention as the most beautiful sight in eastern Massachusetts. A scraggly and disoriented forsythia bush in Mrs. Dennehy's yard next door showed the sparse bloom it usually reserves for April. The candytuft by my fence, having survived the previous December's unremitting subzero effort to transform all perennials into annuals, had three or four white flowers. In a short-sleeved T-shirt and a pair of summer-weight L.L. Bean jeans, I was comfortable, and my dogs probably would have been willing to trade coats, or the absence thereof, with a pair of Chinese cresteds. Even so, Kimi and Rowdy were the beautiful sight. I had them sit together, told them to stay, walked to the end of the drive, and turned to watch them. The true purpose of the long sit in brace obedience is to let the handler step back and admire the glossy coats, bright eyes, and smug smiles of her handsome dogs. Then Rowdy shook his head and shifted his front feet. I corrected him and praised Kimi. He did it again. I reminded him that the dog who acts restless ruins the performance of two other beings who, in case he hadn't noticed, happened to be behaving themselves. Finally, I did what I should have done first: I checked his ears. The left one was fine, clean and shell pink. The right held traces of a waxy, dirty accumulation that I was sure meant ear mites.

In the pre-Steve era, I'd have treated the mites myself, but he'd jettisoned my pharmacopeia of ointments, salves, sprays, and drops. As it was, I had to call the clinic and make an appointment with Lee Miner.

Rowdy had always seemed to believe that Steve's clinic was some sort of multimedia dog-entertainment establishment at which he was the guest of honor. Whenever he marched in, the attendants bowed low to rub his head and tummy. Cats yowled. Dogs yapped. And the atmosphere! Some dogs take one whiff of that veterinary odor, tuck their tails between their legs, and tremble, but Rowdy inhaled it as a tribute to himself. He adored it, all of it, the lingering scent of human tears, puppy urine, kitten blood, feces, vomit, festering wounds, medicine, disinfectant, and sweet, sweet deodorizer: Odormute, Odor Crush, Odo Kill, Nilodor, Outright, Odo Kleen, Citrus II, plain old vinegar, pine oil—you name it, if there's one odor you can't really mask, mute, crush, kill, annihilate, do in, or wipe right out, it's the quintessential scent of pure dog.

That afternoon, Rowdy had fifty-five uninterrupted minutes in which to shove his nose under the crowded benches, follow invisible trails along the linoleum, and make friends or enemies with all of the other pets and owners also waiting and waiting. Rhonda and Lorraine both snuck him treats. After rereading the tattered copies of *Pet Health News*, I leafed through the pamphlets on urinary tract infections, heartworm, fleas, and house-training. The only booklet appropriate to my situation was called "The Care of the Aging Dog": I was beginning to think I'd own one before Lee Miner would finally get around to us.

But he eventually ushered out a woman and her limping collie, raised an arm toward me, and held open a swinging door. Glancing at the file folder Lorraine had given him, he said, "You can bring Rowdy in now."

Once we were finally in the exam room, I was, of course, eager to get the ear mite medicine and be gone.

"He's got ear mites," I told Lee. "He keeps shaking his head, and the ear's got some glop."

Lee rested his back against one of the Formica counters, folded his arms, and began to question me. When did I first notice the problem? When had I last observed the ear? Had I looked in the other ear? Had Rowdy had any previous ear infections? Then he slowly opened Rowdy's chart and spent at least ten minutes memorizing its contents.

"Steve checked his ears the other day," I said. "They were fine then."

He nodded and kept reading the chart. At last, he said, "Well, let's take a look."

He reached for an otoscope, then put a hand into one of the pockets of his white coat and pulled out a brown leather muzzle.

"You don't need to muzzle him," I said. "He likes being here. I'll just hold him. He won't give you a hard time."

But Miner didn't put the muzzle away. "Just to be on the safe side," he said as he slipped it on Rowdy and buckled it. I didn't object. A muzzle isn't painful, Rowdy was undeniably a big dog, and Lee didn't know him. Right after I'd adopted Rowdy, the first time I gave him a bath, I muzzled him, too. But Rowdy loved veterinarians as much as he hated water. My lovely, gentle dog stared at me with puzzled eyes, as if to ask what he'd done wrong. I told him he was good boy, then knelt beside him, my arms wrapped around his shoulders, my hands ready to keep his head still while Lee looked in his ears. After patting the top of Rowdy's head a couple of times, Lee finally inserted the instrument and peered into Rowdy's right ear.

"Mites," I said.

"We'll see," he told me.

Then he spent a long time fiddling around. He took a sample from the ear, disappeared into the back of the clinic, reappeared, checked the other ear, and cleaned out some waxy glop. Steve, I should mention, doesn't exactly rush through anything. He is careful and thorough. Even so, he can diagnose and treat an ear infection in less than thirty minutes, especially when he's an hour behind schedule and the waiting room's packed. Furthermore, no matter how busy he is, he always takes time to visit with the animals and the owners. I tried to chat with Lee, but he said almost nothing. When I asked him about Oscar Patterson, he said we'd talk about it another time, if I didn't mind. He addressed hardly a word to Rowdy. Just as I'd concluded that Steve had hired an associate who'd be a liability to the practice, I got a surprise.

"No sign of mites," said Lee.

I pride myself on my diagnostic skills. "Are you sure?" I asked. Steve doesn't love that kind of question, at least from me.

Lee was nice about it. He nodded. Then, after he'd given me a long explanation and an unnecessary lesson on how to clean a dog's ears and apply Panolog ointment, he removed the muzzle. Rowdy shook his head, then his whole body, and made for the door to the waiting room. We were both glad to leave. It's stupid to take your dog to a vet and announce a diagnosis. I shouldn't have done it. But what had Rowdy done except be himself, a big dog?

"So, I felt like a jerk, and I deserved it," I told Hope late that same afternoon as we sat at my kitchen table drinking tea. She'd stopped in to return my copy of the Ian Dunbar tape. You know the one? *Sirius Puppy Training.* You know who Ian Dunbar is, don't you? The Dr. Spock of dogs, or this being Cambridge, maybe the T. Berry Brazelton. "But he did take forever. Honestly, I was there at least an hour and a half. And I wish I hadn't let him muzzle Rowdy. I was too nice about it. There wasn't a chance in a million that Rowdy'd bite him. I should've said no, but I didn't do anything. I just watched him clamp that muzzle on."

"A lot of them do that," Hope said. "They just do it routinely with big dogs."

Then I heard Rita tapping at the kitchen door. She

often stops in on her way upstairs. If she's just spent the day listening to her patients tell her how they're feeling, she comes in to tell me how she's feeling. Then she asks me how I'm feeling, and—at least according to Rita—I talk about my dogs. Sometimes, though, we just hang out. Rita wears jewelry, and not the ubiquitous Cambridge handmade pierced-ear earrings, either, but chunky necklaces, bracelets, rings, and even pins, if that's what they're still called. Brooches? Anyway, Rita raps quickly and sharply with whatever ring she happens to be wearing. That day, it was a big silver one with an electric-blue stone that matched her suit. Rita always dresses like that. Cambridge people often assume that she lives in New York City because she does things that have nothing to do with the life of the mind. She is the only woman in Cambridge who keeps her hair looking as if she'd just left the salon. The normal thing to do here is to sprint home from the hairdresser to get shampooed before anyone sees you.

Dog people, of course, have no prejudice against the application of gels, conditioners, and mousses to expensively scissored hair, but they never notice it on mere people. If Rita's head had been shaved, or even missing, Hope would still have got down on the floor and spoken gently to Groucho, Rita's dachshund, before wiping her hand on her jeans and offering it to Rita as I introduced them. They'd met once before, but I was sure that Hope had forgotten. Rita hadn't had a dog with her at the time, and, from Hope's viewpoint, a person without a dog is as distinctive and memorable as the average refrigerator.

"What a sweet old boy," Hope told Rita as I was locking Rowdy and Kimi in my bedroom. "How old is he?"

"Older than I want to remember," Rita said. "It shows, huh? I don't like to think about it."

Hope told Rita the same lies I'd been telling her for the past few months: Groucho probably still had a few good years. His eyes looked alert. He was moving around easily enough. Like Rita, I didn't want to think about it. Groucho didn't really even walk anymore. He tottered. Sometimes he leaned against whatever wall he stumbled into. Rita had to carry him up and down the stairs to her apartment, which is on the second floor, directly above mine. His eyesight, hearing, and appetite were just about gone, it seemed to me, but I kept agreeing with Rita's claims that he had seen a cat out the window, heard Rowdy howl, or enjoyed his prescription canned dog food. The one truth Hope told Rita was that Groucho was, in fact, a sweet old boy.

"I feel so ambivalent about leaving him," Rita said. As usual, he was in her lap, but I'm not sure he knew where he was or even *that* he was. "I'm due to go away over Christmas. I made plans a while ago, and I thought I'd take him with me, but I can't see it now. I don't think he could handle it."

"By air?" Hope asked.

"Yes," said Rita, looking down at Groucho and stroking the white fur around his lips.

Hope shook her head in agreement. "And in winter, if the temperature's below ten degrees, they won't take him. Unless he could travel with you? Not with the baggage?"

"I tried that," Rita said, "but no go. They won't let him. He's small, but his carrier's not that small, because I don't want him all cramped up."

"Rita," I said, "you know I'd keep him here if I could."

"Of course," she said and added, to Hope, "Holly's offered to go up and feed him and take him out, but she's going to Maine before I'm due back. Maybe I should scrap the whole thing."

She was supposed to spend Christmas with her mother, her two sisters, and their husbands and children. All of the adults, she predicted, would devote the holidays to cross-examining her about why she wasn't married and when she was going to get married, and the presence of her nieces and nephews would make her ask herself the same questions.

"Hey," said Hope, "I know it sounds like I'm drumming up business, but you could leave him with my sister. She has a sort of kennel. Pet-sitting service. She won't have a lot of room in the runs what with the holidays and everybody going away, but you could probably get her to keep him in the house."

"Is she around here?" Rita asked.

"Haverhill? You know where that is? It's only, like, forty-five minutes. You go straight up 93, and then you cut through North Andover, or else you get on 495. It's not far, and it wouldn't be like boarding him, really. She's there practically all the time. He wouldn't be alone. You want me to call her?"

"Sure," Rita said. "Yes. Absolutely."

Hope made the call, then Rita talked to the sister, who was named Charity. While Rita was on the phone, Hope said to me, "Oh, I meant to tell you. You know that dog, the other night? With the guy who rescued Kimi for you? Well, I was up at Charity's the other day, and she's got one there she's boarding that looks a whole lot like that. The one she's got is a bitch, and she's smaller, a lot smaller, and also she's lighter colored, but other than that, you'd swear they were littermates."

"Well," I said, "there are a lot of shepherd mixes around. You know, probably what they are is mostly shepherd and yellow Lab."

Then Rita hung up the phone, and Hope gave her the directions to Charity's. By the way, the third sister, Faith, died in infancy. Symbolic or what?

6

IT TAKES MORE THAN SITTING in the Garden and licking a Sport Bar to make a real Celtics fan, right? You have to know about Russell, Cousy, and Sam Jones. If you don't recognize Robert's rainbow jumper? If you don't miss Danny's three-pointers, Johnny Most's gravel voice, and every game D.J. ever saved? If you think that French Lick, Indiana, is one more small town in the Midwest? Well, if that's the case, you're no more a real Celtics fan than Rita is a real dog person, or Kevin Dennehy, either. Kevin, who's a good friend of mine as well as my next-door neighbor, had once owned a dog, and Rita had Groucho, of course, but there's more to being a dog person than a mere history of ownership, and if there's one never-fail way to rid yourself of nondoggy acquaintances, it's to include them in a gathering of real dog people, which is to say, people who can discuss impacted anal sacs without gagging on their Brie.

Before scheduling the party for that Sunday evening, I'd carefully and tactfully made sure that Rita and Kevin would have prior commitments. Then I'd invited them. Rita would be safely out of town, vacationing with her family, and Kevin would be at a tree-trimming given by his cousin Mickey De Franco, who makes a big deal of Christmas. Kevin is a Cambridge cop, and his cousin Mickey is a Boston cop. Kevin always points out that the correct generic term is *police officer* and that they're both lieutenants and both in homicide, whereas *cop* suggests that they direct traffic or travel from school to school to deliver little lectures about looking both ways before you cross the street and, while you're at it, not shooting up anything you wouldn't want Santa Claus to find in your bloodstream, either. The problem, though, is that Kevin is built so much like a gorilla that, despite his red hair and blue eyes, he makes me feel like Dian Fossey. Consequently, Kevin looks nothing at all like an *officer* or a *lieutenant* and everything like what he really is: a good Cambridge cop.

As I was saying, even if Rita had been in town, Kevin had been free, and both had accepted my invitation, they'd have had a rotten time. Besides, it was the annual holiday get-together of the Cambridge Dog Training Club, and neither of them is a member. In fact, the party wasn't really mine. All I did was volunteer my place. It isn't very big, but it's so sparsely furnished that it will accommodate quite a few people, at least if they're willing to stand or to sit on the floor. My Christmas tree was already up and decorated. All I had to do was clear the kitchen table for the potluck dishes everyone was bringing, set up a little bar on the counter, and pile a lot of birch logs in the fireplace. Then I carried a big box up from the basement, and unpacked, cleaned, and stuck red candles in all of the glass, silver, and pewter candle holders and ornate, multitiered candelabra won by my mother's dogs and mine.

About ten minutes before people were due to arrive— no dogs invited—I put Rowdy and Kimi in my bedroom, distributed the candles here and there, lit them, got the fire going, and started to worry. Rita once pointed out to me that my two worst preparty fears, that no one will come and that there won't be enough to eat, are mutually exclusive, but before this party, I also worried about whether the three non-club-member guests I'd invited would fit in all right. I'd promised Steve, who was still away at the conference, to do what I could to welcome the Miners, but a veterinarian and his wife aren't necessarily dog people. And John, Kimi's savior? I hardly knew him.

As it turned out, so many people showed up that my apartment was crammed full: Roz and Vince, our instructors, and Diane D'Amato, Ron Coughlin, Arlene, Liz, the Metcalfs, Hope, and all the other present and lots of the past board members, and thirty or forty other people. Everyone who'd promised food brought it. Maybe I should have tried to coordinate the menu beforehand. Real dog people have a lot of things in common, of course, but ethnic background isn't one of them. The spread on the table included a baked ham, a deep-dish casserole version of potato latkes, a bowl of hummus, a platter of tomato and goat cheese salad, a pan of lasagna, a molded cranberry and Jell-O salad, and a big mound of Chinese-style chicken wings.

And I needn't have worried about John and the Miners. John never turned up at the party, and Jackie and Lee fit in fine. Not ten minutes after the Miners arrived, Jackie was popping hors d'oeuvres into her mouth and chatting with Diane D'Amato about stool samples, whipworm, and hot spots; and Lee was happily trading anecdotes with the Metcalfs about bitches in season and testicles that failed to drop. In other words, the party was a success right from the beginning, and once the other guests found out that Lee had worked for Oscar Patterson, I modestly scored it in the mid-190's on a scale that runs from 0 to 200. Mystified by the numbers? You don't show dogs in obedience, do you?

Actually, the party was more like the breed ring than like obedience. Breed is conformation, right? How well each dog conforms to the standard? But there's more than that to winning in breed. In addition to structural soundness, a good gait, and all the rest, a first-rate show dog has a big, attention-grabbing personality that tells the judge, "Hey! Look at me! Me! Me! Me! Hey, I'm the best! Put me up! Me! Me!" Rowdy, right? So I'm not insulting Jackie Miner, who occupied the center of the couch in the packed living room.

Jackie had on red high heels and a silky red dress trimmed with a myriad of tiny red-ribbon bows. Her eyes were keen, her expression was alert, and her black curls glistened so brightly that I assumed that she'd just left the groomer's. "Oscar was a very, very dramatic person, self-dramatizing, if you want to know the truth," she told Arlene, who was curled up on the hearth directly in front of the fire, where she blocked everyone's view of the flaming birch logs and hogged all the warmth. Sometimes I worry about Arlene. Heat-seeking can be a sign of a thyroid problem, especially in an individual who's overweight and has a dull, patchy coat or, in her case, lank, thin hair.

"Well, he *was* a poet," Arlene said.

"Yes, but that's certainly not how he earned his living," said Jackie. "He certainly didn't support himself and Geri by writing poetry. Did he, Lee? Lee! I'm saying that Oscar's poetry was really a hobby. He didn't actually make his living from it. Isn't that right?"

Lee Miner and Ray Metcalf were by the Christmas tree, admiring some of the ornaments, I imagine. Tinsel can foul up a dog's digestive tract—it's as dangerous as panty hose—and glass balls look too much like toys to be safe on low branches. Candy canes and popcorn get eaten, and electric cords are hazardous if you have a chewer like Kimi. Of course, I never pile presents under the tree unless I'm pretty sure that I know what's in them and that it isn't chocolate, which is toxic to dogs, or homemade jelly in breakable jars, or anything else edible, either. The dogs may survive, but it's hard to write a sincere-sounding thank-you note when the present you actually received was a tatter of damp wrapping paper and some drool-sodden crumbs. But, I should add, my tree was far from barren, displaying as it did a rather large collection of small gold- and silver-plated retrievers engraved with the words "Puppy's First Christmas" and eight or ten mock-crystal sled dogs, as well as some ordinary Santas, angels, ribbons, and doves, all of which Lee Miner was fingering.

As I was saying, Lee had good reason to admire the tree, and when Jackie interrupted him to ask whether Oscar Patterson's poetry was a hobby, he looked toward her and said blandly, "Well, yes, I suppose so."

"You see?" she said. "It was really part of Oscar's *persona!*" She studied our faces to see whether we understood the word. "His image," she added unnecessarily. "Like being in the country. Oscar loved to go on about smelling the country and tasting it and feeling it. He could get sort of disgusting about it, if you ask me. He was always talking about smelling and tasting everything."

"California," someone said.

"As a matter of fact, he came from the Bronx." Jackie's tone suggested that she'd just explained everything about Oscar Patterson. For all I knew, she had. Is the Bronx a sensuous borough? I don't know New York well at all. "And," Jackie went on, rubbing one of the little bows on her dress, "he grew up in dire poverty. His father deserted the family, and his mother ran around with *men!*" Jackie paused, then continued. "And she drank, too. Oscar was obviously starved for affection, if you ask me." Her voice dropped. "You could tell because he was always hugging and kissing everyone and putting his hands on people." She crossed her left knee over the right, flexed the arch of the extended foot, and examined either her ankle or her red high-heeled pump.

Arlene looked disappointed. "Was he really from the Bronx? That doesn't . . . I mean, you don't expect . . ."

"Yes, he was definitely from the Bronx," Jackie told her. "He'd lost his New York accent." She added, as if the new information would contradict the old, "But he was very attractive to women, in a kind of Errol Flynn, Lord Byron way, lots of curly dark hair? Except a lot shorter. But when you got to know him, he was very, very bossy. Just ask Lee. Lee, I've been saying how bossy Oscar could be, and I want you to back me up on that. Is that true? Now when you got to know Oscar, was that one bossy, bossy man?"

Lee, who'd been edging toward the kitchen, stopped, turned, and raised his narrow chin about one inch.

"You see?" Jackie said. "Lee says the same thing. But the owners liked it. They like a firm statement. It builds confidence. I always tell Lee: Owners aren't paying to hear what all the possibilities are. Lecture them all about what it could be, and they decide you're guessing, and they aren't one bit happy to pay today's fees for some shot in the dark. That's one reason Oscar was so popular."

"From what I hear," said Ron Coughlin, who was sitting next to me on the floor, "there was one guy he wasn't all that popular with."

"Or one woman he really was," said Barbara Doyle. I remembered that she was a Patterson fan. The one time I'd seen Oscar Patterson, at the poetry reading, he hadn't looked like Lord Byron to me, except that his hair was dark and that he'd forgotten to do up the top buttons on his shirt. But Barbara does look romantic. She has fluffy curls and wears lacy, velvety clothes that are totally impractical for someone with German shepherds.

"No, no," Jackie said. "I don't know why people are saying that, because it was definitely, definitely Cliff Bourque, and if Oscar had minded his own business and let Lee take care of that dog, it never would've happened."

"What kind of dog was it?" I asked. If fate assigns you a role, why recast yourself? Besides, maybe because the story about the young Patterson cradling the newborn puppies had touched me, I felt protective toward him and even toward Geri, whom I didn't know at all. At any rate, I was glad that Jackie hadn't told everyone that Geri was pregnant and that Patterson might have run out on her. I wanted Jackie to talk about anything else, preferably dogs rather than people.

Jackie answered my question about Cliff Bourque's dog. "Some kind of sled dog," she said. "Lee will know."

"A malamute?" I asked. The Alaskan malamute isn't a rare breed, of course. Even so, the number of people active in the breed, people who show or belong to the clubs, is small enough so that I know, or at least know of, a lot of them. I'd never heard of any Cliff Bourque.

"Uh-uh. Something weird. They had a few of them, him and his wife. She was my hairdresser, which is how I know, and she's a very, very nice woman. I feel sorry for her. He must be a very disturbed man. A vet."

I was stunned. Why would a vet have . . . ?

"Vietnam," Jackie said. "For all we know, and I for one think it's very likely, Cliff had some kind of flashback, and when Oscar broke the news that the dog was dead, it took him back to the jungle, and he went completely out of control. And what he did then was take to the woods, if you ask me." She swept a hand wildly toward some imaginary forest.

"That's awful," Arlene said.

"His poor wife," said someone else.

"Could be worse," Ron murmured to me. "If she's a hairdresser, probably she at least knows how to groom—"

But Jackie overheard. "You know, it's no joking matter," she said severely.

I felt chastised. It seemed to me that off and on over the past few days, I'd been guilty of treating Oscar Patterson's unsolved disappearance as something of a joking matter. In spite of her irksome dramatics, Jackie Miner, though, clearly took it very seriously indeed.

Ron apologized. Everyone fell silent. Mostly to smooth over the awkwardness, Ray Metcalf changed the subject. "Well, there's one thing I've heard about Oscar Patterson that I can't help admiring, and that's that he taught Dickie Brenner a good lesson."

"Brenner!" Jackie said. "Well, I can tell you positively everything about him, and none of it's good! Before I knew better, I took Willie to him, and let me tell you . . ."

Both Ron and I had had about enough of Jackie, and as he followed me into the kitchen, he asked, "Who's this Brenner?"

I refilled the ice bucket and tidied up around the sink. "Some kind of dog behavior expert. A consultant."

In Cambridge at least, *consultant* means anything or nothing, or maybe I'm still too much an outsider to understand what it does mean except that consultants tell other people what to do. Can that be right? Why should people pay all these consultants to give them a lot of advice they probably don't want and won't take? Anyway, Vince, our head trainer, and Roz, who does our advanced classes, evidently understood the word or shared my take on it, because they both stepped in to gripe about Brenner.

"Those people make me so *mad!*" said Roz, who seldom looks or acts more than quietly annoyed. In dog training, anger is useful only as a warning that it's time to stop, and Roz is too busy to waste time on anything useless. She keeps her gray hair short and straight, wears indestructible, indistinguishable wash-and-wear clothes, and seldom seems to feel any strong emotion except love for dogs and pride in their achievements. But she can seethe if she thinks they're being mistreated. "Do you know what he does?" She looked slowly around at us.

"What do people expect?" Vince said. "They're too lazy to train their own dogs, and they turn them over to someone else."

"Fine for them," Roz said, "But what about the dogs? They don't deserve it, do they? And Brenner's not the only one, either."

"Would someone tell me who Brenner is?" Ron asked.

"You see?" Roz said. "You people haven't even heard of Brenner, and the reason why is that you won't catch him in an obedience ring, not on your life. You know what he tells people? 'Oh, those AKC types. They don't know anything.' And what he does, Ron, is to get people to leave their dogs there, with him, supposedly to be trained, or else he charges them a fortune for private lessons with the dog, where he does all the training, if you want to call it that. What I call it is abuse, plain and simple." Roz clenched her jaw and pinched her lips together. Her eyes flashed.

"Rubber hoses," Vince said.

"Is that what it is?" I said. "Jesus. Mostly all I know about Brenner is that I've seen the ads. Off-leash training, right?"

"But doesn't the guy have to have some kind of credentials?" Ron asked. "He must've done something."

"Yeah," Vince said. "Brenner's credentials are that he put up a sign and took out some ads, and then he was an instant expert. And then after a while, the ads said he'd been in business a long time, and after a while, it was true enough. He had been."

"So how did Oscar Patterson . . . ?" I started to ask.

"Brenner's up in that area somewhere," Vince said. "I heard about it from Ray, because the dog that Brenner and Patterson had the fight about a couple of months back was a Clumber spaniel."

Ray and Lynne Metcalf raise Clumber spaniels. In case you haven't seen one—they're fairly rare—I should mention that they have long bodies like basset hounds, massive heads, and soft, light-colored coats. A Clumber is about as tall as an English springer spaniel, but much, much heftier.

"What happened," Vince continued, "is that Ray and Lynne sold a show pup to some people in New Hampshire, and he did a lot of winning, and they never had any trouble with him. The dog was great with kids, nice around the house, all that. Then these people heard about this off-leash training, and I guess that sounded like a good idea, and instead of asking Ray and Lynne, they just sent him to Brenner, and when they got him back, it was like they had a different dog. He flew at the woman, then he bit some kid, and then he really did a job on the guy's face. Patterson was their vet, and he'd known the dog all along, and when he heard the story, he figured it out, and he went to Brenner's place and socked him one in the jaw."

"Good for him," I said.

"So what happened to the dog?" Ron asked.

"Ask Ray," Vince said. "Last thing I heard, they still had him. This just happened, maybe a month ago, six weeks, something like that. These people in New Hampshire didn't want the dog anymore and, of course, Ray and Lynne took him back, and what are they going to do with him?"

"Jackie Miner took a dog to Brenner," I said. "She had some kind of bad experience. I'm not sure what. Anyway, she had the sense not to go back. I think I'll ask her about it."

"The *Dog's Life* spotlight team, huh?" Ron said.

That's what the *Boston Globe*'s exposé people are called, the spotlight team. If you're familiar with politics here in Massachusetts—the Vote Early and Vote Often State—you know that there's usually plenty to expose, and when there isn't, the indomitable spotlight team does anyway, or that's what people say.

"*Dog's Life* publishes some anti-pet-shop articles," I said in defense of my employer. "And a few opinion pieces about how the AKC isn't doing anything to close down puppy mills. I could do something about what to watch out for if you go to one of these dog behavior consultants. Some of our readers are new owners or sort of casual owners. They want to be responsible, but they don't necessarily know how. That's one reason they subscribe. If their dogs might be abused, they want to be warned."

After that, Ron and Roz helped me to put out the desserts and coffee. I was really glad that Rita and Kevin weren't there, and although I'd been a little disappointed that John had never arrived, I decided that it was probably for the best, especially when Hope used one of the paper coffee cups and a kitchen chair to demonstrate how to collect a urine specimen from a dog and then added cream and sugar and drank from the same cup. Rita and Kevin would've turned puce. I wasn't sure about John. As it was, though, everyone had a good time and stayed late.

While I was helping the Miners to find their coats, I remembered to ask Lee about the dog that died the night Oscar Patterson vanished. "Cliff Bourque's dog?" I said. "Is that right?"

"Yes," he said as he carefully zipped his parka and did up all of those snaps and Velcro fasteners around the neck that most people ignore.

"I heard it was a sled dog," I said. "I wondered what kind. Because I have malamutes?"

"Oh, it wasn't a malamute," he said.

"No, I heard it wasn't," I said.

"Lee, she already knows what it wasn't," Jackie insisted. "She wants to know what it *was.*"

"Well, I'm not sure I remember exactly," he said. "It doesn't really matter, does it?"

"No, I guess not," I said.

When everyone had left, I put all the food away and starting gathering up crumpled napkins, paper cups, and other trash. As I was snuffing candles and picking up paper plates in the living room, I noticed something odd about the Christmas tree. My family tradition decrees that ornaments belong out of the reach of puppies, but otherwise they go wherever you happen to want to hang them. The dogs will jostle the tree and knock it over a few times, so there's no point in taking pains over a careful arrangement, is there? My random scatter must have bothered Lee Miner. I'd noticed that he'd been toying with the ornaments, but I hadn't expected this meticulous rearrangement. On the exact tips of the branches, I found a "Puppy's First Christmas," then a dove or some other ordinary ornament, then a sled dog, then an ordinary ornament, then a puppy again, and so forth in tedious, equidistant repetition. The slight natural asymmetry of the fir, cut from my father's lot in Owls Head, had probably offended Lee. I was willing to bet that if Lee Miner had happened to be toting a pair of secateurs, he'd have pruned the tree, too.

In need of some healthy chaos, I let Rowdy and Kimi out of the bedroom. While they were snuffling and nosing around after crumbs, I carried two bags of trash outside to the barrels so the dogs wouldn't rip through the plastic and make themselves sick on chicken bones and grease-smeared aluminum foil. Malamutes will eat *anything*. Kimi, for example, had once knocked a jar of blueberry jam off a counter and lapped up the mess, glass and all. The true basis of the Alaskan malamute's low opinion of human judgment is our wasteful habit of always discarding good bread, meat, and milk just when they've ripened to a yummy slimy green and begun to stink like rancid Roquefort.

The only creature I've ever encountered that's as truly omnivorous as the Alaskan malamute is that other agile, persistent, highly intelligent champion trash-raider, the Cambridge raccoon. Raccoons are here by the hundred, maybe by the thousand, and that's why every sensible Cambridge resident has trash barrels with lock-on lids. Nothing really defeats raccoons; the point is simply to discourage them. Raccoons hibernate in winter, but the weird December warmth must have fooled them, because I'd glimpsed one scuttling out of my driveway and down Appleton Street only a few nights earlier.

Anyway, I was standing on the edge of my blacktop driveway, underneath the flight of wood steps that leads up to my back door, when I thought I heard one. I'd dumped the trash bags into a barrel and locked the lid, and I was thinking about the raccoon I'd the seen the other night and wondering whether I should try one of my dozens of useless raccoon-proofing devices. As I was eyeing a pile of concrete blocks and not enjoying the prospect of hoisting them on top of the barrels, I heard something.

The neighborhood was unusually quiet that night. Rita was away, of course, as were my third-floor tenants. On the far side of my driveway, the Dennehys' house was dark; Kevin and his mother were still out, or else they'd gone to bed. The undergraduates who normally wander all around Cambridge had gone home for vacation, and even the traffic around the corner on Concord Avenue was light. Then something rustled. Something stirred. The sound seemed to come from the vicinity of the overgrown lilac bushes at the end of my drive or maybe from beneath my Bronco. In the hope of seeing a raccoon, I moved slowly toward the bottom of the stairs, where I stopped and waited. Yeah, raccoons make a mess of the trash, and I know better than to feed them or try to pat them. And, yes, they can carry rabies, and even though Rowdy and Kimi are always up on their shots, I don't want raccoons around, partly because the dogs would happily kill them. But God damn. Have you ever had two or three raccoons peer down at you from the notch of a tree? They have got to be the cutest animals in the world.

I heard another rustle, then a pleading groan. Raccoons rustle, and when they mate, they shriek like human beings in pain, but they never groan. I ran up the back stairs and into my kitchen, where I grabbed a flashlight, snatched a leash from the collection that hangs on the kitchen door, and snapped it onto Rowdy's collar. Then I smacked my lips to him, tried to explain to Kimi that we were not going for a walk, eased Rowdy out the door, and left Kimi shut inside. I stopped on the landing just outside the door, but Rowdy, apparently unconvinced by my apology to Kimi, headed eagerly down the stairs, his eyes shining in the light of the flood over the door, his beautiful white tail waving back and forth.

"Is anyone there?" I called as I followed Rowdy. It was a stupid question. I knew that someone was there. "Are you hurt?"

At the bottom of the stairs, where I expected Rowdy to head toward the street, he turned and made his way past the Bronco, toward the opposite end of the drive. I hauled him in close to me and called again, more softly this time, "Is anyone there?"

One of the bare lilac branches moved, and I tried to see over the Bronco to the base of the shrubs, but my big car and its shadow blocked my view. Who did I think was there? A victim, I suppose, someone who'd been mugged or a homeless person seeking shelter. Although I'd taken the precaution of getting my powerful, fearless dog, I wasn't afraid. On the contrary, that heartfelt groan had left me with an urgent sense that someone needed help.

A tall figure suddenly rose from the lilacs on the far side of the Bronco, sprang over the ugly barberry hedge that divides the Dennehys' yard from mine, and tore off around the back of their house.

A lot of men in Cambridge have beards, of course. There are plenty of tall men here, too, and I'm sure that lots of them wear light-colored jackets. But if I hadn't recognized the man, I'd have let Rowdy take off after him, and I'd have pursued him myself. I'd have done my best to catch him and demand what the hell he'd been doing hanging around my house. As it was, I patted Rowdy and told him that everything was okay. I never lie to dogs. It was true in the sense that I didn't want Rowdy to do anything. Then I ran the beam of my flashlight over the damp ground under the shrubs and discovered one thing John Buckley had been doing there: When I picked up the empty whiskey bottle, its glass neck was still warm from his hands.

7

DURING MY MONDAY MORNING POSTPARTY CLEANUP, I destroyed Lee Miner's joyless redecoration of my tree. To rehang everything in happy Winter-family jumble, I had to keep stepping over Rowdy and Kimi, who'd prostrated themselves before the Christmas tree. They rolled onto their backs, tucked in their heavy-boned legs, and opened their great jaws to display twin grinning mouthfuls of lupine dentition. Let me tell you, if you've never seen a malamute holding that pose before a Christmas tree, you don't begin to know what silly means.

I got out the camera, snapped a lot of pictures, promised to mail them to *The Malamute Quarterly*, and thus dislodged Rowdy and Kimi so I could vacuum. Then I called Charity Wilson to check on Groucho. Rita had driven him to Haverhill on Sunday morning. I'd half expected her to return with him that evening and announce that she was canceling her trip, but, to my surprise, Charity had passed Rita's inspection. As Hope had suggested, Charity was going to keep Groucho in the house with her, and, according to Rita, the place was more or less a doggy bed-and-break-fast, a country inn. Groucho would sleep in his own cushioned wicker basket from home and eat the prescription food that Steve had ordered for him. Rita's main worry had been that he'd be left alone, but she was relieved to discover that Charity spent most of her time in the house. Rita had found Charity and her business somewhat eccentric, but, as I've mentioned, Rita is not a true dog person. Charity designed and made hand-knit sweaters and hand-sewn, custom-tailored raincoats and parkas for dogs. Eccentric? According to one estimate, Americans spend more than ten million dollars a year on dog clothes.

I'd reassured Rita. "As a matter of fact," I told her, "it so happens that Roald Amundsen's sailmaker made dog clothes. His name was Martin Ronne. He made the tent that Amundsen left at the South Pole, which must've been what let Scott know he'd lost the race. First to the Pole? Anyway, on Byrd's first expedition, Martin Ronne made jackets and booties for Igloo. Byrd's pet terrier? He was very famous. You know he had an incredible funeral? He was buried in a white casket. It was a whole big deal. It must've cost a fortune."

"That's disgusting," she said. "It's decadent."

"Yes, but the point is that if Amundsen's sailmaker could make dog clothes, so can Charity, and there's nothing weird about it."

After allaying Rita's doubts about Charity, I'd also reassured myself by calling Janet Switzer, Rowdy's breeder, whose kennels were in Bradford, part of Haverhill. "The place is no Club Med, if that's what you want to know," Janet said, "and she hasn't got a license, but it's clean enough, and she spends a lot of time with the dogs. She's all right."

Anyway, Rita had left Groucho there, and on Monday morning, I kept my promise to call and ask how he was. I also wanted to make sure that if anything went wrong, Charity would have the sense to yell for help.

"Well, he is one old, old dog, you know." Charity's voice gently warned me to face the inevitable.

"He sure is," I agreed. "How is he doing?"

"How he's doing is kind of hard to say. But if you want to know *what* he's doing, the answer is not much."

"That's pretty normal for him. Is he eating anything?"

"Picks at his food a little. He's not real interested in his dinner. Mostly, he just doesn't want to move from his little beddy unless I'm going to keep him right in my lap, so that's what I've been doing, keeping him warm."

"He does wake up, doesn't he?"

"Well, he opens his eyes. I wouldn't take any bets that he sees much, but, yeah, he opens his eyes, and he knows I'm here. He's a nice little fellow. He's just too old to want to get up and do much, but he knows I'm here, all right."

"Good," I said. "And, look, if you notice any change, call me. You have my number?"

She read it to me and promised to call if she needed help.

Then I did something that may strike you as odd and pointless: I went outside and stared at the ground under the lilacs almost as if I expected to find John Buckley crouched there on the ground. I didn't, of course. I found nothing but a few dead, packed-down weeds. After a few minutes I went back inside to start the research for my story about private dog trainers, the story that was going to focus on Dickie Brenner, maybe by name, maybe not, but at least on the Brenners of the dog world. My first step was to hear what Jackie Miner had to say about him. I wanted her account, but my plan was to present myself to Brenner as a prospective client. Jackie's description was supposed to help me decide whether to present him with one of my dogs as well. I wanted to watch Brenner with a dog, but not badly enough to inflict real abuse on one of mine, or any other, of course. Either Rowdy or Kimi would be easy to pass off as a trouble-maker—people are always ready to believe the worst of a malamute—and I never intended to turn either one over to

Brenner or any other trainer, but I needed to know whether to scrap that part of the plan altogether. Also, if I decided to take one my dogs to Brenner, I wanted to know what to expect.

Jackie invited me to stop in. Although I'd urged Steve to hire a second veterinarian and helped him to move to the little house in Belmont, I still found it disconcerting to ascend the stairs to his old apartment above the clinic and find Jackie Miner in residence. She welcomed me, gave me a cup of coffee, and settled me on Steve's couch, which she or Lee had covered with an unbleached natural-fiber handwoven throw, very Cambridge, and a collection of plaid pillows, very Scottie. The Miners had made quite a few other additions to Steve's spartan decor. The tiger maple end tables flanking the couch weren't Steve's, and he'd certainly never have bought the crystal lamps that sat on them. He pays very little attention to inanimate objects, but if he'd noticed the lamps, he'd have thought of them as something his mother would buy.

Because of Willie's real terrier character, I'd left my dogs at home. I want to stress that Willie did not actually bite my ankles. He didn't even nip at them. What he did was stare at them and ponder. He cocked his head, frisked around, barked, circled, surveyed, salivated, and restrained his impulses. I was glad. You know why terriers are called terriers? *Terra,* right? Earth. They were developed to go to ground after vermin, and although Scotties have been bred almost exclusively as show and companion dogs for over a century, they retain that instinct to go after, dig in, lock onto, and never be shaken off. Most Scotties are thus high-spirited, brave, strong, vibrant dogs, but don't get me wrong: Scotties, in general, aren't biters. Willie was a particular.

"Willie's taken quite a liking to you," Jackie said brightly. "He usually flies at people's ankles."

He'd quit yipping by then and stood foursquare, his black eyes gleaming and flashing at me.

"Really?" I said.

"Oh, yes. He's bitten quite a few people. Twelve, in fact. Well, he hasn't really bitten them. He's nipped them. But they don't like it."

"Oh."

"Visitors, usually, but people really don't like it, especially if they're not used to dogs." Her own dark eyes met Willie's. "And we aren't used to people who aren't used to dogs, are we?"

I interrupted their silent communion. "Was that the reason you took Willie to Dickie Brenner? To get him to, uh, calm down with visitors?"

"Oh, no, no," said Jackie, beaming at Willie. "The only problem is that we take our responsibilities a teeny bit too seriously, don't we? We have to learn that we can keep our teeth to ourselves. Can't we? And we must learn to be a good boy with other doggies. But nasty old Mr. Brenner did not like us at all, and we certainly returned the favor, didn't we?"

Is syntax contagious? I came very close to asking whether we had actually bitten Mr. Brenner, but I caught myself and asked only about Willie.

"Almost!" Jackie replied. "But mean old Mr. Brenner was a little too quick for us."

"What did he do?"

At last, she looked directly at me. "He picked Willie right up in the air and threw him! He threw him right to the ground, just like that."

"Didn't Willie bite him first?"

"Well, of course, he tried, but what good did it do him? Horrid Mr. Brenner was wearing leather gloves. Gauntlets! And he was very, very angry. He wanted me to let Willie loose, and if Willie went for his ankles, he was going to kick him and pick him up in the air and throw him down again!"

"And what happened then?" I asked.

"Well, we left, that's what happened then, and we never went back."

"I'm a little surprised Brenner told you what he was going to do," I said.

"Oh, that was only after Willie tried to teach him a good lesson," she said. "When we first got there, all he wanted me to do was leave Willie there, board him there, and you could tell he really didn't want me around at all. So I said that I was not interested in *that*. We were there for a consultation, period, and I was not leaving Willie, and that was that. So then I started telling him what the problem was, but it was more than obvious that he wasn't listening. And that's when I thought I'd better show him."

"So you, uh, let Willie loose?"

"Yes! And Willie did show him! And then we left, and we are certainly never, ever going back to him!" Black eyes glittering, Jackie held her head high. Willie looked on approvingly.

"Good. Look, there's one thing I don't understand. I heard this story about Brenner and Oscar Patterson? Someone told me that Brenner mistreated some dog, a dog that Patterson knew, a Clumber spaniel, and Patterson went and punched him in the jaw for it. Is that true?"

"Oh, Oscar did a lot more than that! He gave him two good black eyes!"

"So how did you end up taking Willie to him, after that?"

"Because it wasn't after. In fact, if you ask me, that was one of the reasons Oscar did it, because Oscar knew perfectly well what that horrid man did to Willie. I told him all about it. And then when those people brought in another dog! And he had ruined, totally ruined the poor dog's temperament. Well, that was too much for Oscar."

"Jackie, when did this stuff happen? When did you take Willie there?"

"Just a few months ago. October. The end of October."

"And when did Patterson and Brenner have this fist fight?"

"A few weeks later. Maybe two weeks. Not long at all."

"So all of this really just happened," I said. "I didn't know that. Could I ask you, uh . . . do you mind if I ask you how much Brenner charged?"

"Well, I can tell you what I paid him, and that was not one cent." Her eyes snapped. "And I'm perfectly happy to tell you what his bill was, because I could hardly believe that he had the gall to send it."

I probably gasped. For the amount Brenner had wanted for one consultation, I could have trained either or both of my dogs once a week for five months at the Cambridge Dog Training Club.

"And," Jackie continued, "Lee thought we ought to pay it! He said it would easier, that we'd avoid a big fuss if we just paid, but I plain outright refused. Willie could've been seriously injured! Were we going to pay for that? Not on your life, I said to Lee, and don't you dare pay it yourself, either, I told him, and he didn't."

Then we talked about the Monks of New Skete. I didn't know exactly how much they'd charge, but I knew they couldn't be cheap. Well, I thought, the Miners weren't paying any rent, they didn't have to worry about vet bills, and Jackie had at least picked good instructors this time. Also, having recently replaced my old scent-discrimination articles with an extravagant set from Paul's Obedience Shop, I was in no position to accuse anyone else of wasting money on a dog. Mostly, I wished the Monks good luck and hoped that Willie wouldn't bite one of them. As I drove home, I wondered whether a nipped Monk has to turn the other ankle.

8

WANT TO BECOME A PROFESSIONAL dog trainer? Presto! There you go. Don't bother getting certified by the Society of North American Dog Trainers. Don't waste your time putting dozens of obedience titles on dogs. Never trained a dog at all? Never even owned one? Well, that's all right. Just list yourself in the yellow pages, and put in a display ad, preferably one with a picture of a happy-looking dog. Also, be sure to offer everything: complete professional evaluation, obedience training, protection training, puppy training, behavioral consultation, and problem-solving services for any dog of any breed at any age in your home or our homier-than-home professional facilities. Individual lessons? Of course. Classes? Naturally. Residential programs? Make that a specialty. It's very lucrative.

Dick Brenner was listed in the NYNEX yellow pages and had a great big ad there, too. I recognized some of the other people listed under "Pet Training," including a couple of people who'd written dog books and one honest-to-God smart and helpful behavioral consultant who really did specialize in monster dogs. You want to know who wasn't listed? Vince Dragone wasn't there, and neither were Roz, Bess Stein, Tony Doucette, or any of the other first-rate trainers I knew. But wasn't the Cambridge Dog Training Club there? No. Neither was the New England Dog Training Club, Charles River, Concord, South Shore, or any other AKC-affiliated club. But competitive obedience is a sport, some people say, whereas the consultants are dog psychiatrists. Unless the dog is one of those rare fiends with a genuinely rotten temperament, I don't buy that distinction. If you'd never been sent to school and if no one had even bothered to show you what good behavior is, which would you need, education or psychiatry?

NYNEX didn't show Brenner's credentials, but it did give his phone number, and early Tuesday morning, I reached him. All the obedience titles I've put on dogs do not make me a professional dog trainer, but the B.A. in journalism I put on myself does make me a professional writer, and I don't trust secondary sources.

"My name is Holly Whitcomb. I found your name in the yellow pages," I informed Brenner. Whitcomb is my cousin Leah's last name. I borrowed it in case Brenner happened to subscribe to *Dog's Life* or one of the other magazines that publish my articles now and then. "I'm having some problems with my dog? And I thought maybe you could help?" I tried to sound like the kind of person I'm not, someone who'd have problems with a dog and expect someone to save her if she did.

Brenner spoke rapidly for a man with such a deep, full voice. "That's what we're here for," he said confidently.

I feigned a sigh of relief.

"Is this a crisis?" he asked eagerly. "Emergency situation? We can deal with that."

"Oh, no," I said. "Not at all. In fact, you might say, it's, uh, chronic? She's, uh, well, it's a little hard to take her for a walk? Because she pulls on the leash." I hate lying. It makes me feel guilty. "And also, she just won't come when I call her," I added. "Mostly, I just want her to come when she's called, and I want to be able to take her for a walk and not be dragged down the street."

"Well, that's easy enough," Brenner said. "It's simple. It's not difficult." He paused. "For a professional."

Not difficult? Sure. Instill the recall in a cooperative puppy during that chase-anything phase, then keeping practicing and rewarding him ever after, and don't forget to proof the exercise in a few million highly distracting situations, and you've got it made, a dog who invariably comes when he's called. Otherwise? Otherwise, Brenner was right. It's not difficult. It's a real bitch.

"Really?" I said. "Well, that's good news. This is a very beautiful dog we're talking about. She's a thoroughbred. She came from a very good pet shop, and she has papers and everything. One of her ancestors was an American Kennel Club grand champion."

Did you get all of that? Dogs are purebred, not thoroughbred, of course. Reputable breeders never, ever sell to pet shops, and any pet shop salesperson who tells you otherwise is just plain lying. The only truly *good* pet shops are equipment and supply stores that don't sell dogs at all. AKC papers tell you nothing, absolutely nothing, about the quality or even the health of the dog. Finally, there's no such thing as an AKC grand champion. That's a United Kennel Club title. I felt proud of myself: In only a few sentences, I'd managed to sound like a total ignoramus.

"Well," Brenner said, "you've hit it lucky. Right now is a very good time to get started."

"Oh, is there a class starting now?" I asked.

"Holly," he said, "I've got to tell you. What we're seeing here? The way the dog's pulling you down the street? Well, what we're seeing here, Holly, is the first little step, the first little peak of the iceberg."

"Really?" I tried to sound alarmed.

"You know, you'll find people who might disagree, and my opinion may be no better and no worse than anybody else's, but I'm convinced that if you don't latch onto a problem like this and get right to the root as soon as it rears its head, you're making a big mistake, and it's nothing you want to tackle yourself."

"Oh," I said.

"You know, right now, it might seem kind of complicated, because you're in over your head with this dog, but maybe it's not as complicated as you think."

"Maybe not," I said.

"So what you want to do, Holly, is, really, you want to wipe the slate clean. You have to understand that what the dog's doing is directly tied into what you're doing, and you don't have to be a rocket-ship scientist to figure out that once the dog's behavior's straightened out, it's going to unlock a whole new world for you. What you want to do is get a nice clean break, take your vacation, whatever, give us a couple of weeks, we can pick her up and deliver her back to you, and when you get back, we teach you a couple of simple commands, and you and the dog are two happy campers chugging off down the tracks."

"Actually," I said, "I'd been wondering about training her myself. . . . Or maybe somebody could show me what to do?"

"Well, of course, we can do that, but I've got to warn you, maybe eight times out ten, it's a waste of time."

I persisted, and we worked out a plan: I would take my dog to Brenner for a one-hour evaluation and consultation. After that, I hinted, I might decide to board my dog with him for two weeks. His fee for one hour would be exactly what he'd tried to charge Jackie.

As soon as I hung up, while I was congratulating myself on saving hundreds or even thousands of dollars a year by training with the club instead of going to an expensive private trainer—there *are* some good ones around here, including some who give classes—the phone rang. Charity Wilson was worried about Groucho. Should she call Rita? Or did I want to?

"No, don't call her," I said. "Let me hear about him first, and then we'll decide."

"I feel awful," she said. "I hate to bother you, but I just don't know. Maybe he gets like this sometimes. It's like he's half awake. But the thing that's got me most worried is, he's not eating, and if you ask me, that's a bad sign. Isn't it? You always know, don't you? If a dog puts away a good dinner, then there's not too much wrong with him?"

"Groucho doesn't have much of an appetite anymore," I said, "but he does eat. He hasn't eaten anything?"

"Not today," she said. "Not a thing. To tell you the truth, I'm not sure he even notices the food's there for him, and, like, yesterday? Well, he kind of picked at it, but today, I keep offering it to him, and he's not interested. And I'll tell you another thing. Sometimes, when I get a dog here, it takes him a day or two to get adjusted. For a day or two, he might go off his food, or act nervous, or not pay any attention to me, withdraw. But then, when he sizes me up and figures out I'm all right, he perks up, and lots of them, by the time the owners get back, I'll tell you, lots of them would just as soon stay."

"I think I'd better come up and take a look at him," I said. "I know him pretty well. If he's different, I'll be able to tell."

"Well, I hate to bother you, and if Dr. Patterson was still around, I wouldn't. He was the only one I could get who'd come and take a look, and if he knew that the dog wasn't mine, if it was a stray or something, not one of my boarders, half the time he wouldn't charge me, either."

I shouldn't have been surprised. Haverhill is on the New Hampshire border, as I already knew.

"I used him for years," Charity went on. "Look, you want me to take the little guy to someone else? I can try and get him to someone, if you want."

"No, don't," I said. "I can leave now. I'll be there in, what? Forty-five minutes? An hour at the outside. And if it looks serious, I'll bring him back with me."

And then? And then hope that I didn't have to call Rita. If Groucho died while she was away, she'd blame herself. Therapists are like that. Groucho was an old, old dog with a chronic liver problem. As Steve had explained to Rita a few dozen times, the condition wasn't painful, but it wasn't curable or predictable, either. Groucho could go on for a while with his usual vague old-dog symptoms—nothing specific except that yellow tinge in his eyes—or he could fail anytime.

As I kept warning Steve, that business about failing *any* time is the wrong thing to say to a therapist, because if there's one thing that therapists believe, it's that *any* time is not just any old time. Look at it this way: Einstein said that God does not play dice with the universe, right? According to Rita, God may not, but we do, and what's more, we play with loaded dice, and worse yet, we not only load them ourselves, but, a lot of the time, against ourselves, too. Thus therapy. Thus Rita.

9

Route 93 took me to 495, which follows the Merrimack River northeast through a valley dotted with famous birthplaces. Patrician Andover is the home of Phillips Andover Academy and the Raytheon Patriot missile plant, strategic-weapons establishments that mass-produce projectiles to precision-fire at their respective targets, namely, Ivy League admissions committees and enemy rockets. Beyond Andover lies plebeian Lawrence, which gave birth to the Bread and Roses strike and is now the whelping place of Blue Seal Feeds, dam of Gentry Premium Formula Dog Food. Next came Haverhill, ex-Shoe City, U.S.A., now down at the heels, setting of the Archie comics and birthplace of John Greenleaf Whittier, author of "Snowbound" ("The sun that bleak December day . . .") as well as that extant canine blizzard himself, my own Rowdy the Arctic Wonder Dog, who was back in Cambridge keeping Kimi company.

Actually, Rowdy was whelped in Bradford, on the south side of the river, and Charity lived north of the city, almost in New Hampshire. You know the area? From 495, I took that recently widened, rough-shouldered road lined with dozens of brave, seedy new business establishments that repair lawn ornaments, reglaze kitchen appliances, sell giant, splintery wooden salad bowls, and offer lots of other services and goods that nobody wants. The half-finished stores behind the raw parking lots, carless even at Christmastime, reminded me of home, except that many Maine by-the-road retailers are married partners who combine divergent interests in a single weirdly assorted but sometimes prosperous small business. Not far from my father's place in Owls Head, for instance, there's a farm with a dangling sign out front that advertises "Worms, Crawlers, Ceramics." In the summer, the same people also offer homemade bread, live bait, and raspberries, presumably not all layered together in sandwiches. In brief, the route to Charity's had the familiar look of a privately funded, courageously inventive antipoverty campaign.

On a narrow street off the main drag, I passed a sprawl of corrugated-metal machine shops and found Charity's house, a white near-Cape with a disfiguring front porch, a couple of misplaced dormers, and a scatter of whitewashed outbuildings: an ex-toolshed, a once-garage, a former guest cottage, and a low, slant-roofed hut originally built, I suspect, for pigs or sheep. The setup reminded me of the clusters of overnight cabins you still see now and then in coastal Maine, except that December draws too few tourists for most proprietors to bother with wreaths and red velvet bows like the ones that adorned Charity's guest house. Also, of course, her guests consisted entirely of a multitude of my own heavenly host: large and small, longhaired and shorthaired, young and old, fat and thin, yapping and silent dogs. The kennels were a little rough and small, but the runs were paved, and everything looked and smelled clean.

The barking summoned Charity from one of the outbuildings. She looked younger than Hope, maybe thirty-five, and suffered from the dry skin, ragged nails, and undone hair of a woman who grooms her dogs better than she grooms herself (and probably loves them more, too). The top button of her blue-flowered, round-collared blouse was fastened to the second buttonhole, and so forth on down the front. Her jeans were heavy-duty work denim and too big— not baggy, just big—but both knees had ripped anyway. She greeted me, then suddenly self-conscious, stooped to tie an undone lace on her mud-stained Nikes.

"Now you'll think I've been leaving Groucho all alone," said Charity as she hung an industrial-size pooper-scooper on a hook near the back door of the house. "But some of them don't like to soil their pens, like that little lady there." She pointed to one of the runs attached to the refurbished garage. A rather heavy, shepherdlike golden-yellow bitch watched us wide-eyed, evidently the one Hope had mentioned, the one she'd said looked like John's dog, Bear. "They aren't used to it," Charity continued, "and it's not fair, is it? A house pet doesn't want to dirty his own quarters. So I take them out, and then I've got to scoop up after them. I'd take her in the house with me, but I don't have the room, and I didn't want them pestering Groucho, not now. And, you know, I did tell Rita, he's not my only dog, and I do grooming, too, besides boarding and my sewing. Well, come in and see what you think."

Green and purple must have been that winter's colors in dog wear. Glazed cotton swatches of kelly and deep rose violet lay on the kitchen table. Most of the other surfaces were stacked with cheerful piles of miniature parkas and bright jackets. Groucho's pillow-lined wicker basket rested on the floor near the table; Charity must have been keeping him at her feet while she worked. As she'd said, he was asleep, his long, fragile, loose-skinned body slightly curled, his short legs limp, his head immobile. I knelt down and lightly held an ear and cheek to his chest. Wirehaired and longhaired dachshunds need grooming, but smooth dachshunds like Groucho, the shorthaired ones you're apt to see on the street, usually remain shiny and odorless. Except in unusual circumstances—a wallow in mud, an encounter with a skunk—they don't even need brushing and bathing. Now, though, Groucho had the musky, thick odor of an old, old dog. But he was still breathing.

"Groucho?" I whispered. "Groucho, wake up! Groucho?" He looked so weak that I was almost afraid to touch him again. I put a hand on his head and lightly stroked him. I raised my voice a little. "Groucho? Can you hear me?"

His heavy, yellow-tinged eyes slowly opened. Rita, I might add, had bought Groucho as a pet-quality dachshund. With his thickish hair and bowlegs, he'd never had the makings of a show dog, but his keen sight, acute hearing, and sharp sense of smell, plus his bold disposition, were exactly what's wanted in a small breed meant to hunt big adversaries. *Dachs hund.* Badger dog. Until chronic disease had dulled his perception, his effervescent red-brown eyes had been his best feature, and Groucho himself had been a vivacious little sparkler. Stuporous and probably sightless, his drooping eyes now stared blankly.

I got to my feet. "I'll take him," I told Charity. "He probably needs to be on intravenous something or other. At least they can get some food into him that way. He might pull out of it."

In the Bronco on the way back to Cambridge, through Lawrence, Andover, Tewksbury, Wilmington, and Woburn, I kept giving Groucho orders that he couldn't have obeyed even if Rita had ever civilized him. I didn't yell at him, of course. Like a beginning handler begging a pup not to get up on the long down, I pleaded softly. "Don't you dare die before Rita gets home! Just hang on, and we'll get you pumped full of medicine. You don't have to wake up, and you don't have to get healthy. You just have to stay alive. Got that?"

As we approached Boston on 93, I was tempted to head straight into the city and cut across to Angell Memorial, but we were closer to Cambridge than we were to South Huntington Avenue. Steve would be back from Minneapolis late that evening, but, in the meantime, if he trusted his practice to Lee Miner, I should respect that trust; the impulse to run to Angell felt disloyal. I squelched it.

Before long, I was glad I had. When I hustled Rita's little withered dog into the waiting room, Lorraine and Rhonda didn't ask who we were or demand my Visa or MasterCard. I didn't have to explain that this was an emergency. In fact, I'm not sure that any of us spoke a word. While Lorraine was pulling Groucho's chart, Rhonda held open the swinging door to the back of the clinic, then the door to an exam room, and waved me in. Almost as soon as I'd settled Groucho's bed on the exam table, Lee Miner appeared and checked both Groucho and his chart. For a few seconds, I was afraid Miner would dither around memorizing Groucho's medical history, but he scanned the record and examined the limp, dozing little dog pretty quickly. While Miner washed his hands, I told him that Groucho had refused food and water today and that he seemed much worse than I'd ever seen him before, almost comatose.

"Don't worry about him," Miner told me. "He'll be fine."

Then, although I felt that I should stay with Groucho, Miner took him away. I was standing in the exam room wondering whether to insist on special privileges when Lorraine came in. She has a sturdy, compact body and round everything, and she keeps her long, somewhat frizzy brown-gray hair clamped to the back of her neck in a big leather fastener. Even if she wore makeup, I suspect that her face would have a bare, scrubbed look.

"You okay?" she asked.

"No," I said. "Steve warned me this might happen. Rita knew, really. She knew that it could happen any time. And Steve keeps saying this liver thing is not painful."

"It really isn't, you know," said Lorraine. Her official title is veterinary technician, I think, but she's Steve's administrator, business manager, and chief clinical assistant. She worked for Dr. Draper before Steve took over the practice a few years ago, and she's had lots of clinical experience. Also, she does speedy, neat, legible ID tattoos on dogs and artistic ones on her friends, or so I've heard, but I think the people part is illegal, so don't pass that on.

"Lorraine," I said, "I have to call Rita. If she isn't here when—"

"Hey, give it a few hours," Lorraine said. "They can pull out of it sometimes. At least wait until you have something to tell her. Dr. Miner'll go over it with you."

She still called Steve "Dr. Delaney," too, and he called her "Lorraine." The inequity bothered only me, but the crisis with Groucho made me understand it. If a magical honorific could have magnified Miner's power over death, I'd've been happy to call him Dr. God.

"Lorraine, does he know what the hell he's doing?" I asked.

"Yes," she said. "He really does. Dr. Miner can be sort of a cold fish, but he loves animals, and he's got the patience of Job. He's really very thorough. He'll come and talk to you about him. He's pretty good at that. It may take him a while, though."

As Lorraine had predicted, Lee Miner was good about explaining Groucho's condition, not as good as Steve is at that kind of thing, of course, but not bad, and he was warmer and gentler than I'd expected. We both stood leaning against the counters in one of the back rooms of the clinic, a cabinet-lined cubbyhole where Steve, or perhaps I should say Lorraine, keeps instruments, cotton swabs, gauze, tape, boxes of latex exam gloves, disposable hypodermics, medications that don't require refrigeration, and other veterinary paraphernalia.

"But he *is* still alive," I said.

Lee nodded. "There are things we're doing. There's a medication we use, Lactulose, and antibiotics." He spoke with quiet, confident authority.

"He belongs to one of my best friends," I said. "She's out of town."

"Lorraine said."

"But I know she'd want you to do everything you can, if you're sure there's no pain."

"Of course." To my amazement, he moved next to me, put a bony arm around my shoulders, and gave a paternal squeeze.

10

I FELT GUILTY ABOUT LEAVING GROUCHO, but Lee Miner, Lorraine, Rhonda, and the rest of Steve's staff could do more for him than I could, and Rowdy and Kimi needed to be fed and taken out. They greeted the sound of the Bronco so enthusiastically that I had to shove against a hundred and sixty pounds of thrilled malamute to open the kitchen door. Malamutes, of course, are ungodly strong, and when two of them wiggle, dash around, bump against you, and scour you with their tongues, you can feel like a minisubcompact trapped on the conveyor belt of an outsize automatic car wash designed to lather moving vans. I staggered to my feet, held both arms straight out from my shoulders, braced myself, and said, "Dogs, up!" Well, I wish you could see this trick, which wasn't all that easy to teach. Rowdy learned immediately to rise gently and rest his forepaws on my left arm, but it took a while to convince Kimi to put her feet on my right arm and not to throw her weight on me or dig in her nails. Once she got it, though, the performance looked spectacular.

The dogs got a minute in my fenced yard, then raced each other back inside, where I tied Kimi at one end of the kitchen, Rowdy at the other, and gave Kimi a helping of Science Diet Maintenance. Rowdy, the would-be world's first gray-furred sumo wrestler, got a skimpy portion of Iams Light. Ten seconds later, I picked up the empty bowls and unleashed the dogs.

By the way, if you're worried, scared, or sad, does a fish care? And if you force your cat to go on long antidepressant walks, be honest: He hates it, doesn't he? And with a person, it always all depends. But a dog? Two Alaskan malamutes? On a cold December day? At the sight of my tattered navy blue Maine warden's parka and their Christmas-red leashes, Kimi and Rowdy were all smiles and prance, even when I told them about Groucho. In brief, late that afternoon when I should have been phoning everyone who'd ever known the missing Oscar Patterson, forcing myself on his pregnant common-law presumed widow, penning *Dog's Life*'s welcome to the Chinese crested, and otherwise earning our daily kibble, we went for a walk.

And that's how I happened to run into John Buckley. Rowdy, Kimi, and I were trotting down Huron Ave. in the direction of Steve's clinic, not to visit Groucho, but to be near him. Just after we'd crossed the Fresh Pond Parkway, I caught sight of John and Bear. They appeared suddenly, when it was too late for me to execute a swift about-turn and pretend I hadn't seen them. As it was, I decided that unless John brought up the Sunday night episode, I'd act as if it had never occurred. That kind of deception does not come easily to me, and I felt momentarily dizzy. But you understand, don't you? Well, if my lovely Kimi were *your* dog, you'd understand. Maybe you'd have done the same thing.

Even in the bleak winter dusk, the contrast between

John and his dog was sharp. Among other things, Bear hadn't been drinking and didn't seem morose. Don't get me wrong. As on the day he saved Kimi, John wasn't drunk; he'd been drinking a little.

John had on a dark warm-up jacket with a small, colorful, reassuring rectangular patch on the left breast. I always trust a person who wears L.L. Bean. "Sorry I didn't make it to your party," he said.

"That's okay. It was only an invitation. It wasn't a summons or anything."

"I'm not all that social a guy," he said.

I wanted to inform him that if he kept training Bear, that would change fast. Make it through basic obedience, join a club, start Novice work, enter a fun match or even a show-and-go, and you'll find that you've unwittingly completed the initiation rites of a unisex fraternity-sorority. Henceforth, your persistently gregarious brothers and sisters in caninity will unremittingly ask you to steward at shows, invite you to annual dinners, remind you of upcoming trials, call you to chat about dogs, and eventually draft you to serve as a board member. Creatures of the pack, we tolerate few lone wolves. No more shrubbery, no more hand-warmed bottles of cheap whiskey.

Bear, who was no lone wolf, was politely nosing Rowdy, who was returning his own friendly sniffs. Dog friends greet each other exactly the way people do, but scent replaces sound: Each dog finds out how the other is, where he's been, what he's been doing. They really can smell all of that, you know. Kimi, however, skipped the small talk to announce that she was toughest kid on the block. So she was a girl. Wanna make something of it? I'd recently watched her introduce herself to a male Great Pyrenees by chasing him, leaping on him, and pinning him to the ground. He must've outweighed her by more than fifty pounds, but he'd groveled in submission. Bear, though, took the one tactic that defeats her: When she circled him, then rose up and rested her chest on his back in a doomed effort to stand over him, his hackles didn't even rise. His tail moved neither up nor down, but held its sickle curve. He didn't display his teeth. His lips didn't twitch. In brief, this true gentleman refused to acknowledge that Kimi was no lady. Disappointed, she scrambled off him and, for once, minded her own business for the rest of the walk, which took all five of us around Fresh Pond, then back down Huron and around the corner to Appleton and home.

Maybe John somehow looked ready to hear about death. Maybe I simply needed to talk to someone who, regardless of anything else, obviously loved dogs. Possibly I hoped that in revealing myself to John, I would persuade him that it was unnecessary to lurk around outside. As we walked our dogs, I told him about Vinnie and how I feel about old dogs: They're messengers, my link to Vinnie and the others I've lost, including, foolish as this may sound, my mother, who is certainly wherever good dogs go, and if they weren't good when she arrived, they are now. If John found my confessions strange or silly, he had the grace not to say so. Then I told him about Rita and Groucho.

"He's the worst-acting dog I ever liked," I said. "It's not his fault. Rita would *not* do anything with him. Well, she did housebreak him, but he doesn't even understand *sit* or anything. So, when you consider Rita, he wasn't too bad, and, of course, lately, he hasn't been able to do anything, anyway. I mean, Rita takes good care of him, food, all his shots, that kind of thing, and since he's been sick, she's been taking him to Steve all the time, not that there's all that much he can do."

"Nice guy."

"Yeah, and a good vet, too. He'll be back tonight." Was that a warning? I'm not sure. I went on. "The new guy he's hired seems okay, I guess, and everyone there knows Groucho, so he'll get lots of attention, but . . . Shit. I should probably call Rita. The damn thing is, though, even if he makes it this time, he's not going to last much longer."

"Yeah. There you have the one bad thing about dogs."

"It's why I won't get a giant breed," I said. "Like Irish wolfhounds? I love them, but you're lucky if they live, what? Seven years? I can't go through that all the time. In fact, I can hardly make it through as it is. You know, if you hadn't been there . . ."

"Hey, forget it. Like I told you. I know what it's like. As a matter of fact, I went through it not all that long ago myself."

"I'm sorry," I said. "Hit by a car?"

"No, nothing like that. And the damn thing was, she was pregnant." He jerked his thumb at Bear. "His."

Do you have any idea how many healthy, friendly, unwanted dogs and cats are killed each year in this country in humane society shelters? About fifteen million. *Shelters?* God's arms, I guess. Even so, it seemed an inopportune time to deliver my usual spay-and-neuter lecture.

"That's awful," I said. "I'm really sorry."

He shrugged and looked away. "You sure this dachshund's in good hands? You don't want to, uh, go take a look at him? Keep an eye on him?"

"Maybe I should," I said. "I thought about it, but, for one thing, I'm half sure he wouldn't know I was there, and he does know the technicians and everyone. He's not in pain. It's not as if I could do anything." What? Watch him die. There was that, wasn't there?

"You trust this guy?"

"Lee? I guess so. Jesus, I hope so, because Steve's coming to Maine with me the day before Christmas, so if Groucho makes it till then, I'd better trust him. Why? Did you hear something about him?" I paused. "At dog training?"

If you don't do obedience, you might imagine that dogs constitute our exclusive topic of conversation. Not so. We also discuss judges, top handlers, other clubs' instructors, traveling dog experts, and local vets. I'd heard the latest on which judges never to show under, which top handlers ought to have their AKC privileges suspended, whose classes I ought to try, and whose seminars were worth the money. But vets? Except for having accidentally overheard what I assume was a facetious proposal on how to raise funds for German shepherd rescue—auctioning off a weekend with Steve Delaney—I hadn't been privy to the raw vet talk for a while, except for the usual complaints and debates about how much Angell charges. If human dogdom had started growling and whining about Dr. Miner, I wanted to know.

But John denied it and added, "Somebody said Delaney's good and doesn't charge too much. And they say he likes big dogs. You know a lot about this other guy?"

"Steve says he's got good credentials. I know his references were good. It was mostly one of Steve's assistants, Lorraine, who hired him, more than Steve. She pretty much does the administrative stuff. And I took Rowdy to him for ear mites, and it turned out I was wrong. It was one of those mixed bacterial things, not mites. I don't think he's crazy about big dogs, but lots of vets aren't, or at least they're nervous around the ones they don't know. And today, he seemed fine with Groucho. In fact, he was good, as far as I could tell. With Groucho. And he was sympathetic, too."

"Huh," John said.

"You sure you didn't hear something?"

"No, I swear."

"Would you say if you did?"

He laughed.

"He doesn't have a long-term contract," I said. "If people are unhappy . . . I mean, you wouldn't be getting him fired or anything. Is there something Steve ought to talk to him about?"

"Don't ask me," he said.

I took him literally and changed the subject. We were on Huron, near the corner of Reservoir. "We're almost

home," I said. "You want to come in? You want some coffee?" The best defense?

"Can't," he said, "but thanks. Okay if we walk you
there?"

We turned left onto Appleton and when we reached my
driveway, I opened the outside gate to the yard and hustled
in Rowdy and Kimi so I could say good-bye to Bear without
their help. By then, the dusk had turned to murky December darkness, and the floodlight over my back door didn't let
me see much of Bear except the tawny radiance of his thick
coat. In lieu of looking at Bear—or the barren lilacs—I
pulled off my gloves, gave Bear my palms to sniff, then, with
his permission, gently ran my hands over him. As you probably know, dog massage is trendy these days, especially something called TT.E.A.M., The Tellington-Jones Every Animal
Method, which is based on TTouches with your fingers and
hands. Alternatively, you can buy special pet-massage tools
with plastic teeth or rubber fingers. In any case, the dogs of
au courant owners are now getting systematically stroked
and rubbed, so if your dog has to settle for a tap on the head
and a few thumps on the back, he may justifiably feel
cheated.

Anyway, I didn't TTouch Bear or whip out a massage
brush, but aimlessly ran my hands over him and gently
worked my fingers into his coat from head to tail. His head
felt broad and a little rounded between the ears; his neck,
muscular; his ribs, well sprung. By the time I'd worked my
way to his tail, he'd let its sickle curve relax a bit, and I
stroked it very lightly and tentatively. Some dogs hate to
have anyone touch their hindquarters. Bear, though,
wagged his tail between my hands. Have you ever seen an X
ray of a dog's tail? Or an anatomical drawing of a dog's
skeleton? Well, if not, go find a cuddly, relaxed, long-tailed
dog, and check out his tail from base to tip. What you'll
notice is that the tail bones near the base, where it joins the
body, are large and that as you move toward the tip, the

subsequent bones become narrower and narrower. Like the tails of other dogs, Bear's started out wide at the base, but it didn't taper. Rather, it stayed wide for maybe four inches. Then it abruptly narrowed.

"What a strange tail he has!" I said. "Have you ever noticed this? It doesn't taper. It just suddenly gets narrow. Did something happen to him?"

John shook his head. "It's always been like that."

"Well, it's very unusual. When you touch him, you can't miss it." I looked at John, who was shuffling uncomfortably, eager to leave.

Hey, what were you doing lurking around under my lilacs? I wanted to ask. But I didn't want to accuse him of doing anything, especially something so silly and so weirdly menacing.

11

Last August, the Becker County Humane Society, an all-volunteer organization in northern Minnesota, helped the local sheriff to raid a puppy mill. If you swear never again to buy so much as a rawhide chew toy from a pet shop that sells dogs, I'll spare you the details except to say that the rescued dogs included a malamute mother and her litter of two-month-old puppies. One of the daughters found a good home in New England, and I'd been responsible for picking her up at Logan, all of which is a roundabout way of explaining that I'm an expert on Northwest flights from Minneapolis to Boston. I'd expected Steve to call and say he was taking the one that arrives at nine-thirty P.M., but, as it turned out, he not only caught the one that gets here at six o'clock, but sat next to one of his human clients, who gave him a ride to Cambridge. I suspect that even if I'd picked him up or if he'd taken a taxi, he'd still have gone directly to the clinic instead of going home first like a normal person.

Anyway, at seven forty-five, when I answered the

phone, I was surprised to hear Lorraine say brusquely, "Holly? Hold on. Steve for you." Then I got five minutes of an AM radio station playing the end of "Away in a Manger" and the beginning of "God Rest You Merry, Gentlemen." I've tried to convince Steve that, hey, this is Cambridge: The average client has had five to ten years of higher education, hence can presumably use an interlude of silence to solve the mind-body problem or decline irregular verbs in Aramaic, if it has any, while waiting to hear how little Simone and Jean Paul did in surgery. Failing that, I've argued, these people want Terry Gross, Beethoven, the BBC, or, in December, a tape of John Fahey or the Christmas Revels. But, as I've mentioned, Lorraine really runs things there.

The music cut off suddenly, and Steve said, "Holly, you there?"

"Yeah, hey—"

"I'm real sorry," he said. "He just slipped away. I'm real sorry. There was nothing anyone could've done. You want to give me Rita's number? Or you want to do it?"

If you love animals, people are always telling you that you should've been a vet. Come on! The first owner who asked me to euthanize a healthy pet would've got a swift injection of sodium pentobarbital himself. When devoted owners lost their pets, I'd have found it so hard to break the news that I'd have ended up searching the adoption wards of Angell and the Animal Rescue League for identical animals to substitute for the deceased. *("Yes, I've noticed, too. Fluffy's never been quite the same since, has she? Much friendlier and almost rejuvenated, isn't she? But we often see that happen, you know.")*

"Could you?" I said.

"Of course."

"No. No, it's really not fair. You have to do it all the time, and I . . . How do I tell her? Is there something . . . ?"

"Just tell her what happened. Look, I'll do it."

"No. Really, I can do it. Were you, uh, with him?"

"Yeah. In fact, I was holding him. I'd just got in. Tell her he didn't even wake up."

"I don't think she'd like that," I said. "She'd want him to be *aware*. That's very important to Rita. Not in pain, but awake. She wouldn't want him to just vanish. I think he opened his eyes and looked at you."

"Holly—"

"And you were sure that he knew what was happening. He took it all in. And he voluntarily decided to leave. You realized that he was making an active choice."

"This is crazy," Steve said. "Could you just tell her the truth? It isn't like he'd died in agony. He didn't feel anything. We did everything we could, and we lost him anyway, okay? You don't have to lie about it."

"I won't," I said. "I'll tell her the whole truth. From Groucho's point of view."

"For Christ's sake."

"Trust me," I said. "I know Rita, and what does it matter? I mean, he's gone, and she isn't, and God didn't make me a dog writer for nothing, so just don't contradict me, okay? It's a small gift, but it's what I've got, and I don't intend to waste it. And I won't lie. I'll tell her the emotional truth. She doesn't believe in historical truth, anyway. She believes in psychological truth. She's always talking about it."

"Jesus. Okay. Look, when you talk to her, ask her what she wants done."

It took me a second to understand. "Cremated," I said. "We talked about it."

"Are you sure?"

"Positive. We talked it over."

"Private?"

I didn't want to imagine the alternative. Public cremation? God! "What?"

"Does she want his ashes?"

"No, of course not. Actually, don't even mention it to her, because if you do, she'll keep them here and spend years in analysis trying to decide what to do with them, and, in the meantime, she won't get another dog because she hasn't come to terms with losing Groucho."

My pride in my craft compels me to admit that there was only one thing wrong with the death of Groucho: For obvious reasons, it wasn't publishable. Imagine, if you will, the death of Little Nell collaboratively rewritten by Jack London and Albert Camus, but with a male dachshund subbing for the girl, of course. Maybe I overdid it, though: Rita was so moved that she decided to come home to say goodbye.

"Rita," I said, "don't you think it would be better to remember him the way he was?"

"I don't want to . . . Is that what you thought? No, I don't think I want to do that. I mean, it's not as if . . . No. It's important for me to remember that that's not Groucho. It's only his body."

"That's right," I said.

"But I can't stay here now, anyway. I knew I shouldn't have come, because, you know, he did feel abandoned, and how could he not? I abandoned him. How was he supposed to feel?"

"Loved," I said. "And not a nuisance. When he was healthy, he liked to go places. He would not have wanted to keep you stuck at home because of him. And you didn't abandon him, Rita. He was very old and very sick. Until the last few minutes."

The part of her argument that made sense was that her family wouldn't understand her grief. Most people don't. According to Rita, Freud did. He apparently realized that our love for our dogs is the only unambivalent, unconflicted, entirely positive, perfectly pure feeling we ever have. Obviously, then, when your dog dies, you lose the one being that—even deep in the disgusting depths of your unconscious—you never wished dead. And then most people expect you to keep your dinner plans for the same night, enjoy your meal, show up at work the next day, and, in short, express about as much grief as you'd feel for the last house-fly you swatted. Rita said that she wasn't going to deny her loss by "falling into the old trap of socially sanctioned, familially induced dissociation" (can that be right?) and was coming back to Cambridge. She also announced that she was going to call Steve. Fortunately, I reached him first.

Rita arrived home late the next morning. When she tapped on my kitchen door, I still hadn't decided what to do with Rowdy and Kimi, whether to let them offer comfort or try to keep them out of sight. In the dogless month between the day Vinnie died and the evening Rowdy chose me as his companion animal, I'd found other people's dogs a source of comfort and pain. Sometimes I'd start to feel as if Vinnie had somehow been the only dog and that, in losing her, I'd had all dogs ripped away from me. Then Groucho would jump on me, or a free-range yellow Lab that used to live down the street would appear in my yard with a tennis ball in her mouth and beg me to toss it for her, or another dog would force its way into my loneliness and remind me that they hadn't all died, that, yes, I'd have another dog some day. Whenever the pain began to lose its edge, though, I'd be ambling through Harvard Square or waiting stuck in the traffic on Memorial Drive, and I'd see a golden retriever, any golden, not necessarily one that looked remotely like Vinnie. Tears would roll down my face, and I'd feel heart-sick and furious, especially if the dog happened to be with a woman, a woman I'd hate because she'd gotten to keep her golden, but mine had died.

The presence of two big dogs would've been tricky to disguise, and the second Rita walked into the kitchen, I was glad I hadn't hustled Rowdy and Kimi out to the yard or shut them in another room. Although Rita's coat was navy blue, a color that rivals black for displaying dog hair, she sank to the floor and threw her arms around Rowdy's neck. Kimi, slightly less huggable than Rowdy because she was incapable of holding still, nonetheless couldn't endure being left out; she poked her nose into Rita's face and shoved

Rowdy aside. Exactly how our species first came to domesticate the wolves that evolved into today's dogs is one of those moot questions that keep dog writers in business, but I'm positive that as I watched Rita and my dogs, I witnessed one basis of the complementary bond between people and *canidae:* Dogs like the taste of human tears, and people find comfort in having their faces licked. As it happens, Rowdy and Kimi also love moisturizer and foundation makeup, a preference that's clearly a recent product of deliberate selective breeding.

Or did they actually perceive her sadness and try to console her? I am supposed to understand dogs. I know nothing about them.

It seemed to me that the silent comfort of the dogs went beyond words, but either because she's a therapist or because she's not a real dog person, Rita needed to talk, and not to Rowdy and Kimi, either. Tea always feels more healing than coffee, so I made a big potful, let it steep, and filled two mugs Vinnie had won at matches when she was only a puppy.

"Vinnie won these," I said.

"I know," Rita said. "You've mentioned it."

"Would you rather have brandy or something?"

"Holly, it's what? Eleven-thirty in the morning?"

"It's what you're supposed to drink to buck yourself up, isn't it? If you don't want tea."

"Buck," she said. "What an odd word for you to choose."

"I didn't choose it. I just said it."

"It's your father's first name."

"No, it isn't," I said.

"Okay. It's what everyone calls him."

"Yes," I said. "So what?"

"Never mind. Anyway, I don't want to buck myself up, and I don't see how getting drunk before noon would do it, anyway."

"Sorry," I said. "I was only trying to help."

"Well, more denial won't do it." Her eyes were dry now, but red and tired. She rubbed at them. "It went on for so long, you know, that I started to let myself think it wouldn't ever end. It's ridiculous. What did I think? That he was going to live forever? On the way back, on the plane, I was looking at an old picture of him, and it hit me that I hadn't looked at it for a long time. If I had, I couldn't have kept on refusing to see what was happening. You've seen it for a long time, haven't you?"

"What? That he was old? Of course he was old. Rita, you knew that. And you also knew he was sick. But the truth is, he could've died last year, and he could've lived another year. Or more. It just wasn't predictable."

"Oh, yes, it was," she said.

"Rita, he did not die because you left him."

"He did, you know," she said. "That isn't why he got liver disease, but it's why he died now and not some other time."

"Possibly," I said. "But what were you supposed to do? Cancel your life?"

"Stay with him," she said quietly.

"Look, Rita. Maybe you know some word for it that I don't, but to anyone except you, it's fairly obvious that what you're doing is taking all your grief and turning it into guilt. You could have held him in your lap and never left the house, and one of these days, he would've been too sick to keep going. You did not kill him, no matter how it feels now. And he didn't die all alone. Steve was with him. I told you all about it. He didn't feel any pain. He didn't suffer."

"I know. I really do know that." She sighed.

"Rita, is there anything I can do to help? Do you want to take one of my dogs? For a day or two?"

"Thank you," she said, "but I don't think that would help."

"Is there anything that would? Anything I can do?"

"Well," she said, "this may sound stupid."

"Okay," I said.

"Actually, maybe it won't. To you."

"It probably won't," I said. "I've done a lot of mourning for dogs. Are you thinking about another one? Is that what it is?"

"God, no. Of course not. Not now."

"Well, it does help," I said. "It's the only thing that really does."

"Maybe sometime. But not now. He isn't a replaceable part, you know. He isn't some appliance that broke."

"Did I say that? Of course not. No dog you love is ever replaceable. You might not even want to get another dachshund. It might be better to get some breed totally different from Groucho."

"Holly, look. I am not ready to think about another dog. I am nowhere near ready, and I'm not going to be for a long time, okay? I have a lot of grief work to do first, which is what . . . This is going to sound silly, but I don't think it is. Anyway, it feels right."

"Good. What is it?"

"I can't just let him disappear. I leave, then I come back, and he's just gone? He's vanished? If I leave it like that, then basically, it's more denial. I can feel it. I half expect to walk upstairs and find him."

"It's always like that," I said. "Everybody goes through that."

"No," she said. "Or if you do, you need to do something about it, which is where rituals come in."

My voice was very soft. "Rita, do you want some kind of funeral for him? Because, if you do, I'm the last person to think that that's stupid, you know."

She started to sob, then reached into her purse, pulled out a tissue, and blew her nose. "I told Steve that I didn't want the ashes."

I nodded.

"And now I do. Do you think it's too late?"

"Probably not. I don't know. But, you know what? I'll find out. I'll ask Steve. I'll take care of it. Is there anything else . . . ?"

"Well, there is one thing. It's just something I've been wondering about."

"Yeah?"

"How did Steve know that Groucho was making a *decision?*"

"He's very intuitive about dogs," I said.

12

As soon as Rita went upstairs, I phoned Steve at the clinic.

"Look, this is very important," I said. "I know Rita said just routine final care, but now she's decided she needs Groucho's ashes, and if it's too late, don't tell her. Just give her *some* ashes."

"No," he said. "Anyway, it's not necessary. The body'll still be here."

"So you can. . . ."

"Yeah, we can do it. This's happened before."

"Steve?"

"Yeah?"

"Where *is* . . . ?" I should've known, but there are certain matters upon which no dog lover likes to dwell.

"In the freezer," he said matter-of-factly. "In a plastic bag. Lorraine's brother hasn't been here yet."

The company that employs Lorraine's brother—yes, indeed, nepotism—is called Perpetual Pet Care, and if the name strikes you as silly, you're clearly a newcomer to dogdom, otherwise known as the land of foolish euphemism. I mean, there actually exists a liquid worming product called Evict. Prefer pills? You can buy, I swear to God, Good Riddance.

"So you can ask him to, uh . . ." I said.

"We'll have to tag it," Steve said. "But it's okay. Don't worry about it. Owners change their minds now and then."

"So . . . ?"

"So if she wants private cremation, I need to find the right bag and put an ID tag on. That's all."

"They aren't . . . ?"

"They aren't clear plastic," he said.

"So somebody has to open—? Look, don't. It's not really necessary, is it? I mean, how's she going to know?"

"Hey, Holly, we'll take care of it. Don't let it bother you."

Then, as if to prove that the topic and task weren't really unappetizing, he suggested that we go out to dinner that night, and we did. To celebrate his return, we ate at Michela's, probably the only expensive restaurant in Cambridge worth the cost, which is more than Steve or I can afford. If we'd gone to one of the little Thai or Indian places, he might have told me about that business with Groucho. As it was, although Michela's is not pretentious, you still get the message that you should probably discuss something other than body bags and canine cadavers over the house-cured *bresaola* with caponata and roasted potatoes. Also, the tables aren't crowded together, but our neighbors might still have overheard, and if they had and then had lost their *pesce*, I wouldn't have blamed them and might even have joined them.

So, having said something vague like, "It's all taken care of," Steve told me the big news: Jackie Miner had left Lee.

"She took Willie, didn't she?" I said. It's one thing to walk out on a husband, but what kind of woman deserts her dog?

"I didn't think to ask," Steve said.

"You didn't *ask?*"

"Well, he wasn't the one who told me," Steve said. "And if he had—"

"Who did? Did she?"

"No. This was while I was gone. Lorraine told me."

Michela's bakes what is undoubtedly the best bread in Greater Boston. Steve tore off a piece of it, dunked it in the plate of olive oil you get there, and ate it. Does that sound disgusting? It isn't. He wasn't being uncouth, either. That's what you're supposed to do. In Cambridge, peasant is forever in.

He swallowed and said, "Lorraine says Lee told her he thinks Jackie's with Oscar Patterson."

"What?"

"Lorraine says that's what Lee said, and then he told her to forget it."

"I guess he doesn't know Lorraine very well yet."

Should you ever find yourself vetless in Cambridge with a dog that's contracted an embarrassing social disease, let me reassure you that you may safely go to Steve. Neither Lorraine nor Pete, the most talkative of the aides, ever violates the confidentiality of animal patients or human clients. Steve isn't a client, of course, and they apparently distinguish between me in my capacity as dog owner and the other, discussable me, so to speak.

"In this case, it doesn't make any difference," Steve said, "because Geri's got the same idea. Patterson's, uh, friend. It seems like she's been treating the whole thing like some kind of last fling, but now she thinks it's not so funny. She's coming down here to check it out."

"Really? Everyone was so sure. But how did she . . . ?"

"How'd she find out about Jackie? For all I know, Lorraine called her. Lorraine's the one who told me about it."

We talked about Lorraine, then about Jackie and Lee

Miner. I said nothing about John Buckley. When Steve turns
protective, he overreacts.

When you hear how I slept that night, don't blame the
food at Michela's. If you need to blame something or someone, blame Admiral Byrd. At about three A.M., I awoke from
one of those long, confused dreams that seem to have been
produced, directed, and cast by some maddened Cecil B. De
Mille. I was in Little America, Antarctica, and I was franti-
cally searching for a lost dog. The landscape was vast, white,
and semidark, but lurid images of green and blue castles
filled the sky. Burly figures in bulky, fur-trimmed parkas
wandered among shabby huts and drifted off on brief and
evidently futile treks. Admiral Byrd lounged in a doorway.
Although heavy fog and thick sheets of falling snow hid
most of the faces, I somehow knew that this was Byrd's first
expedition, but I wasn't surprised to recognize Oscar Patterson and Jackie Miner among the wanderers. The shriek
of the wind blended with human voices crying: "Gone!
Gone!" A man who looked like John wept for his lost dog. I
felt very cold.

Then I was fully awake but still cold, and the howling
hadn't stopped. Steve lay on his back with one knee bent
upward to form a sort of tent frame for the top sheet, blankets, and comforter. I was lying naked. The radiator in my
bedroom doesn't work very well. The temperature in the
room may have been as high as forty-five degrees. I climbed
into Steve's tent, fastened my chilled fingers around the
edges of the bedclothes, and yanked. Then I nestled up to
him, pressed my icy body against the hard heat of his, and
hoped that the dogs would shut up.

Even for a malamute, Rowdy had always singled himself out as a howler of feature-soloist caliber, but he and
Kimi rarely performed, and I have no idea what got them
going that night. They didn't like being locked out of the
bedroom, of course, but they were used to it, and it was
absolutely necessary, because the murmurs, cries, and odors
of human lovemaking drive them completely wild, and when

they get wild, they yowl, yip, and bay even more loudly than they were howling that night. Mostly, though, malamutes are people: Making love in their presence feels like some kind of perverse group sex. So maybe they'd heard a cruiser or an ambulance with some extraordinary lupine siren. Or maybe, in fact, they were singing a lament for Groucho.

Even if they weren't, I had to make them stop. In a way, it seemed a shame. Their voices were melodious, their tones happy, not at all mournful, but that's not how their calls would sound to Rita, whose apartment is, of course, directly above mine. The wood floor of the bedroom felt like permafrost under my bare feet, and even when I'd grabbed a robe from the closet, shoved my arms in the sleeves, and knotted the belt tightly around me, I was shaking. As soon as I opened the kitchen door, though, the dogs quit howling and ran over to me. I hated to set a precedent by rewarding them for the middle-of-the-night chorus, but what choice did I have? In a high cupboard over the sink was a collection of brand-new chew toys. I tore the heavy plastic wrapping off two Souper-size Nylabones, thrust them into the gaping but silent jaws of the dogs, and stumbled back to bed. As you've probably gathered, Steve can sleep through almost anything, but by that time, I was so desperately cold that I did a bad and inconsiderate thing: I eased my hands under him and wedged them between the small of his back and the warm bed underneath.

"Jesus Christ!" he hollered.

I removed my hands and slithered to my own, cold side of the bed. "I'm sorry," I said, still shaking. "I'm frozen, and I had a bad dream. You took all the covers, and the dogs were howling, and I dreamed I was in Antarctica."

His voice was low and bleary. "It's all right. Come back here. Give me your hands." He wrapped them in his and pulled me toward him, then under him. Is it possible that missionary women were simply the ones who had to get up with the dogs?

13

"IT WAS A TERRIBLE DREAM," I said over breakfast.

"Sounds awful," Steve said. "You were cold, and you heard the dogs." Rita says that on a psychological-mindedness scale running from zero to infinity, he would score zero.

"I like hearing the dogs, if they aren't bothering anyone. The bad part was Antarctica. And the lost dog. And the man crying. And that son of a bitch, Byrd."

"Hey, okay," he said soothingly.

In August of 1928, the dogs of Byrd's first expedition traveled by train from Wonalancet, New Hampshire, to Norfolk, Virginia, where they were loaded onto the Norwegian whaler *Sir James Ross Clark* for the voyage to New Zealand. In Dunedin, New Zealand, the dogs were transferred to the *City of New York* for the final leg of the trip to Antarctica. Ninety-seven dogs left Wonalancet, or maybe only ninety-five. No one seems to know for sure. At least four died on the way to Antarctica. No one kept count, but about twenty-six surviving pups were born in Little America, which makes about a hundred twenty-seven dogs, right? Some died in dogfights. Some froze to death. At least twenty-five were killed and fed to their teammates. Of the seventy-seven still alive at the end of the expedition, seventeen were shot, and only sixty taken on board the ship. Our national hero, Richard E. Byrd. Steve knows about all that.

"It's not okay," I said, reaching for a piece of toast and then tearing it up. "It's a nightmare. Hey, Steve? I just realized something. That crying man? You know who that was? The one who looked like John. That was Arthur Walden. And the lost dog was Chinook. That's what the dream was about. It was about looking for Chinook."

If this were the 1920s, I wouldn't have to explain who Chinook was, or Arthur Walden, either, because Chinook was the most famous dog in America, and Walden, his owner, was pretty famous, too. Walden wrote a popular book, *A Dog-Puncher in the Yukon,* and he and his Chinook dogs—the famous sire himself and a team of his offspring— won the first Eastern International Sled Dog Derby in 1922.

"Did they ever find him?" Steve asked.

I shook my head. "Chinook died in Antarctica. They never even found his body. That part of the dream was true, that he wandered away, and that they looked for him, but he was gone. And Walden never got over it, I guess, even though he had the other dogs, the rest of the team. He took a whole team of Chinooks, sixteen, I think, and probably there were more back here. But I guess it just tore his heart out when he lost that dog." Then I made the connection. "I have to call my father."

"Your father'll just get you more worked up," Steve said. "He's worse than you are about it."

"No, it's not about Byrd," I said.

Even so, I waited until Steve had left before I called my father. Their relationship is complicated. Buck raises wolf dogs, whereas Steve maintains that hybridizing wild and domestic animals is a big mistake. Steve is right, but Buck is my father. That's one complication. Another is this: Despite Buck's prejudice against veterinarians ("thieving charlatans"), every time Steve and I go to Owls Head, Buck wants Steve to examine the dogs, clean their teeth, immunize them against everything, and perform miscellaneous minor surgical operations. Buck's requests would be okay if he had only three or four dogs, but he has eighteen: seventeen hybrids and one golden retriever puppy. My parents raised goldens, but this is the first one Buck's had for a long time. Her name is Mandy, she looks like a stuffed toy come to life, and I hope she's a sign that Buck is finally coming to terms with my mother's death. It's been more than twelve years since Marissa died. Vinnie was her parting gift to me. If a golden retriever puppy could console me for the loss of either of them, I'd get one tomorrow.

Anyway, ten minutes after Steve left, I was saying to Buck, "So I have this vague memory about their tails. . . ."

Buck swore a lot about the deficiencies in my knowledge of God's Country, the beautiful State of Maine, home of the Perry Greene Kennels. He also cursed out Perry Greene and thus explained this gap in my expertise about my home state and Chinook dogs.

"And," my father bellowed, "the fellow maintained a monopoly! A monopoly on the breed! You know how Perry Greene billed himself? 'World's Only Breeder of Purebred Chinook Dogs.' And that's how he kept it. The only dogs that left there were males and spayed bitches, so he didn't get a lot of competition, did he?"

"Evidently not," I said.

"Nearly exterminated the breed. And God help you if you wanted to buy one."

"You had to spend the night there, right?"

"*I* didn't," he said defensively.

I corrected myself: "The potential owner. If Perry Greene didn't like you, you didn't get a dog. I heard that. Or I read it somewhere."

"No, no," Buck said scornfully. "It wasn't if *he* didn't like you. It was if the *dog* didn't like you! Or if he decided the dog didn't." I have heard Buck refuse to part with puppies on precisely the same grounds.

Do you ever have moments of sharp recognition about your parents? I don't mean flashes of insight into feelings or character, but swift, clear perceptions of simple facts that are probably obvious to everyone else. Perry Greene, I suddenly realized, had once refused to sell Buck a dog. Furthermore, Greene's explanation had been an intolerable insult: He'd said that the dog in question didn't like my father. I'm convinced that it happened. Buck, I am sure, agonizes over the possibility that, after all, Greene might have been right, that in this universe of Buck-loving canines, one dog just didn't take to him.

"So, look," I said, tactfully keeping this vision to myself, "about the tail—"

Buck does know more about dogs than I do, and he's always loved to pontificate about them, but ever since *Dog's Life* hired me, he's gotten worse than he was before. I'll spare you most of the lecture on the six principal features that distinguish Chinooks from all other dogs. Among them is the distinctive structure of the tail, which consists of a thick section that abruptly narrows about four inches from the base.

"Sixth," Buck finally said, "and you can't miss this one, their front teeth interlock. So the result is that you look into a Chinook's mouth, and what you see isn't like a dog's mouth at all. Looks just like a bear's. If you bother to look."

The accusation was fair enough: I hadn't examined Bear's teeth. Yes, Bear. Most of the other distinctive features weren't readily observable, either, but the general description fit perfectly: the beautiful, thick, tawny double coat, the size, the overall look of the dog. So how had I missed it? Oh, haven't I mentioned this? In 1966, the *Guinness Book of World Records* listed the Chinook as the world's rarest breed of dog. There were only about a hundred and twenty-five purebred Chinooks then. Later, the population dropped to about twelve breedable dogs, then rose again. I'd seen small pictures of Chinooks in atlases of rare breeds and faded old photos of the team Walden took to Little America, but there are hundreds of rare breeds. Although I'd've picked out a fila Brasileiro, a dogue de Bordeaux, or a Leonberger, I probably wouldn't have spotted a Fell terrier, a New Guinea singing dog, or a Nova Scotia duck tolling retriever, either, and I can't even pronounce Owczarek Nizinny, Owczarek Podhalanski, or Xoloitzcuintli, never mind recognize one. I still should have known Bear, though, especially because Rowdy and Kimi were Kotzebues, the strain of Alaskan malamute that originated at the Chinook Kennels. Arthur Walden didn't develop the malamute, of course. Either he sold the kennels in 1930 when he returned from Antarctica; or, according to some accounts, his wife sold them while he was still there. In any case, it's a poor excuse. The Chinook is a sled dog, too.

John Buckley's dog was a Chinook, and John was grieving for a bitch he'd lost, Bear's mate. Cliff Bourque owned what Jackie had called "some weird kind of sled dog," and Bourque had lost a bitch, too, the one that died the night Patterson vanished. A "weird" breed of sled dog? A rare breed. Not a malamute, not a Siberian, not a Samoyed. A Mackenzie River dog? So far as I knew, the breed was extinct. An American Eskimo dog? An Alaskan husky? Not exactly rare, not like a Chinook. Two men with unusual sled dogs who've lost two different bitches? Maybe. But the owner of a gorgeous Chinook who deliberately passes off this stellar rare-breed specimen as a shepherd mix? As a *mutt?* Well, in case you reside outside the land of purebred dogdom, let me welcome you to the shameless kingdom of brag, brag, brag. *Mutt* was John's word, not mine. *Mutt?* Are you kidding? Never. Never in purebred dogdom. Well, never without a good reason. And it seemed to me that John Buckley had a very good reason. So did Cliff Bourque, I thought. The same reason? More than that. The same man. But it was only a guess.

An hour after I'd finished talking to my father, Geri

Driscoll knocked on my front door and, as I discovered later, shook about half of the needles off the Yuletide swag I'd fastened there. My front door has a bell. She didn't use it. Have I ever told you that Vinnie could press doorbells? Golden retrievers have great aptitude for that trick. Vinnie, I might add, not only could announce our arrival in a civilized fashion, but often did.

Let me add that from the moment I first saw Geri Driscoll standing there on my front porch, I felt small. I also felt ashamed of my kennel clothes—a stained sweatshirt, ragged jeans, and running shoes with holes in the toes. In retrospect, though, I'm quite sure that Geri didn't notice what I had on. In fact, within an hour after she left, she'd probably have been unable to pick me out of a lineup.

"Holly Winter?" Geri didn't ask. She told me my name.

She was dressed entirely in black, and her skin was thick and creamy. Like Oscar Patterson, she had wavy dark hair, but hers fell to her shoulders, and, in all other respects, she and Patterson had obviously consisted of a dog of one breed and a bitch of another. Geri had a massive head, a wide, deep chest, prominent haunches, and sturdy, strong-boned arms and legs. Standing next to her, Patterson must've looked like her pet chihuahua.

I invited her in. Refusing my offer of coffee, she strode into the living room, seated herself in the center of my couch, and arranged her black draperies. She glanced briefly around at the fireplace, the Christmas tree, and the absence of furniture. She admired nothing and made no small talk. I should have brought in a kitchen chair for myself, but I made the mistake of sitting on the floor facing Geri. I felt about six inches tall.

Have I mentioned that Geri was beautiful? She had immobile features, a wide mouth, and dark eyes with long, thick lashes and overplucked brows. Her voice was like her skin, thick and creamy. "I read your column," she said, without adding what she thought of it.

"I didn't know you had a dog," I said eagerly.

"Died." I was about to offer condolences and ask what breed, but she firmly switched to the topic she apparently wanted to discuss. "Delaney says you're writing a story about us."

I realized that I was kneeling in a pose easily mistaken for a posture of worship. I shifted around, but didn't have the sense to stand up. "My editor asked me to write something." I understated Bonnie's insistence. "She wants a story about Oscar Patterson."

Although Geri looked only about my age, her presence made me feel not only undersized but juvenile. She wore a strong, musky perfume with an unnaturally ancient odor, and she reminded me of those prehistoric statues of faceless pagan earth mothers. I almost expected to see her features dissolve. If they had, her face would've expressed as much feeling as it did now.

"I don't have to write the story," I went on, "but my editor wants it, and if I don't do it, someone else probably will."

Her voice was strong, commanding rather than pleading, when she said, "Leave me out of it."

I'd never intended to do more than mention her, if that. "I can try," I said. I pulled my shoulders up high. Holly Winter, girl dog reporter. "Why don't you tell me what's going on, and I'll do my best with the story. You're probably better off with me than with—"

She interrupted me, but her question sounded almost casual. "You know what everyone's saying?" Her eyes showed a hint of pain.

"If someone disappears, people are going to talk about it," I said.

"The joke's gone far enough. I don't want to see it in print." Geri's expression was impossible to read, but her voice sounded false.

Even so, I don't like to be ordered around. "Could we get something straight?" I said. "I don't write a gossip column." One of my readers should have known that, it seemed to me. "And when I do articles, including articles about people, they aren't about gossip, either. Anyway, most of the talk is about this client, Cliff Bourque—the guy whose dog died that night."

She waved a hand in dismissal. "That's bullshit. I know Cliff Bourque."

Yes, I thought, *but I don't know you. And I'm not exactly getting to know you, either.* I looked up at her. "Then why did Bourque run away? I heard that as soon as the police started questioning him, he disappeared."

"I know Cliff," she repeated impatiently, as if her word should have been good enough the first time or as if I'd misunderstood her. "You can forget Cliff Bourque." She leaned back, raised her arms, and embraced the back of the couch.

As I've mentioned, I don't like being told what to do. "The other thing people are saying is that Oscar Patterson might've been, uh, interested in someone else," I said. Geri's face showed nothing, but I'll swear that if she'd had hackles, they would have risen. "I've heard people say that he might've run off with someone. So now that Jackie Miner's left Lee—"

Geri interrupted me, but she spoke languidly. "Let me tell you something. Oscar was a born sniffer, and he could smell a bitch in season from a mile away, and they could smell him." She removed her arms from the back of the couch, dropped her wide shoulders, lifted her chin, elongated her neck, and ran the long red nails of one hand lovingly down her throat. She had what's called a "dry" neck, no loose skin and no wrinkles. "Oscar might've been sniffing around, and Jackie might've been sniffing around. You can't blame her. You can bet she wasn't getting any at home. Myself, I like a male with all his organs intact."

Unless I'm assembling a chorus of male sopranos, I do, too, but I don't usually announce my preference to strangers. I thought about Jackie Miner and Oscar Patterson. Jackie irked me, but there was nothing crude or distant about her. And Jackie Miner and Oscar Patterson were both small, physically suited to one another, it seemed to me. Jackie wouldn't have made Patterson look—or feel?—like a lap dog.

As if Geri had read my mind, though, she added, "Oscar's always liked big women." She lowered her voice. "And, in case you wondered, I like small men. They try harder."

If Oscar Patterson had been a male malamute I was considering as a prospective stud for Kimi, I wouldn't have hesitated to ask whether he was an ardent male with all his organs intact. If I'd had any doubt, I'd have checked with my own eyes and hands. As it was, I felt embarrassed, more for Geri than for myself.

"Geri, you said something about how the joke had gone far enough. I don't understand the joke part."

"Let me tell you a story about Oscar." Geri fixed her huge dark eyes on the ceiling above my head. "This is something that happened when Lee Miner first got there. The poor little shit. You had to feel sorry for him. Lee'd hardly settled in when Oscar sent him out to one of the farms. Shit." She was staring with apparent pleasure at the overhead light fixture, which is too ugly to please anyone. "First of all," she went on, "if there's one thing a veterinarian's got to not mind, it's dirt. And on top of that, it turns out, Lee's scared to death he'll get kicked. So Oscar goes and sends him out to this farm." She paused, glanced toward me, and resumed her study of the ceiling. It's possible that she wasn't ignoring me or avoiding eye contact. Probably she was just performing a throat-beautification exercise, the secret of that dry neck. She continued: "What happens is, there's this bull. That's the animal Lee's supposed to look at. And the bull gives him a kick, and he ends up in the manure pile." She paused, lowered her head, and moved it slowly back and forth. Her beautiful mouth formed a wide, rich smile, and her eyes danced. "And, of course, the guy that owns the bull is standing right there." She chuckled.

"And he thinks it's the funniest thing he's ever seen in his life. Shit. And so the last thing he does is keep it to himself. Everyone up there knows about it." She looked vaguely in my direction.

"Well, it seems to me that you do have to feel sort of sorry for Lee," I said. "But, yeah, it happens. If you work with animals, you're going to get kicked and bitten and scratched, and they're going to make a fool of you. Lee Miner should've known that."

Geri leaned forward, toward me, and said in low, knowing tones, "But Oscar did. He knew when he sent Lee there. He knew the bull kicked, and he knew where the manure pile was. He knew everything." She narrowed her eyes and brought her hands together as if in prayer.

I wished she'd come right out and say she was pregnant. "So," I said, "this is, uh, a joke at your expense?" I waited for her to answer. When she didn't, I added, "Only the joke's gone far enough? Or too far, I guess, since Jackie left."

Geri raised her right hand, brought it to her mouth, stuck in her thumb, and sawed the thumb nail back and forth across her bottom teeth. "I don't enjoy being the one that ends up in the shit. I'm three months pregnant, and I've been through that other before. I'm not exactly wild about going through it again."

Geri seemed younger now and a little less like a statue. I still didn't like her, but I did feel sorry for her. She was pregnant, of course, but that was only part of it. Mostly, I pitied her because of how she explained her lover's disappearance: She assumed that Patterson had vanished as a way of doing something mean to her.

I finally got to my feet. I took a step forward, looked down at Geri, and asked, "Where do you think Oscar is?"

"You ever hear of a book called *On the Road?*" she said scornfully.

Of course I had. Jack Kerouac was born in Lowell,

which happens to be—what did I tell you?—on the Merrimack River. "Sure," I said. "Jack Kerouac. Oscar is, uh, on the road?"

"Shit," she said. I expected her to continue, but she said nothing and paid no attention to me. Instead, she began to buff the nails of her left hand with her right thumb.

I wanted to offer her some explanation of Patterson's disappearance that would have nothing to do with her. "Geri," I said, "Cliff Bourque *was* there that night. From what I've heard, he loved his dog. Isn't it possible that when the dog died, he really went berserk?"

Now that I was standing up, she was looking downward. She shook her head. "Cliff? He might've started blubbering, but when Oscar lost that bitch, he probably started blubbering, too. Then they both decided they needed a good stiff drink."

"And then?" I folded my arms and waited. Once again, she ignored me. I don't like the sense that in someone else's eyes and ears, I'm not there. Dogs pull that sudden-deafness ploy all the time, of course. *Rover, come!* Rover ambles away sniffing the ground. *ROVER, COME!* Rover continues to meander away, nose to the ground. Unfortunately, Geri didn't happen to be wearing a training collar attached to a long leash. I raised my voice and asked, "Geri, is Oscar's car gone?"

I must at last have sounded like a person who expects to be answered. "No," Geri said, "but that doesn't mean a damn thing. He probably borrowed one from one of the farmers, or more likely a truck."

"Would a farmer just . . . ?"

"Oscar does a lot of trading back and forth," she said. "If a guy owes him, and Oscar shows up and wants a truck? There must be twenty guys'd let him have one and keep their mouths shut. They all owe him." She sighed. Now she looked weighted down.

I moved toward her and took a seat at the end of the couch. I looked for redness in her eyes, enlarged pores, a white hair or two, any sign of imperfection, but even up close, she remained distantly beautiful. "Geri, if he's really playing a joke on you," I said, "it's not a very funny one."

She studied her hands, but her face gained some animation. "Well, if he's not back by New Year's," she said, "the joke's on him." She leaned back and rubbed her abdomen. "Would you believe he wants to deliver this kid himself? With his own hands?"

"Really?" I wasn't surprised, of course.

"Yeah, really," she said, mocking me. "But if he's not back by New Year's, the joke's on him. There won't be any kid to deliver." She gave a low, gloating chuckle and patted her belly. "You seen Jackie Miner lately?" she asked casually.

For a second I thought she was suggesting that Jackie, too, was pregnant. Then I realized that Geri had arrived at the real point of her visit. Before Jackie Miner vanished, Geri had thought that Patterson was letting her squirm and that he'd be back. Now, despite her protestations, she was convinced that he'd left her for Jackie.

"No," I said, "not since Monday. I haven't seen Jackie since she left Lee. I don't know where she is."

"I just wondered," Geri said. "She ever talk to you about Oscar?"

"She mentioned him," I said.

"Delaney must be some stud." Geri's expression was flat, her voice was matter-of-fact. "Jackie ever show any interest in him?"

"No," I said truthfully.

"In Oscar?"

"No," I said.

Geri must have realized that I knew nothing. As she rose to leave, I asked her about Cliff Bourque's dogs.

She confirmed my guess. "Chinooks, they're called," she said. "Chinook dogs."

As soon as Geri Driscoll left, I opened a window to let in air and to let out the musky scent of her perfume, and I brought Rowdy and Kimi in from the yard. For once, though, the dogs were no help at all. I didn't know exactly what to make of Geri, and even if Rowdy and Kimi had met her, they wouldn't have known, either.

I once had a friend who could have helped me to understand Geri. Her name was Elaine Walsh. She died not all that long ago. Maybe you've heard of her? She wrote books. She was a radical feminist. She owned Kimi before I did. Anyway, Elaine believed that all marriage is slavery, and she'd certainly have defended Geri's right to an abortion. She would have had a lot of other things to say about Geri, though. I wanted to ask Elaine why Geri assumed that Patterson's disappearance was a cruel joke he was perpetrating on her. Then I knew what Elaine would have answered: Because that had been Geri's experience of men. And why had Geri treated me as if I weren't really there? Because that's how Geri had been treated, Elaine would've said, like an object whose voice wasn't heard.

14

GERI DRISCOLL'S THEORY THAT PATTERSON was deliberately letting her squirm had the paradoxical effect of convincing me that he was dead. Patterson might have found the prospect of a family uncomfortably bourgeois, but I couldn't believe that he'd have risked losing the opportunity to deliver a human baby with his own hands. He'd known Geri for years; he'd have known that to take to the road was to run that risk.

But I cared more about Cliff Bourque—John Buckley—than I did about Oscar Patterson. I called Hope, who had temporary charge of the battered old wooden file box that contains the Cambridge Dog Training Club's current records. She checked the index cards for the beginners' class and found one for John Buckley. In place of an address, he'd written "Moving." If I'd had all day, maybe I'd have started to search the streets of Cambridge for my lone ranger, but I had an appointment late that same afternoon with that famous dog behavior consultant, Dick Brenner, and I intended to keep it.

New Hampshire information gave me Cliff Bourque's number. I dialed it. A woman answered. I told her my name, explained that I wrote for *Dog's Life,* and asked to speak to Cliff Bourque. He wasn't available, she said, but she liked my column. Could she help? I told her that I wanted to do a story about Chinook dogs. By then, I did.

You know anything about rare breeds? As has been demonstrated, I'm no expert, but I do understand what moves a breed from the faceless hell of nonrecognition to the heaven of acceptance by a major registry. In the words of the American Kennel Club, what's required is proof of fanciers' "substantial, sustained nationwide interest and activity in the breed." People, not dogs, right? Fair enough. Dogs already recognize themselves, and they admit the existence of their brethren, too. Anyway, for admission to the happy purgatory of the AKC's Miscellaneous class or for recognition by the United Kennel Club (no purgatory there, just damned or saved), you need a national breed club with a registry, as well as sires and dams to enter in the stud book. And you'd better promote the breed. For example, get it written up in *Dog's Life.* Thus Anneliese Bourque was delighted to hear from me. I didn't have to fish for an invitation, and although she must have been surprised that I not only accepted hers but said that I could arrive in an hour, she seemed pleased.

The Bourques lived not far over the New Hampshire border, but far enough north of Cambridge so that our previous night's rain had crystallized and fallen in a light dusting of snow that clung to the pines surrounding the lime-green fifties ranch, a tract house with no tract. Like all peace-loving kennel owners, the Bourques had no near neighbors. As if to create the illusion of suburbia, though, someone had installed an iron lamppost at the bottom of the long drive, where I parked the Bronco to prevent my traveling companion, Kimi, from clawing up the interior in a frantic determination to introduce herself to the Chinooks. As maybe you know and maybe you don't, I'm Kimi's third owner, but that's a long story. The point is that if she'd spent her puppyhood with me, she'd have had plenty of opportunities to socialize with other dogs. As it is, she's pretty good except when she finds herself staring through a window at a lot of strange dogs that she can see, hear, and smell only from a distance; the mystery of who they are drives her crazy. Her reliably horrible behavior in that situation was the reason I'd brought her with me: Kimi was going to be the monster dog I'd present to Brenner. His place would be directly on my route home from the Bourques', and I'd decided to bring Kimi with me instead of having to drive all the way back to Cambridge to get her.

I walked up the Bourques' driveway and approached the house. A shingle suspended by the door of a small addition read: "PINE TREE SALON," and a row of slats hanging from a post announced:

PINE TREE KENNELS

Purebred

Chinook Dogs

Yet another sign, this one nailed to a garage door, advertised, "PINE TREE ELECTRIC. SUPPLIES AND SERVICE." As I've mentioned, economic survival efforts in rural New England generate these oddly juxtaposed enterprises.

From the first of four immaculate chain-link runs attached to the garage, a smaller version of Bear barked softly and wagged his tail at me. His voice carried no menace.

"I'm here," he told me.

"Me, too," I answered. "Nice to meet you."

Kenneled next to him was a pretty, fine-boned bitch with a rich, tawny coat. The other two runs were empty. I rang the bell by the front door and studied the Bourques' wreath while I waited. It was much more elaborate than my plain swag of evergreen with its simple red bow. Wired into this wreath were real pine cones and a few dozen sprigs of artificial holly. Responsible people, I decided. Real holly is poisonous to dogs. Leaves, berries, everything. Talk about irony. I told you it was a bitch.

Anneliese Bourque must have been in her midthirties, and, in case you're one of *those* people, let me add that she looked nothing whatsoever like a Chinook. Her eyes were blue, her hair was shiny black, and she had lots of it. A gigantic mane of ringlets, either natural or credible, softened her thin oval face. Perhaps because Anneliese was very slim, everything she wore looked a little too big for her, as if bought with the expectation that she'd keep growing. Her round-collared white blouse had been starched and pressed, and the long skirt of her loose blue denim jumper covered the tops of highly polished, flat-heeled tan boots. She had delicate hands with short nails buffed to a high gloss. I admire anyone who manages to raise dogs without simultaneously lowering standards, but what I immediately liked most about Anneliese Bourque was the gentle way she spoke when she welcomed me in. Although her accent was definitely north of Boston rather than pure Southie, she greeted me as Miss *Wintah,* and then, at my insistence, switched to *Hawley.* Especially when she pronounced my first name, she sounded exactly like the best teacher I ever had, Miss Ginty—fifth grade, a collie fancier from Manchester, New Hampshire, who not only accepted ten separate reports on the same book but gave me an A on every one. (You're joking, right? *The Call of the Wild.*)

When I entered the Bourques' living room, I realized that Anneliese didn't merely observe Christmas, but really did it up. A sparsely branched tree held an extraordinary number of tiny blinking lights and plain round ornaments, glass globes up high, unbreakables on the lower limbs. A pristine white skirt masking the base of the tree displayed a collection of artfully wrapped packages; the Chinooks were either kennel dogs never allowed indoors or else paragons of non-leg-lifting and non-present-chewing. Mistletoe, also poisonous, of course, dangled safely above the archway to the kitchen. On every windowsill, a ceramic elf or two danced around, little reindeer pulled a sleigh, a Santa silently ho-hoed, or an electric candle awaited the dark. On a low table, a miniature forest of pine surrounded a tiny manger. Pink-cheeked plaster figures of Mary and Joseph smiled ambiguously down at an unnaturally red infant. Also admiring the baby were the usual Wise Men, donkeys, sheep, and shepherds, the latter unaccompanied by the multitude of china sheep dogs my mother always added as guardians of the flock and, in her theology, the true intended recipients of the good tidings of great joy. The room smelled of pine and coffee against a subdued chemical background of perms and beauty-shop color.

After I'd taken a seat on the couch and accepted some coffee, I asked, "So how did you get started with Chinooks?"

Perched primly on the edge of a vaguely modern but overstuffed chair, she said, "Cliff did. My husband." She settled back in the chair. "This was, like, seven years ago, he's walking down the street somewhere in Boston, and he sees a guy's got two of them. And Cliff says, 'Hey, Chinooks.' And the guy's surprised that Cliff knows what they are. So they get talking. And a couple of months after, Cliff buys a puppy, which is Karluk, he's out there. And we got married."

"Oh," I said. "How did he know? I mean, how'd he know they were Chinooks?"

"Well, once you know what they are, you can't miss them, and he knew one in, like, the strangest place to find a Chinook, when you think about it, which was Vietnam."

"Vietnam?"

"Yeah, it seems like a crazy place to send a Chinook. It was a crazy place to send anyone, if you ask me. It was a mascot, I guess. They've been used for a whole lot of things. Maybe that's something you want to write about? There's one that's been trained to be a helper to a handicapped person, and they're basically sled dogs, of course, but you can teach them to do anything. They're so smart, and they really want to please you. One time we saw one that'd been trained for obedience. Utility? And this dog was really amazing."

I nodded. You want to know how hard Utility is? One year not long ago, when there were about 11,000,000 AKC-registered dogs in the United States, the AKC awarded 785 U.D. titles. Even if you add in the dogs that already had their U.D.'s, the proportion of dogs who finish graduate school is minuscule. I haven't gathered the statistics, but there are probably more Ph.D.'s in Cambridge alone than there are U.D.'s in the entire country, which explains the mess we're in. Have I digressed?

Anneliese went on. "We'd never seen anything like it. We'd read about obedience and all, and we've got good dogs, but when we saw that? It was amazing. This was at the roundup last summer. You know about that?"

"Yes." A Chinook roundup is the equivalent of a national specialty, an annual show limited to one breed that draws entries from all over the country. She looked a little embarrassed when she used the term, as if a basically AKC specimen like me might find "roundup" silly. Silly? Hey, this is the world of doggie bagels, Happy Breath dental powder, and See Spot Go. Yes, it's a stain remover. We're used to dogs with polish on their nails and snoods on their heads who've been perfumed with Rodeo Drive cologne: Beverly Hills ("Giorgio type"), New York ("Chanel type"), Rio ("Obsession type"). We don't look twice at the ruffled britches on the hindquarters of a bitch in season. "Roundup" might sound silly? Not a chance.

"It's too bad you weren't there," Anneliese said. She pointed to one of the framed photos that rested amidst the greenery on top of the television. "That's from there." It showed a smiling, suntanned John Buckley kneeling down in a field with one arm around Bear and the other around a much smaller Chinook. "But there's still lots to write about anyway," she assured me. "And I have to tell you, everyone'll be glad to have you do it, because most people have never even heard of a Chinook, and they used to be famous. You know they almost became extinct?"

Chinooks could be registered with the American Rare Breed Association, and, mostly because of a long-ago AKC rebuff, Chinook owners were more interested in UKC than in AKC recognition. She gave me some reprints of old articles and a copy of the breed standard. Then I followed her through the kitchen and out the back door to the kennels. As Tolstoy remarked, more or less, all good kennels resemble one another; every bad kennel is bad in its own fashion. These were good: large paved runs giving access to shelter, spotless pails of fresh water, one dog per run, a really big fenced exercise area, and clear-eyed, tail-wagging, well-fed, carefully groomed dogs eagerly wiggling all over in expectation of love and attention.

The inhabitants of Pine Tree Chinooks consisted of the two I'd seen when I arrived—Anvik and Kaila, they were called—plus a half-grown puppy bitch named Taku, and Karluk, the foundation stud, who occupied the run of honor closest to the kitchen door. Those are pretty common names for malamutes, too. Why? Study the map of Alaska. Kasegeluk? Ouzinkie? Kwigillingok? Thus all the Anviks, Karluks, Kodiaks, and Kobuks. Four runs were empty, the two I'd seen earlier and two in the back. An empty dog run isn't a sad sight unless you know that the dog who left is gone forever.

Anneliese must have read my face. "We lost a bitch. And our big male isn't here right now."

I shifted my gaze from the dogs to her blue eyes. "Bear. Is that for Bering?"

"Yeah. It is. Did you hear about him?"

"I met him," I said. "With Cliff, only I didn't know his name. In Cambridge."

She understood. Her voice was angry. "Who are you?"

"I really am going to do this story," I said. "But, look. I

owe your husband a big favor. He saved one of my dogs. You can see her if you want. She's in the car. I have two mala-mutes. You read my column, right?"

She nodded.

"Then you know about them. You know how I feel about them. This one, Kimi, got loose. She ran into heavy traffic, and your husband went after her."

I told Anneliese most of the story: Kimi's rescue, dog training, Bear, his tail, the talk about Oscar Patterson, what I'd heard about his client and the dog that died, Geri's story, all of it.

"So," I concluded, "what's Cliff doing in Cambridge?"

"He actually went and took Bear to a dog training class?" She made a wry face, then smiled. "He's not half as crazy as he used to be, but he's pushing it again. Most of the time now, he's just crazy about dogs is all." She stopped smiling. "How much is he drinking?"

"Some," I said. "Not a lot." I rubbed my nose. It wasn't growing. Yet.

"Damn. You mind if we go back in?" She opened the latch on Karluk's run and whistled to him. He followed us. "It's kind of a long story."

15

I'M STILL NOT SURE WHY Anneliese trusted me. *Dog's Life?* My forthright manner? But she did. We sat in the kitchen this time, drinking too much coffee and patting Karluk, who was about seven, but so playful that he was almost puppy-ish. He was a good-looking dog, but his color was paler than Bear's, and he had one ear up and one ear down, like Walt Disney's Tramp. Bear's ears were both pricked. I wondered whether they'd gone up on their own or whether they'd been taped. Malamute breeders do that sometimes, anyway.

"Let me tell you about Cliff," Anneliese said, her hand resting lightly on the dog's head. "Like I said, he was in Vietnam, and what I know about that is two things. One was, like I said before, the Chinook. The other was that he lost a lot of buddies. Oh, and three: He came back a mess. I didn't meet him for a long time after that—I'm a lot younger—but he pretty much stayed a mess for a long time, except that he did get through a program and get his elec-trician's license, not that he worked a lot. He doesn't talk about Vietnam, but he'll talk about after, at least to me he will. So then a couple of things happened, which was the two of us." She smiled at Karluk and stroked his lopsided leathery ears. "But the Chinooks came first, before me. And that's pretty much the way it is."

I may have looked sympathetic. It's a response I've learned to feign whenever a nondoggy spouse complains that the dogs always come first.

"But that's okay," she said quickly. "It's more than okay. The dogs basically keep Cliff in one piece. Then my job is to keep him on track. But they're, I don't know, what got him over it? Not that it's totally gone or anything, but . . ."

"There's a Vietnam vet I heard about once," I said, "or maybe I saw him on TV. Anyway, what he does is study bears, in Yellowstone or some place like that. He spends his whole life out with a video camera. He photographs the bears, observes them. So that's his life. Is it anything like that?"

"Yeah. Actually, it's a lot like that. Except, partly it's the dogs, always having somebody other than himself to take care of, somebody he can totally trust. And these dogs, Chinooks, have got to be the sweetest dogs in the world, and they're so friendly. Nobody can stay isolated with a Chinook around. A Chinook really, really needs people. Don't get one if you're gone all day, because that'll practically kill a Chinook. But the other thing is that once Cliff got started with the Chinooks, he started talking to breeders. And then he'd go and visit them, to see their dogs. That's when he really got involved with the breed. And these weren't the kinds of people he'd been hanging out with before. You can't imagine how nice these people are. They're wonderful, most of them. Before that, most of the time, he was either by himself, or else he was with these people who were basically worse than nobody, if you ask me."

"So when did you . . . ?"

"Uh, Karluk was two. So it was five years ago." Thus

spoke a real, if recently converted, dog person. My father never forgets the date of my birth because he knows precisely when the preceding litters were whelped.

"So he was already . . . ?"

"Yeah. Sort of. He was at least speaking to people, and he wasn't drinking all that much because he'd mostly quit hanging around with those other people. And he was working some—he had to, because of the dogs—but it was more like, you know, odd jobs. But he was still living . . . Well, I won't tell you how he was living, except it was not like this. So, basically, what he needed at that point was somebody to get him organized."

"That doesn't always work, does it?" I asked tentatively.

"No," she said, "but, basically, he was ready, because . . . You know, it's like, not that it really happened, but in a way, it's like he got his buddies back. With Cliff, these are not just dogs. Not that they are with me, either, but, with Cliff, it's different."

"So the night Patterson—?"

"No. Yeah, I know maybe it sounds like that, but actually that's how I know Cliff didn't have anything to do with that."

"But if . . . ?"

"No." She shook her head emphatically and looked directly into my eyes. "Because he would never, ever have just left her body there. He'd have brought her back home, to bury her, here. Cliff loved Mattie. We both did. So one thing I'll swear on any Bible is that when that man got back here that night, he did not know she was dead. In fact, he still wasn't all that worried about her."

"Anneliese, what was wrong with Mattie?"

For the first time, she sounded bitter. "Good question. If you ask Cliff, he doesn't know. That's half of what's eating him now, you know. Like she's missing in action. He's had about as much of that as a person can take. That's what's killing him, you know. Like, did she die in pain? Was she all alone? And what *was* it?"

"Can you tell me what you do know? About what happened that night?"

"Sure, but it's not all that much." She paused and took a deep breath. "This was maybe, I don't know, one in the morning? And Cliff woke up. Yeah, I know everybody wakes up, but not like Cliff. First he'll start to moan and roll around, then . . . it's like when the nightmares start, he can wake himself up instead. And what he'll do then is get up and go and check on the dogs. So that's what he did. Bear and this guy here were in the bedroom with us, but Cliff went out to check on the others, not that there's ever anything wrong with them, but, basically, it gives him something to do, when he doesn't want to go back to sleep. So this time, though, Mattie was sort of gagging and trying to vomit. So he carried her into the house, and that's what woke me up. And I really panicked, because I'd just read this article about bloat, like that day, and one of the things you're supposed to watch for is when the dog does that and doesn't bring anything up. But Cliff was, like, sure that it wasn't bloat."

"Had she been—?"

"I know what you're going to ask, but, no, that's what Cliff said. She hadn't been drinking a lot of water, and there's no way she could've raided the food bags or anything like that. And the other thing was, I was afraid her stomach was swollen, and he said it looked exactly the same, but it really was hard to tell, because she was pregnant."

"That does make it hard to tell, I think. But retching without vomiting? When it's a big dog?"

"Yeah. That's what the vet said. I made Cliff call the vet. Dr. Miner. He said if a dog keeps doing that, you have to assume it's bloat, and he told Cliff to get her there right away, to the animal hospital, and he'd meet them there. And when Cliff left, he was like, 'Oh, this is mostly to calm you down. There's nothing that wrong with her, because if there was, she'd look a lot worse.' And that was true. She didn't look all that sick."

"Maybe with bloat, they don't always. I don't know. Anyway, and then? You stayed here."

"Right, because we thought, so if it isn't bloat, maybe they're all going to get it. Like something contagious? Or maybe they did eat something. So I stayed here."

"And did any of the others . . . ?"

"Not a thing. And I'm positive, because I brought them all in. I had all of them in the bedroom with me. I went back to bed, but I was still listening. And then when Cliff got back, we took a good look at all of them, and they were fine. They would be. I mean, bloat isn't contagious."

"And what did he say? About taking Mattie in."

"Just that Dr. Miner was there, and he said not to worry. They'd call, and Cliff could probably go pick her up the next day."

"One thing I've been wondering is, is there some reason why Cliff didn't stay there at the clinic? I mean, why he left and came home?"

"Mostly in case the other dogs had started with the same thing. If it'd been Dr. Patterson, maybe he would've. Dr. Patterson practically lets you move in. He doesn't exactly want you breathing down his neck when he's doing surgery or anything, but he'll let you take your dog home the same day, most of the time. And one of the things we like about him is that he doesn't just treat your dog. He'll explain what he's doing, and he'll teach you about it. The woman who's there now—she's the only one of them that's left—she'll do that, too. But with Dr. Miner, it was like, 'I'm the doctor, and you don't know anything, so get out of my way.'"

In presenting Lee Miner with my own misdiagnosis of Rowdy's ear infection, I'd invited the conclusion that I didn't know anything. But with Groucho? Although I'd been relieved to have Lee Miner, D.V.M., take charge, I'd felt brushed aside.

"But you called Dr. Miner?" I asked. "Not Dr. Patterson?"

"We would have, except Dr. Miner was the one the answering service got. It was his night. I guess we could've called Dr. Patterson or just gone and showed up at his door, but it didn't seem right, to go and wake him up. And we didn't like Dr. Miner a whole lot—he didn't exactly fit in around here—but there wasn't anything wrong with him. People laughed at him, 'cause he was kind of a sissy, but he was a good enough vet. And some people did like him. Like, one of my clients has this cat that got into a really bad fight with something, maybe a raccoon, and got all torn up. And Dr. Miner sewed it completely back together. She thought she was going to have to have it put to sleep, and now I guess you can hardly tell. So she thought he was great, and some other people did, too."

I nodded. It was easy to imagine Lee Miner spending hours on the cat, meticulously cleaning and suturing every wound and tear.

"Anyway," Anneliese continued, "Cliff wasn't exactly happy when he got back, and we were both kind of worried about the other dogs, just in case. But he did not know Mattie was dead. And he didn't expect her to die, either."

Her eyes filled with tears. We talked about losing dogs you love.

Eventually, I asked, "So when did you hear about Mattie?"

They'd learned the next day, when they'd also heard Miner's story about overhearing a fight between Cliff and Patterson.

"What do you make of that?" I asked.

The hollows beneath her cheekbones seemed to deepen. She looked directly into my eyes. "That it wasn't Cliff. It was some other guy. That's all. Because Dr. Miner never *saw* Cliff, you know. He just *heard* them—the man who was arguing with Dr. Patterson—when he was leaving. After Cliff left and came home, I guess, Dr. Patterson showed up, which is like him. You know their house is right there? The animal hospital is right on the road, and their house, his and Geri's, is back down a dirt road, so there's just a field between his house and the animal hospital. And he does have a tendency to sort of butt in."

"With Dr. Miner's patients?"

She smiled affectionately. "With everybody's, the woman, too, and the vet who was there before Dr. Miner. But he doesn't mean it like that. They're a lot younger than him. You can't blame him if he wants to make sure they're doing everything right."

"Oh." I envisioned Oscar Patterson charging in to play God, D.V.M., while Steve Delaney was working on an animal or explaining something to an owner. The picture that came to mind was of Steve stooping down to Patterson's level, scooping him up, and tossing him out the door.

"Which is one of the things I don't understand," Anneliese said. In spite of the masses of hair, her face seemed almost bony now, thin and tired. "When Dr. Patterson came and took over and told Dr. Miner to go home, he must've thought Mattie was okay or at least starting to get better. Otherwise, wouldn't he've told Dr. Miner to stay?"

"Hold on a second. What does Dr. Miner say? Does he say it was bloat?"

"Yeah, now he does, because that's what she died of, I guess, but he didn't know then. I mean, he didn't know yet, because Dr. Patterson came right over, right after Cliff left. He must've seen the lights on in the animal hospital, and then he came right over. And he told Dr. Miner to leave. And then when Dr. Miner was going out, that's when he heard yelling, which is what he thought was Cliff having a fight with Dr. Patterson. But it wasn't."

"So Lee Miner thought that Cliff had turned around and come right back?"

"Yeah. And, you see, everybody believes that—that it *was* Cliff he heard. Look, you asked me, right? Why didn't he stay with her? And the cops asked the same thing, when they came here the next day, and they've asked me again, and you can tell they don't believe me. And I can sort of understand it, because if you know Cliff and how he feels about the dogs, it'd make sense that after he left Mattie, he'd change his mind and go back."

"How sure are you that he didn't?"

"He didn't have time! I was here! He did not have time. And I explained about the other dogs, that it was mostly Cliff who thought she didn't have bloat, so it was mostly him who was worried that the other dogs might be sick. But you can tell they don't believe me, which is partly because of how it ended up. I mean, if the other dogs had got sick, too, and we'd had to take them all to the vet or get Dr. Patterson to come here, then there'd be some proof that, you know, Cliff really did feel like he had to come home. And with Mattie dead, it looks like he had a good reason to go back there. Only he didn't know, not then. Dr. Miner told him Mattie'd be okay and not to worry."

"Anneliese, what about cars? If Cliff went back, his car would have to have been there. Did Dr. Miner say that he saw Cliff's car?"

"No, but he wouldn't have, even if it was there. You haven't been there? Well, like I said, the animal hospital is right on the road, but the entrance and the parking lot we use are on the opposite side, next to the field. But where the people who work there park *is* on the road. There's like a little staff parking lot between the road and the building, and there's a back door there, for deliveries and stuff. So when Dr. Miner went out to his car, he used that door, and the only car he could've seen was his own."

I drew a mental map of the scene and studied it: the road, the staff parking lot, the animal hospital, then the clients' parking lot. I darkened the map; the events had taken place in the middle of the night. Even if Miner had glimpsed the clients' parking lot as he drove away, he'd probably have seen nothing more than the outline of an unidentifiable car, anyone's car. Anneliese's account made sense.

"So what do you think happened?" I asked.

"Somebody else showed up, and when Dr. Miner heard them yelling, he just assumed it was Cliff. And, you know Dr. Miner?"

"A little."

"Well, can you see him going to help Dr. Patterson?" She gave a quirky little smile. "If there was a fight? What he'd do was run away." She jerked her chin down once as if to say, *So there! That's what happened.*

"Even with Mattie there? If Dr. Patterson was fighting with whoever it was, he couldn't have been paying much attention to Mattie."

"Which is what happened, you see. That's mostly why she died. So, in a way, you could say that it was Dr. Miner's fault, for leaving her. But Cliff . . ."

"Is that why he's in Cambridge?"

"He thinks Dr. Miner *knows.* If you listen to Cliff, Dr. Miner wouldn't run out and leave her like that. We both think he wouldn't've run in and helped Dr. Patterson, but Cliff says he's lying. Dr. Miner knows what happened. And Cliff does have sort of a point. Dr. Miner was the one who saw her body."

"So you never—?"

"No, which is part of Cliff's problem right now. When Dr. Miner got to the animal hospital the next morning, she was dead. And, of course, he thought Dr. Patterson was home asleep. Anyway, he didn't really know us, so he had her body sent away to be cremated, which I guess is sort of the normal thing they do. Dr. Patterson would've known that Cliff would want to bury Mattie here. But how was Dr. Miner supposed to know? And besides, it's sort of against the law. Probably Dr. Miner would've thought he was committing a crime or something. He's kind of like that. Anyway, meanwhile, the cops keep asking questions about Dr.

Patterson, what happened, where he was, all that kind of thing. And, you know, I thought Cliff would go totally wild, about Mattie, but he didn't. He just got *so* quiet. So when the cops finally figured out that Dr. Patterson actually was gone, which took a while, and when they started leaning on Cliff, he just took Bear and left."

"So Cliff followed Miner to Cambridge?"

"That's not what he calls it," she said. "He calls it *tracking.*"

16

ACCORDING TO THE AMERICAN KENNEL CLUB, every obedience judge "must carry a mental picture of the theoretically perfect performance in each exercise and score each dog and handler against this visualized standard." *Mental picture.* An abstraction? Never. There is nothing abstract about a golden retriever, and make no mistake: The real standard is a golden. In developing that mental picture of the perfect golden, every judge also ends up with a photographic negative, the visual representation of monstrously rotten performance, this, too, embodied in the image of a particular breed. Again, make no mistake: The Alaskan malamute sets the real standard of ultimate disobedience.

All this is to say that it probably didn't matter which dog I presented to Dickie Brenner: An experienced obedience judge—something Brenner certainly wasn't—swiftly looks beyond the breed to the individual dog, but everyone else is ready to see *any* malamute as a monster. I'd chosen Kimi and taken her with me to the Bourques' mainly because I predicted that Brenner would have a few dozen barking dogs, and, as I've said, in that situation, I trusted Kimi to act worse than Rowdy would.

To guarantee naturalness in my own handling, I pulled in briefly at a shabby shopping mall located about five miles south of the Bourques' and maybe ten miles north of Brenner's. In the pet supply section of a sprawling, depressing discount department store, I found what I needed: A bad collar and a worse leash. The right collar for a malamute is rolled leather. The one I picked was flat and wide, the kind that ruins a thick double coat. It was studded with silly, undignified blue and orange costume jewels. A good training lead is strong and soft. Whether it's made of cotton webbing, nylon, or leather—the old-timers swear by leather —it folds easily and feels comfortable when you loop it neatly or just crumple it up in your hand. I tested one short, thick leash made of hard, scratchy braided plastic, but settled on the kind of chain leash that I'd always assumed to be good for one thing, namely, scraping the skin off your palms. Inadequately attached to the chain was a flimsy hard-leather handle designed to cut into your flesh and then fall off.

In the parking lot, I changed Kimi's attire, replacing her good collar with the piece of junk and hiding it, together with my good leash, under the front seat of the Bronco. I opened the thermos of water I'd brought for Kimi, filled her water bowl, and, as she drank, delivered a rousing preshow pep talk. Then we set off.

We reached Brenner's about twenty minutes later. He had quite a spread. A white sign with green lettering hung in front of a great big white farmhouse with neat, freshly painted green shutters. A gravel drive wound around the house to a long, low cinder-block structure reminiscent of a prefab barn but with row after row of chain-link dog runs along the sides. There were at least sixty runs, perhaps more. I didn't count. The setup reminded me so much of a modern, professional dairy operation that I half expected to see someone attaching a milking machine to one of the dogs. Even with that detail missing, the effect remained professional. Despite the pervasive, damp, dirty gray of New England in December, when the lifeless brown earth reflects the mucky slate sky, the paint looked dead white; the gravel, newly raked.

I deliberately parked as close as possible to one of the rows of runs, thus offering Kimi the stimulating sight and sound of an entirely black male German shepherd dog in ardent defense of his territory. At a guess, he stood thirty inches high, four to six inches above the standard. German shepherd dogs, GSDs, are supposed to be longer than they are tall—the ideal ratio of length to height is ten to eight and a half—and this one's proportions weren't bad. Oh, and in case that all-one-color rings a bell, it's white shepherds that can't be shown in breed. All black is fine. Attempting to bite the judge, though, is definitely disqualifying. I was glad that I didn't have to examine this big guy, but Kimi was growling, scraping, and clawing for the chance.

While I was debating whether the hapless Holly Whitcomb should leave her dog in the car to shred the interior (would *Dog's Life* pay for the repairs?) or whether a bona fide know-nothing would enter by malamute power, a man who turned out to be Brenner appeared through one of the doors to the building.

His command to the shepherd was loud enough to warrant a substantial penalty in the ring: "Sultan, down!"

The big dog hit the ground, quit barking, and stared at the man.

"Place!" the man shouted.

The dog slunk through a low door into the building. Obedience? Tyranny. Steve's shepherd bitch, India, obeyed as quickly, but, when she did, her eyes radiated loyalty and self-confidence, not fear.

Nonetheless, I forced my face into an expression that said, "Wow! Just look at that!" I flashed a nervous smile of helpless admiration and edged my way out of the car as if expecting Kimi to leap ahead of me. Just before I shut the door, I softly cleared my throat, and Kimi, who'd been un-cooperatively quiet since Sultan's disappearance, responded on cue with the throaty roar that usually translated as her polite request for what dogdom euphemistically calls "exercise." "Growl on Command" is an easy trick, no harder than "Speak."

"You must be Mr. Brenner," I simpered. "That was really amazing, the way that dog did exactly what you said."

"That's what we do here." He shrugged—Aw, shucks, ma'am, it ain't nothing—but his strange build spoiled the effect. As I've mentioned, proportion is important in the GSD, and it was one of Brenner's most striking characteristics, too. In his case, though, the significant ratio was width to depth. As befit the pastoral setting, he was built like the door of a low barn: short, broad, and almost flat, as if he'd started out round and bulky but had been sat on by a genetically engineered mammoth cow and been permanently squished. Also, he was either naturally hairless, a gigantic Chinese crested, or else U.S. Marine bald. He had opaque pale-blue eyes.

After verifying that I was, indeed, Holly Whitcomb, he offered me his pudgy right hand, and I took it briefly. Then, without even asking to look at Kimi, who remained in the Bronco, he led me indoors to a small office paneled in knotty pine and plastered with framed photographs of German shepherds interspersed with important-looking certificates purportedly awarded by institutions of canine this-and-that. I'd never heard of any of them, which is not to say that they didn't exist. Some, I suspected, were diploma factories offering mail-order dog training. About a third of the floor space in the office was occupied by a long, wide fake-walnut desk. Quite unnecessarily, it seemed to me, a sheet of glass protected the top of the desk. What harm can come to wood-grained plastic? And even if it does? A throne-shaped pseudoleather black chair with a high back and broad arms sat behind the desk, and on the wall above hung a set of those shelves that kids make in junior-high shop classes. The wood was cheap pine, but at least it was real, and someone had made a laudable effort to cover it up by layering on at least ten thick coats of high-gloss polyurethane. On the shelves, like brand-new gilded tenpins arranged on the lanes of a virgin bowling alley, stood a display of ornate trophies. I was curious to know where they'd come from. Although I never got a close look, my bet is that Brenner acquired them all at the same place, and not an obedience trial, either, but a trophy shop.

Brenner enthroned himself behind the desk. I plunked down on one of the simple, hard wooden chairs facing the desk and said, "I really don't know what to do about Juneau."

"Well," he assured me, "you've come to the right place. There's a lot of people out there that'll tell you they're experts, you know, but just look around." His hand swept over the display. "And, you know, Holly, you want to ask yourself something, and you want to take your time and give yourself an honest answer. Because there's no sense trying to fool yourself, is there?"

"No. Of course not."

"Well, then," he said happily, "what you want to ask yourself now, Holly, is you want to ask yourself this. Ask yourself, 'Have I honestly got the hours and hours every single day of the week, week after week, that it's gonna take me to train this dog?' Holly, do you have all those extra hours?"

"No," I said. "Actually, I don't have a lot of free time."

"Well, then, you see? You've answered your own question, haven't you? Much as you hate to admit it to yourself, you don't have the time it takes to train a dog."

I wondered whether he had ever sold something door to door, vacuum cleaners or maybe knives that never need sharpening; or whether he'd ever demonstrated multifunction kitchen devices at home shows and country fairs, magical chopper-shredder-slicers that really, really work.

"I guess not," I conceded.

May I digress? Amy Ammen is a legendary young trainer and handler who's now up to three O.T.Ch. dogs, pronounced "otch", Obedience Trial Champions, and not golden retrievers, either: a flat-coat, a Japanese chin, and—get this—an American Staffordshire terrier, yes, an O.T.Ch. AmStaff. For those O.T.Ch. results, Amy Ammen trains a dog on a schedule of twenty minutes three to five times a week, less time each week than most of us spend blow-drying our hair. No time to train the dog? Amy Ammen's real achievement has been to ruin that heretofore perfect excuse. She knows how, of course. Brenner got to that part next.

"And maybe you want to think of it this way, Holly," he said sympathetically. "You need your appendix out, okay?" The happy expression on his pudgy face suggested that acute appendicitis was a delightful condition for which I was probably longing at that very moment. He went on: "And, sure, maybe you know that's what's causing this pain in your belly." He punched his fist into his gut. "And, sure, you know it's gotta come out, okay? But even if you've got all the time in world, you aren't going to do it yourself, are you?" He nearly rose from the chair, stared directly at me, and pointed an accusing finger toward what I assume was supposed to be my inflamed appendix.

I smiled, crossed my legs, and said, "Hardly."

Brenner smiled as if trying to convince me that I'd said something clever and surprising. Then he wrinkled his brow and, with a slow, solemn nod of his head, said, "And I know it might not hit you straight off as the same thing, but when you get right down to it, when you get to the heart of the matter and yank it up by its roots and take a good, hard look at it, it *is* the same thing, and I'm going to tell you why: You want it done right, and you want it done painlessly, you go to a *professional*." He sank back in the chair and waited.

I tried to smile appreciatively.

"So what you want to do is," he confided, "you want to give us a couple of weeks to work with her, and, then, before you practically even know it, you've got a fully trained dog." He gave me a few seconds to contemplate that happy prospect, then went on. "We spend a couple of minutes with you, we show you a couple of easy commands, and that's all there is to it. You don't even have to come all the way back here. We deliver her right to your own door. It'll be just like getting a brand-new dog."

"You can really get her to come when she's called?" I asked.

"Like a shot," he promised. "Piece of cake." He stood up. "Let me show you something."

I was hoping to get a close look at the kennels from indoors, but, according to Brenner, strangers upset the dogs' routine. He had me wait in a large bare room while he got Sultan, who turned out to be what's called a "robot," a dog that works with more precision than joy, and not even a very good robot. Brenner dropped him a few times, and, each time, Sultan hit the floor promptly. Brenner also had Sultan retrieve, first a handkerchief, then a glove.

"Wow!" I gushed. *Big deal,* I thought. On command only, of course, Vinnie would answer the phone for me by picking up the receiver and depositing it politely in my hand. Rowdy, for God's sake, could retrieve handkerchiefs and gloves.

The real test of an obedience dog, of course, the exercise that breaks a tie in any obedience trial, is off-leash heeling, which isn't a test of the dog at all, but the ultimate evidence of teamwork. Yes, the dog never forges, never lags, never heels wide, never crowds, but so natural and so apparently effortless is his perfection that even the astute observer is temporarily persuaded to forget that such faults exist; and to the confident handler, they are evidently unknown. Never so much as sneaking a glance at the dog, the handler stands tall and straight, head high; smoothly follows the judge's orders; glides into a brisk walk, a fast pace, a slow pace; halts; turns right and left; makes an about-turn; and, all the while, moves and stops as unhesitatingly as if that perfect score were preordained. Flawless off-leash heeling is one of the most beautiful sights in dogdom.

One of the ugliest is the mockery that results when a self-aggrandizing handler mistakes terror-driven outward compliance for the joyful half of the relationship that we foolishly call "dog obedience." Ordered to heel, Sultan slunk; when Brenner stepped forward, the dog did, too; whenever the man halted, the dog sat. In that sense only, the dog heeled, and heeled quite well. I acted impressed and said how good the dog was. I hoped that Sultan was listening. He might never have heard the word *good* before, but he'd understand it, anyway. All dogs do.

Brenner saved the highlight of Sultan's performance for last. With no warning to me, Brenner gave the dog some signal that I missed, and the shepherd crouched low, bared his teeth, unleashed a monstrous and terrifying combination of growls and roars, and twisted his face into a mask of menace. Just as suddenly, on signal, the dog quit, and I started breathing again. I was half sorry I'd ever taught Kimi or any other dog that harmless warning growl. I was glad that I'd never trained beyond it.

"We can teach Juneau that, too," Brenner offered. "Course, it takes a little more time."

Finally, for the first time, he asked to see my dog. While he returned Sultan to his run, I went out to get Kimi.

"This is going to be strange, and it might get scary," I warned her as I opened the tailgate and snapped on the chain leash. "And I know it's a lot to ask. But if I don't see for myself, I can't write about it very well, and if I don't write about it, this crazy son of a bitch is going to keep on duping people into leaving their dogs here. And I know you can handle it. I have perfect confidence in you." I stroked Kimi's face. Direct eye contact makes some dogs uncomfortable. She met my gaze. I know I'm biased, but I'll swear that the Alaskan malamute is the strongest, sweetest dog on earth, iron and honey.

To protect my hands in case I needed to grip the leash, I grabbed a pair of leather gloves from the front seat and pulled them on. Then I let Kimi move ahead of me to the barnlike building and deliberately trailed after her. Once we were inside, the scent of all the other dogs keyed Kimi up. When Brenner appeared through a door to the kennel area, I nervously said, "Now be a good girl. Sit down, Juneau?"

The dog's name, preferably her own, comes first, of course. Besides, even a golden retriever, for God's sake, won't obey a question, and did I want Juneau to sit or to lie down? Except to pull happily toward the kennel door, Kimi ignored me.

"It isn't time to play with other dogs now," I said feebly. Then, still fighting the temptation to grab Kimi, beat it back to Cambridge, and settle for Jackie Miner's story of how Brenner had treated Willie, I told him that I was sure I didn't have the money to have him train Juneau for me. But I *did* need help. Couldn't he give us just one lesson? He agreed. It galled me to pay cash, but the name printed on my checks is my own.

A good instructor occasionally borrows a dog to demonstrate something, but a genuine expert, if forced to work with only one half of the dog-handler team, will choose you, not your dog. Dogs learn fast. Real pros enjoy a challenge. Brenner led us back into the big empty room, pulled a standard six-foot leather leash and an ordinary metal choke collar from his pocket, and slipped it over Kimi's head. He snapped on the leather leash, removed that stupid flat collar and the chain leash, and handed them to me. I hadn't expected him to teach like an expert, of course, but I was so inexperienced with really bad instructors that I'd thought I'd be the person at Kimi's side. She kept her soft, intelligent eyes on me. More quickly than I'd expected, Brenner stepped to heel position on her right side, and I knew that the second she heard the word *heel,* she'd blow our cover.

Brenner was watching Kimi, not me. I cleared my throat and, catching her eye, raised my arm slightly and mouthed, "Up!" She growled and rose.

Over the years, I'd heard a lot of stories about barbaric methods employed and recommended by a few high-priced private trainers: If the dog jumps on you, slam your foot on his hind feet. If he barks and growls, squirt ammonia in his eyes. Ammonia! Jesus. If he challenges you, lift him up in the air and hurl him to the ground. Only now did I realize that I'd never quite believed the stories. I'd expected Brenner to act, but not to overreact so strongly and certainly not so quickly. With one sharp upward yank on the leather leash, he started to string up my dog.

You know what that means? It's also called "hanging." The choke collar is the noose, the leash is the rope, and the human arm is the gallows. Is it ever okay to string up a dog? Maybe, if it's the only way to break up a dog fight or if it's a last-resort effort to save a dog's life by convincing him that biting people is absolutely taboo. Desperate? A pinch collar looks like an instrument of torture, a series of linked prongs, but it won't damage the dog's larynx.

I wasn't packing a pinch collar, but those cheesy chain leashes turn out to have a use after all, at least if you're wearing heavy leather gloves. Before Kimi's front legs left the floor, I had a solid grip on the length of chain. As I've mentioned, an experienced handler glides into a fast pace. A few rapid steps positioned me directly behind Brenner, and with a single sweep over his head that was as smooth and natural as even the AKC could want, I wrapped the chain around his neck and yanked hard enough to remind him that *canis familiaris* isn't the only species with a larynx. One firm jerk on a training collar works better than a hundred weak little tugs. When I want to yank, I yank *hard*.

"Brenner, you son of a bitch," I told him, "drop that leash." Training Rule One: Name first, then the command.

He complied. Although the chain must have hurt, I suspect that my effective weapon was, in fact, surprise. I do not look or sound like the kind of person who goes around half garrotting people with crummy chain leashes from discount department stores. Even so, before Brenner had time to recover from his state of shock, whether physical or mental, and before he could fetch Sultan, who really did scare me, I released my grip, left the chain draped around his neck, and swooped up Kimi's leash. Then, with what the AKC calls "the utmost in willingness, enjoyment, and precision," Kimi and I beat it out of there. *Front and Finish* is always publishing scrappy exchanges about what that key word, *utmost,* really means. Now I know.

Oh, except for Sultan. If you really love dogs, you'll understand that I hated to leave him there. There must be a curse on German shepherds that makes them attract the human extremes, the best and the worst, Steve Delaney and Dickie Brenner. A German shepherd or any other dog who's been bred or trained to act vicious is a desecration. I mean that. A sacrilege. Ever read the Bible? Every dog wants nothing more than to play Ruth to your Naomi: "Whither thou goest, I will go; and where thou lodgest, I will lodge; thy people shall be my people; and thy God my God."

About Sultan? The moral of the story is that if you own a German shepherd, be careful how you choose your God. Here endeth today's Lesson.

17

GOD DOES NOT LIKE MODERN ENGLISH and holds a grudge against the whole twentieth century, or so you'd gather from how Cambridge celebrates Christmas. In normal places, people invite you to go out caroling and get together for a few drinks. But not in Cambridge. When I first got here, a guy asked me if I wanted to wassail. I thought he was propositioning me to do something so perverted that I'd never even heard of it.

Not long afterward, though, I lost my innocence: I went to the Christmas Revels in Sanders Theater. If I'd never met Steve, I'd probably have come home from Brenner's and immediately gone out to spend the evening of December twenty-third decadently frolicking around in puff-sleeved peasant garb while an accompanist piped out a winter solstice tune on some cumbersome but authentic protorecorder with a range of three notes. Oh, well, the life wouldn't have suited me anyway, and I've renounced it entirely, except to drag Steve down with me while I walk the streets of Harvard Square.

A heavily festooned giant evergreen loomed in front of the kiosk in the center of the Square. The subway entrance was moved years ago, and the Out of Town Newsstand is a substantial business housed in a building that's too big to be called "the kiosk," but that's exactly what it's called. Kendall Square, near MIT, may be scientific, but Harvard Square is metaphysical. You have to be a visionary to find your way around; the evidence of your senses tells you nothing. Anyway, suspended over the streets that radiate out from the kiosk were the same kinds of silvery giant-candy-cane decorations and strings of multicolored lights that were swinging over a million American Main Streets. According to the sign flashing above one of the banks, the temperature was sixty-three degrees. Steve and I were wearing jeans and T-shirts. We hung around in front of the Coop for a few minutes to listen to a small Salvation Army band play a brassy "O Come, All Ye Faithful" or, Cambridge being Cambridge, "Adeste Fideles." When the carol ended, we threw some quarters into a big kettle suspended on an iron tripod.

Then we rounded the corner at Nini's and strolled into the Cambridge of Brattle Square, the atavistic, anglophile Cambridge of mimes, jugglers, sword swallowers, fire-eaters, acrobats, storytellers, and street musicians, including street musicians with Ph.D.'s who take offense if you mistake their viola da gambas for mere cellos. Violas da gamba? Damn. I'll never fit in here. I mean, this is a place where you can state your occupation as bard, fifer, ballad-monger, or busker, and most people won't even laugh. If you get asked what you want to drink, it's perfectly okay to call for a tankard of mead. There are people here who not only can speak fluent Elizabethan English, but who never speak any other kind, for God's sake. I love Cambridge. It's a human dog show.

"So what did you want me to do?" I indignantly asked Steve over the din of a female choir fervently caroling in what sounded like Russian. I'd filled him in on my visit to

Anneliese, but he was more irked at my visit to Brenner than he was interested in the Bourques. "Take Jackie's word for it? Look, when you want to make a diagnosis, you want to see the animal, don't you? You don't just want to hear someone else describe the problem. You want to see for yourself. It's the same thing. I wasn't going to leave Kimi there, you know, and obviously, I wasn't about to let him hurt her. I didn't, did I?"

He shook his head. "Did you have some plan in mind if he went back and got the dog? You know what a dog like that could've done to Kimi?" He added as an afterthought, "Or you?"

"But he wouldn't have. That's the other thing I confirmed, besides Jackie's story. Look, if Brenner'd been going to retaliate against someone, he'd have done it with Patterson, wouldn't he? The second Patterson punched him, he'd have punched him right back, and he didn't."

"Nothing happened to Patterson, he's in great shape, so nothing's going to happen to you, either. Is that it?"

"Yes," I said. "Appearances to the contrary. What was he going to do? Slug me? Sic his dog on me? No, and for the same reason he didn't punch Patterson or get the dog, which is that he couldn't afford the bad publicity. Look, if Brenner had kicked the shit out of Patterson, what would've happened? The first thing is that it would've ended up in all the papers. Patterson'd probably have pressed charges, and it could've ended up in court. And you know what? You can bet Patterson would've really played it up, first of all, because he dramatized stuff anyway, and, second of all, because he'd've been glad to see Brenner exposed, and Brenner probably knew it. And me? His showpiece dog mauls a client? Or a client's dog? Yeah, sure, I was scared. Who wouldn't be? But so what? And so what if it's just his pride that's hurt? Other people must've called him on things before, and it hasn't hurt his business."

"Sure," Steve said. "All he did was get kicked in the

balls. Twice. But, hey, he's the only guy in the world that didn't give a damn."

"You're wrong," I said. "Because, look, you of all people ought to know that when they don't descend, they can be a lot of places, or they can not be there at all, right? So Brenner's are in a really weird place, which is a safe deposit box at the bank. So if you really want to kick him where it hurts, that's what you go for. Jackie Miner didn't exactly stroke his macho image, and what about whoever owns that Clumber spaniel? The people I told you about who bought the dog from the Metcalfs. They're the ones who told Oscar Patterson about Brenner. It was their dog that made Patterson go after Brenner in the first place. So presumably they didn't exactly tell Brenner they were thrilled with him, either, and nothing's happened to them, at least as far as I know."

"He wouldn't just take it," Steve said.

"He didn't. Or I don't think he did. He acted out of self-interest. He did what he had to do to avoid bad publicity. If he'd put on a John Wayne act, all it would've done would be to cost him a lot of money, maybe even ruined his business. Stringing dogs up and the other stuff doesn't hurt his business because most owners who go to him don't know any better. But hurting a person would hurt him. So he didn't do it. Besides, not everyone feels compelled to be John Wayne, and if you don't believe me—"

It isn't polite to point at people, no matter how silly they look, so I nodded my head. Right in the middle of the paved area in the dead center of Brattle Square, right there in public where everyone could see them, six or eight grown men were leaping and thudding around. They wore stupid costumes and had bells on their ankles. They seemed to be having fun. I tried to imagine going to bed with a morris dancer. Would he take off his bells? Leave them on and let them jingle?

"Hey, Steve," I said. "You know how your mother's always telling you that you need a hobby? All you do is work all the time, and what are you going to do when you retire? Well—"

"Jesus Christ," he said.

"Gotcha," I said. "You see? And when you get to know them, they're probably okay. Actually, they look pretty tough. In fact, at Red Rover—"

"Holly, enough," he said. "No one who practices veterinary medicine in this crazy place needs this lecture."

"I wasn't lecturing. I was demonstrating, right? Morris dancing is all men, you know, and from their point of view, it's probably very macho. It happens to be Ye Olde English Macho, and you'd just as soon pirouette around in a tutu, but they don't care. It's probably what they like about it. And with Brenner, if you ask me, macho is that big, impressive place and the shepherd putting on the vicious dog act. It's probably other things, too. Expensive cars or something. Anyway, I think it's mostly the dog. You could teach India to do that, right?"

"Yeah, but—"

"So why don't you? Because if someone punches you in the jaw, you punch back. Or maybe you don't, but you know you could."

"I'm not so sure it's such an either-or situation." Steve shook his head. "As a matter of fact, a lot of the time, it isn't. If a guy's got a guard dog, it doesn't automatically mean he hasn't got a gun, too."

"So maybe the general principle is wrong, but I still think it's true about Brenner. You know what it is? The hype. The sales pitch. The barking dog? You just don't get the feeling that there's a lot of punch behind it. I humiliated him, you know, and he just watched me walk out of there. Why not? I'd paid, and cash, too."

Steve looked skeptical. "And you also got some kind of guarantee out of him that he's not going to show up later and—"

"Okay! For all I know, he's the one Lee Miner really

heard with Patterson. It's possible that the guy he heard was Brenner, not Bourque."

A young couple with the strained, educated eyes of graduate students rose from their seats on a length of high granite curbstone. Steve and I took their places. They strolled toward WordsWorth. After watching the morris dancers, they'd browse for books and then go for espresso and bend their heads together in ardent dispute about Heidegger. Another wild night in Harvard Square.

"What's his voice like?" Steve asked.

"Brenner's? There's nothing special about it, at least that I noticed. Or about John's, either. Cliff Bourque's. I still half feel as if he's two people. Anyway, if you heard them one right after the other, you'd probably notice some big difference, but they both have kind of ordinary voices, not deep, not high, nothing that you couldn't miss. And their accents are sort of the same, not Boston, but Massachusetts, southern New Hampshire, that kind of thing. Speaking of Bourque, maybe there's something you can straighten out. I'm not sure what was wrong with the dog."

Steve smiled a little. "A couple of minutes ago, I was the guy who wants to see the animal."

"Yeah, but, failing that, you can at least take a better guess than I can."

"The ultimate tribute," he said. " 'The man can even take a better guess than I can myself!' "

"I didn't mean it like that. Anyway, here's the story. This is a Chinook bitch. She's pregnant. She starts retching, but she doesn't vomit. The wife has just read some article about bloat, and she's scared, but her husband, Cliff, thinks it isn't bloat, because, except for the retching, she doesn't look all that sick. So?"

"So the wife is right. Especially with a large dog, you pursue it as bloat."

"That's what she said that Lee Miner said."

"Lee was right."

"But that doesn't mean it *was* bloat. It just means that the safe thing to do is assume that's what it is."

"Because if it is, and if you don't treat it real quick, you'll lose the dog."

"Soon?"

"Within a few hours. But, look, what you're talking about is two things. One is gastric dilatation, and the other is volvulus. G.D.V. syndrome. People say 'bloat,' but all that means is the dilatation. The abdomen's distended because the stomach's full of something. Food, water, gas. Something. Dilatation with volvulus means torsion. The stomach's also twisted. Okay? So there's pressure on the vena cava, which means that no blood's getting to the heart."

"So the husband is right, too, in a way," I said.

"You can't assume—"

"Okay! I understand. But, look, if you get a dog brought in and it really is G.D.V. syndrome, what do you expect? Ordinarily? What do you usually have to do?"

"Decompress the stomach. And, yeah, treat the dog for shock. What did this retching look like? Was it like gagging or—"

"I don't know. I wasn't there, either. But Anneliese says that the dog hadn't got into any food and overeaten or something like that. Oh, and she says she thought the abdomen was distended, but he didn't."

"Anything else they noticed?"

"No. Except that the other dogs were fine. And they stayed fine. So obviously, it wasn't something contagious, and it wasn't something they'd all got into, you know, something rotten they'd all eaten or whatever. So probably it was bloat."

"Isn't that what Miner . . . ?"

"But he wasn't the one, was he?" I said. "That's what Jackie told you, right? Patterson barged in and took over before Miner'd started. Patterson told Miner to get out, he'd take care of it himself. And Miner did. He left. And the next day, the dog was dead. And Patterson was gone, of course. Besides, Geri thinks Patterson was the one taking care of the dog, and she says that when Patterson lost Bourque's dog, both of them would've been really broken up. They'd've had a drink together and cried in each other's beer or something like that."

"Did Lee examine the body?"

"I guess so," I said. "Hey, this jingling is starting to hurt my ears, and I'm getting cold. We should've worn better clothes. We could've gone to Harvest and sat at the bar."

"They won't kick us out."

"There's a line a mile long at the X-Press machine, and I don't have any money. Do you?"

He slipped his wallet out of the back pocket of his jeans, and while he was opening it and searching for bills, I kept watching his jeans. Our relationship is really very simple.

"Maybe we should go home," I said.

"If we stick to beer, I've got enough," he said. It kills him to use credit cards.

I shook my head. "No. If we show up at Harvest in kennel clothes, we'll have to do something to redeem ourselves. Mead."

18

Tourists won't pay for dead history anymore. Visit Old Ironsides or Plimoth Plantation, and you'll find scads of college students in colonial costume who've been coached to answer your questions in stilted dialect. Exhibits of living history, they're called, these unfortunate Henry David Thoreaus who hoe away summer vacation in the steamy bean fields of tourism, these saddle-sore Paul Reveres whose professional daytime cries that the British are coming must turn into heartfelt private midnight pleas that the Redcoats would finally arrive.

On Brattle Street in Cambridge, no sinewy-handed, brawny-armed undergraduate interprets Longfellow's village smithy, but only a few steps from where the spreading chestnut tree stood, the would-be future-famous daily portray themselves. Harvest is hence no mere restaurant and bar, but a vital museum of local culture obligated to display its animate artifacts in their natural setting. When the proprietors of lesser dining and drinking establishments ripped down the Marimekko fabric, tore up the butcher block, composted the spider plants, and tinted the all-white every-thing else shell pink and pale gray, the wise curators of Harvest had the foresight to leave fashion-pandering to mere restauranteurs. Fads be damned. The Marimekko stayed.

I don't know why I worried about our jeans and T-shirts, which were indistinguishable from those of several people at the bar, although the other patrons had doubtless paid dearly to have theirs prefaded, shredded, and ripped by the Banana Republic instead of waiting to have them wrecked gratis by Canine Enterprises. A distinguished-look-ing gentleman in black tie was leaning across a little table to whisper in the ear of a handsome woman wearing a heav-ily embroidered deep-blue velvet dress, a flower-trimmed straw hat, and wooden clogs with two-inch soles, probably the traditional sixteenth-century festival costume of some long-defunct European principality.

Seated alone at a table for four, Rita was the least Cantabrigian-looking person there, which is to say that she'd done her face, hair, and nails and was wearing a Lord and Taylor Christmas-red dress with matching pumps. As if to announce where she belonged, she was drinking a Man-hattan.

"This is going to sound very sour," she warned us when we'd seated ourselves at her table, "but this is Holly's fault. The man who was supposed to meet me here—exactly fifty-five minutes ago—is one of your single dog owners." I am the one who told her about the dating service, but its mem-bers are not, of course, *mine*. "What the hell," she added morosely. "I don't even qualify anymore. I'm here under false pretenses. Maybe he intuited that I wasn't on the up-and-up."

"Of course you are," I said emphatically. "He probably just got lost or something."

"Let him stay that way," she said.

As Steve told Rita, the man was obviously a fool. Even so, as if to prove herself a wonderful person and generous friend, she refused to let us order beer and insisted on paying for our brandy.

"So, Rita, what kind of dog does he have?" I asked, mostly in the hope that the no-show's breed would be accident- or illness-prone and hence explain his absence.

"Something I've never heard of," she said. "A Chinese something."

Steve began offering suggestions. "Chow. Shar Pei. Pekingese."

Rita shook her head and ordered another Manhattan.

"Are you sure it isn't Japanese?" I asked. "An akita! I'll bet that's what it is."

Akitas aren't clumsy or sickly. They're big, tough, and interesting. They promise well of their owners. If the guy had one, I hoped he'd finally arrive.

"No," Rita said. "It was a Chinese something."

"Crested," I said reluctantly.

"A Chinese crested! That's it!" Rita said.

Steve's normal expression is serious, and he never chokes. I tried to hide the smirk on my face by leaning over to thump his back, but Rita is hard to divert.

"Okay, both of you," she said severely.

"It's a small dog," I said. "It's just been recognized by the AKC."

Steve pulled himself together and gave Rita a factual description of the breed and a technical explanation of why the hairless variety tends to lack the full dentition possessed by powderpuffs.

When Steve had finished, Rita said, "I don't see what's so bad about it. They sound cute."

"Oh, they are," I said.

Rita sounded defensive. "So what do you want? Someone who's got, what? A giant attack dog?"

"I was hoping for an Airedale," I said, not that there's anything wrong with Airedales, either. Far from it.

"Yeah, any kind of terrier," Steve said. "It doesn't have to be large. A Cairn, a Norwich."

"A Scottie!" I said.

Steve looked as if I'd gone mad. "Not . . . ?"

"Oh, God, of course not," I said. "Rita wouldn't like him at all. Besides, Willie's gone. She took Willie with her." After a few seconds I added, "Didn't she?"

"No," Steve said.

"That's impossible!"

"Would you mind . . . ?" Rita said.

Steve and I apologized and filled her in.

"Hey, Steve," I said. "If Jackie didn't . . . I don't understand. When she left, where did she go?"

He said he didn't know. He'd been out of town.

"Well," I said, "it's one more thing that doesn't fit with Geri's theory." Then I had to stop and tell Rita about Oscar Patterson, Geri Driscoll, Geri's Kerouac theory, and what I assumed to be Geri's fear that Patterson had left her for Jackie Miner. "Actually," I continued, "you'd think that would be one of the major benefits of leaving your husband for another vet: You'd be more or less guaranteed that you could take your dog."

"That happens not to be most people's major consideration," Rita said.

"Rita, you didn't know Jackie," I said. "If you had, you'd realize that the whole idea is completely off base. It's practically a joke. If there's one place Jackie Miner isn't, it's on some bohemian cross-country trip. Her idea of being on the road is driving to the nearest upscale shopping mall. Not that I didn't like her. I did. But, Jesus, I never thought she'd leave Willie, either. Jesus. I can't believe it. I never thought she was that kind of person at all. I mean, if she'd do that, she'd do practically anything. Steve, has anyone run into her since she left? Lorraine? Pete?"

"No," he said, "but don't think they haven't been looking." As the last word left his lips, his face paled.

"Are you all right?" Rita asked him.

"No," he said as he stood up.

Therapists have a lot of practice in making their voices

convey nonjudgmental interest. "Are you going to be sick?"
she asked.

He didn't hang around long enough to answer.

When he'd dashed off, Rita said, "Don't you want to go
with him?"

"To the men's room?"

"He didn't go there. He went outside."

"He did? Maybe he . . . This is totally unlike him.
He's never sick." The practice of veterinary medicine requires a strong constitution and, in particular, a stomach
that will take anything. I'd actually once watched Steve eat
curried shrimp on rice while he read a color-photo-illus-
trated journal article about how to treat maggot-infested
wounds. He didn't so much as burp.

"Anyway, he hates having people hover," I added.

"He doesn't take very good care of himself," Rita said.
"You know, maybe I'll give him my membership in the
Mount Auburn Club. I wonder if I can do that."

The Mount Auburn Club has tennis courts, a pool, exercise machines, sauna, steam, and all the rest. Two days
after Rita joined, she was swimming laps and accidentally
frog-kicked a guy who turned out to be one of her patients.
When she went to the steam room to meditate about
whether she'd unconsciously recognized him and kicked out
her repressed impulses, two of her women patients walked
in and found her lying there in the mist, naked and guilty.
She's never returned.

"Or maybe you'd like it?" she offered.

"Thank you. That's really generous. But why don't you
just wear something in the steam room? Just wrap a towel
around yourself."

She shook her head knowingly.

"Or, look," I said. "You're the one who's in charge. The
next time one of them walks in naked, just tell her to get
dressed. Or you could use the sauna instead."

She lowered her voice. "They're in there, too." She
made them sound like cockroaches: in the kitchen and in

the bathroom, too. "Sometimes it feels like they're every-where. There's one in here now."

I looked around.

"No," she said. "In the dining room."

Rita maintains that *paranoid* doesn't mean what people think it means, but she was beginning to make me uneasy. "Speaking of your profession," I said, "what do you know about Vietnam veterans?"

"What everybody else knows. I've read a little bit about Post Traumatic Stress Disorder. That's about all. Why?"

I told her Anneliese's story about Cliff Bourque. When I'd finished, I asked, "So, does that make sense?"

"I guess so. I don't know him, of course, but there are a couple of things that strike me."

"Such as?"

"Some of the words you're using. Phrases. I don't know whose they are, but take 'recognizing the breed.' You said that. Did she?"

"I think so."

"I wonder if it's his. If it is . . . He saw the same kind of dog he'd seen in Vietnam, and he 'recognized the breed'? To me, that connotes something in addition to breed of dog. It's also, you know, special breed? The Vietnam vet. Him-self. Himself as a Vietnam veteran. Member of a special breed."

"So the Chinooks are . . ."

"Himself. And the other members of the breed, includ-ing the ones that died? So, yes, when she says they're the buddies he lost, probably they are. Is that his word? *Buddy?*"

"It's what she said. I don't know whether he says it."

"Don't you call your dogs that sometimes? Buddy?"

"Once in a while. Actually, I picked it up from a dog training book. Pearsall. That's what the Pearsalls call the dog. 'Have Buddy sit,' that kind of thing."

"I wonder . . ." she started to say. "Anyway, the other parallel I'm hearing is *training*. Didn't it seem strange to you? Here's a man who's more or less a fugitive from jus-

tice? He's presumably got some vaguely paranoid suspicions? He's doing something he calls 'tracking'?"

"Yeah. She said that's what he calls it."

Rita nodded. "And all of a sudden, in the middle of
this, he takes up *dog training?* Didn't you find that peculiar?
Well, no, you wouldn't, but—"

"Oh, I understand that," I said. "They saw an obedi-
ence-trained Chinook, and obviously, he saw that it was a
way to promote the breed, right? Get the breed recognized.
Oh, yeah. Get what the Vietnam vets didn't."

"Exactly. But what you've missed is *training.* It's no
more than a hypothesis, of course, but for a man who was in
Vietnam? Holly, 'basic training'? For this character, *training*
is not a neutral word."

19

WHEN YOU'RE SICK TO YOUR STOMACH, a loyal hunting dog will hover around pleading to retch and vomit in your stead. In contrast, the Alaskan malamute views your relationship as a partnership of equals: He throws up for himself, and he expects you to do the same. A malamute may even take advantage of your prostration to steal, demolish, and comfortably digest the rest of whatever made you sick. If he decides that you're too weak to ban dogs from the bed, he'll vault in next to you. Once he's there, though, he'll train deep, gentle eyes on you, thrust his big paw into your hand, shove his wet black nose at you, and scour your smelly face with his wet red tongue.

You are what you pat. When I was a solicitous golden retriever, I'd have gone trailing after Steve the second he left. As it was, I didn't look for him until I'd finished his drink.

"He hates being fussed over," I told Rita, "and if he's throwing up, he's going to want privacy."

"I can't believe you're saying this," she accused me. "What if he's passed out?"

"From one drink? Or two? He hasn't passed out. He probably ate some bad curry. He'll be back in a minute."

"He could have the flu," she said.

"He doesn't get the flu. He doesn't even get colds."

"This is ridiculous," she said. "To maintain this Superman image of him that you like to cultivate, you're leaving him all alone out there?"

"Okay," I said, "but I'm warning you. All he'll do is growl."

"That's his problem. Let's go." She'd apparently forgotten about or entirely given up on the Chinese crested owner.

When she'd paid our bill and retrieved her coat, we went out and scanned the area around the entrance and checked the maze of narrow, dark alleys and footpaths that weave around behind Harvest. The temperature had dropped at least thirty degrees since Steve and I had sat in Brattle Square watching the morris dancers, and the air had turned damp. Mark Twain got it wrong. If you don't like New England weather, the thing to do is enjoy it while it lasts.

"He probably went home," I said.

"And just left you here?"

"What was going to happen to me? But you're right. It isn't like him. The only thing is, maybe he wasn't sick? It's possible that if he suddenly thought of something about a patient, he could've just bolted for the clinic. That's possible."

"Well, he looked sick," she said.

Rita had parked in the garage under the Charles Hotel, and by the time we reached her car and she got the engine going, I was shaking from the cold. Have you ever noticed that the chills and fear feel a lot alike?

"Let's just go home," I said. "I'll try calling him."

Once I penetrated the guard of his answering service, however, Steve turned out to be easy to reach. As I'd guessed, he'd gone directly to his clinic.

"I'm real sorry about that," he said. "But Jesus Christ. Once it hit me . . . Anyway, you want to come over here? No, don't. Stay there. I'll be right over."

What had hit him was not, of course, the flu, and he wasn't begging for help. When I heard the bell and opened my back door, he was leaning against the frame, and his skin retained that green tinge it had had when he'd dashed out of Harvest, but he didn't look sick.

"Christ, Holly," he said. "It's so goddamned obvious. It was all I could think of. I'm sorry. You got home all right?"

"Apparently." I stretched out my arms to make an exaggerated appraisal of my hands and lowered my head to gaze at the rest of me and verify that I was all there. "Yes. All of me seems to be here."

But it was no time to get cute. After a token smile, Steve wrapped his arms around me, buried his face in my hair, and groaned. His breath made a warm spot on my scalp. He hadn't even put anything on over his T-shirt. It smelled faintly of dogs and bleach.

"Christ," he said. "It's like something my grandfather used to say. He used to say, 'They left the door open, and the wrong dogs came home.' When I was a kid, I could never understand what it was supposed to mean."

"What *is* it supposed to mean?"

"Right now it's supposed to mean that my grandfather's grandson is the major fuck-up who left the door open, that's what it's supposed to mean."

I'd seen him in this mood only a few times before, once when he'd made some trivial, inconsequential misdiagnosis, once when he'd blamed himself for failing to save a dog that had been crushed by a car. The dog's owners had always let it run loose, and, as Ian Dunbar says, dogs that live on the street die on the street, but Steve hadn't even wanted to hear about that. "You lost an animal?" I asked, looking up at him.

"Jesus, no." He let go of me, stormed around the kitchen, raised his arm, made a fist, and looked ready to slam it into one of my heavily mortgaged walls or doors.

"Don't you dare!" I said. "If you want to break something, including the hand you use for surgery, fine, but go outside and do it, and don't put a goddamned scratch on anything that belongs to me."

Whenever Rowdy and Kimi decided to chase each other around indoors, I told them the same thing, minus the reference to surgery, of course. Alaskan malamutes are remarkably intelligent and dexterous, but they have their limits. Steve recognized the words and the tone of voice. "I'm not one of your dogs," he snapped, but he lowered his fist.

"Go out and kick someone else's trash cans," I suggested.

"God damn it, don't condescend to me," he yelled.

I yelled back. "What the hell is this about?"

His voice was suddenly soft and rumbly, but still enraged. "Goddamned son of a bitch! He put her in *my* goddamned freezer! He killed her, and then he put her in *my* freezer, and he counted on it. He figured I'd be too dumb to figure out what was going on, and he was dead right." Then he caught the gruesome pun and said, "Oh, shit."

"Jesus," I said. "Steve, look. Could you start talking to *me?* I don't know what's going on, you know. Except . . ."

I didn't really want any coffee, but I needed something normal to do. I filled a kettle with water, put it on to heat, and nervously got out filters and French roast. "Sit down," I added.

"You do talk to me like one of the dogs," he said, turning toward me.

"It's a compliment. You should know that." I fished in my pocket, pulled out a hunk of freeze-dried liver, held it up pertly, and said, "Speak, boy!" Then I sobered up. "Christ, Steve, is that really true? That can't be true."

"Good," he said flatly, still pacing around. "That's real comforting."

"Hey, all right. But if this awful thing really happened, and if I have to hear about it, I need you to quit stalking around. Just sit at the table, we'll have some coffee, and I'm going to let the dogs in. Okay? And don't growl at me. I didn't stash any bodies in your freezer."

"Holly, do me a favor and don't kid around about it."

"I'm sorry," I said. "Rita says that compulsive joking is a defensive—"

"Never mind. I don't want to hear about it. Just don't do it."

"Sure. I'm sorry. I guess it's just hard to believe, but if it's true . . ." In the freezer, for God's sake? The impulse to get cute was nearly irresistible. In the freezer? Well, it sounded like a joke to me, albeit a sick joke, which is to say, no joke at all. My skin was crawling.

Steve made coffee while I let in Rowdy and Kimi. Then I tied them at opposite ends of the kitchen and gave each one a big Iams dog biscuit. Rowdy's disappeared so fast that he must practically have swallowed it whole. The second Kimi saw that he'd finished every crumb, she ostentatiously dropped hers on the floor, picked it up, dropped it again, and then lay down and began licking it very slowly. Her eyes never left Rowdy. Eventually, she began to nibble on the biscuit. He stared at it. She grasped the biscuit between her paws and very deliberately chewed. I was, of course, tempted to give him a second biscuit, but she'd probably worked it out: If I gave him one, I'd give her one, too. If there were a canine version of chess, all of the grand masters would be malamute bitches. And, yes, I'd rather tell you about my dogs than talk about what really happened to Jackie Miner.

"One of these days, Rowdy's going to figure it out," Steve said. "It takes some of us a while."

I unleashed the dogs. After each had checked to make sure that the other hadn't overlooked any crumbs—dream on, guys, you're both malamutes—Kimi sat primly in front of me in the hope that I'd feed her some of the Christmas cookies from a plate I'd put on the table, and Steve started tossing a greasy potholder for Rowdy to retrieve.

"Use two if you want," I said. "Or three. He can do a directed retrieve. Then when you're done training my dog, you can tell me what's going on, unless you want me to set up the high jump and get out his dumbbell."

"Dumbbell, right," he said.

"When did you get so hypersensitive?"

"Do you want to hear about it?"

"Yes," I said. "No, not really." I closed my eyes and held my breath, as if vision- and oxygen-deprivation would blot out all sensation. Finally, I said, "Look, Steve, first of all, what was it? At Harvest?"

"That was just what triggered it. You remember what happened? What we said?" He'd returned to his normal way of talking, slow and patient. "You were asking if anyone'd seen Jackie, Lorraine or anyone, and so I said something like, no, but it wasn't because they weren't looking. Right?"

"And?"

"And then it was like I was hearing my own voice. Here's where we need to back up."

"Good," I said. Asking him to hurry up and spill a story is a waste of time.

"You remember you asked me to see about getting a tag put on Groucho's body. Rita'd changed her mind. She wanted the ashes back after all."

I nodded, but as Steve uttered the words, they'd seemed to catch in my own throat: *body, ashes.*

Steve went on: "So I said, sure, no problem, I'd do it."

"And you did, right?"

"Wrong," he said. "It got done, but not by me. That's the point. This was Wednesday, right? I'd just got back, things had piled up, and then an emergency came in, so I mentioned it to Lorraine, not to let me forget, because her brother was due there, and I didn't want to get busy and then find out he'd already come and gone. So late in the afternoon, damned if I didn't remember, and Lorraine hadn't reminded me. So I got after her, but she said it was all taken care of. She knew it was important to Rita, and I was tied up, so she decided she'd do it herself. She didn't mind that much, but she was sort of . . . They'll talk about that kind of thing. They have to, or they can't manage it. So she was telling Pete, and Miner stepped in. And when he heard what was going on, he said, no, he'd do it. And he did."

"He was being a nice guy?"

"I should've got it then. *Nobody's* that nice a guy. Especially him. And he's always so damned slow that the waiting room's full, he's way behind schedule, so for sure he didn't have a lot of free time. And doing favors for Lorraine isn't his idea of what he's supposed to do, anyway. I should've known something was way off. Lorraine should've, too."

"Probably she was just glad she didn't have to do it herself."

"She wasn't the only one." He stroked Rowdy's throat. "Hell, if he'd offered while I was on my way to do it, I'd've said, sure, thanks. So that's what did it. At Harvest. No one'd seen Jackie. And then I hear myself talking, and what I hear is, they haven't been looking. Jesus, was I slow. Why would he've volunteered?"

"Yeah. It's not an upbeat job."

"And Rita isn't a friend of his. Anyway, Lee doesn't do favors. So it fell in place. He did it so none of us would look in the bags."

"But what about Lorraine's brother? After he, uh, takes the bags away . . . ?"

"Rumor has it that sometimes they do check, but he knows we're not going to try and pull anything."

"What could you possibly pull?"

"Two bodies in one bag. Charge two owners for their animals and then put both animals in one bag. Pay him for one. Keep the difference."

"Steve, is that what you think Lee did? He killed her? And then, Jesus, he must've had to bend . . . God. And then he put her body in with . . . ?" A horrible song began to run through my mind, a nasty children's ditty I'd managed to forget for a couple of decades. Remember? "The worms crawl in, the worms crawl out. . . ." I could feel them, invisible beneath my skin. I hope I never again say that my skin is crawling unless I really mean it. I reached across the table for Steve's hands and held them tightly. "Steve, did he put her with Groucho?"

He shook his head. "The fee depends on the size of the animal, roughly. Not the exact weight, but small, medium, large. So if it was supposed to be a small dog, it wouldn't match up. And if there was already, say, a large dog, the bag'd weigh so much that someone would notice." He paused. "Jesus, when it hit me, I honest to God did feel sick. But that's what I had to check, how he pulled it off."

"And?"

"And according to our records, on Monday night, somebody showed up with the body of a Saint Bernard mix and paid cash for routine final care."

"Could that have happened?" I wanted him to promise me that, sure, that's exactly what happened, that and nothing more.

"Yeah," he said, "but most people aren't going to pay cash. It's not all that cheap."

"So whose name was it? Was it someone we could call?"

"Sure. The name's John Kelly, and the entire address is South Boston. What's there is *Kelly* with a *y*, no *e*, but you'd want to check *e y*, too. You want to start?"

There are more Irish people in Boston than there are

in Dublin. In Southie alone, there must be hundreds of John Kellys, maybe more.

"It would be a lot of fun trying to prove he didn't exist," I said. "Or for that matter, that Jackie doesn't. Anymore. But why?"

"Patterson. Jackie added things up. Why else?"

20

"DIEHARD," I SAID. "It's a nickname, right? For Scotties. Diehard."

"She probably didn't, you know," Steve said gently. "Any veterinarian . . ."

Doctors are supposed to make the best murderers, but let me warn you: If your own M.D.'s office is stocked with the means of rapid euthanasia you'll find in any D.V.M.'s and if your own doctor has anything approaching the average veterinarian's hands-on experience in granting swift demise, mute those complaints about aches and pains, and don't confess that your life isn't worth living, unless, of course, you really mean it.

"If you decided to get rid of me," I said, "that's probably what you'd do, isn't it? In fact, if I ever—"

"Holly, look. It's not funny, and you know it's not. But, yeah. If the whole thing was calculated, yeah, that's what he did. It wouldn't look like a natural death, but he had that all worked out. With a half-empty freezer waiting, it didn't matter. He'd've sedated her first. There's no shortage of sedatives back there."

"Otherwise, she'd've been a little curious about the needle, I guess."

"If you can't put a lid on it, I'm leaving." He sighed loudly, got up, and poured himself some more coffee.

I apologized. "Steve, I liked her. She was irritating, in a way, and I didn't exactly want her for a good friend, but there was nothing wishy-washy about her. She was very definite. Like a Scottie. And I would never want . . . Steve, I need to ask you something. Maybe it'll help if I don't just have to imagine . . . Steve, the, uh, the bags the bodies go in. What are they . . . ?"

"What are they like?"

"Yeah. What do they look like?"

"They're ordinary plastic bags, like trash bags. But a lot heavier." He drank some coffee.

"I keep wondering if . . . This is going to sound stupid."

His voice was low and gentle. "Say it anyway, huh?"

"I wonder if he—" I got up, found a tissue, and blew my nose. "This is stupid."

"What is it?"

I sat down and rested my elbows on the table. I found myself staring at my big kitchen wastebasket, which was lined with a heavy green trash bag. The cover of the wastebasket was ajar, propped open by an empty Lipton tea bag box and an out-of-date L.L. Bean catalog. "I keep hoping he, uh, closed her eyes. You know? Instead of just shoving her into a trash bag." The tune of the disgusting schoolyard dirge was still running through my head. The worms crawl in, the worms . . . I tried to remember that Jackie hadn't even been buried, for God's sake. Her body had been cremated.

"She honest to God did look like a Scottie." Steve made it sound like the beginning of a eulogy. "And she acted like one, too. You never want to admit it, but it does happen."

"Yeah, well, she was an exception. Steve, what about Patterson? Do you . . . ?"

"Occam's razor," Steve said ponderously.

Under normal circumstances, I'd've asked him whether it was some kind of specialized veterinary scalpel, but I managed to keep quiet.

Steve must have misunderstood my silence. He started to explain: "The basic principle that—"

"The simplest explanation is the best."

"More or less," he said. "Don't multiply your elements."

Steve isn't callous, you know, but how much raw sensitivity can he afford? If your dog ever needs a leg amputated, do you want to have to do the surgery yourself because your vet is too busy sobbing and wailing?

"So?" I asked.

"To explain what happened to Oscar Patterson," he said laboriously. "Minimize the elements. Miner arrives. Cliff Bourque and his dog arrive. Bourque leaves. Patterson shows up, Bourque returns, or maybe someone else does, Brenner, whoever. Miner goes home. So?"

"So? Okay, so there's no mysterious stranger. Or no Brenner?"

"Keep going."

"Well, Miner *was* there," I said.

Steve nodded.

"And Cliff Bourque did leave Mattie. And Patterson did disappear."

"So?"

"Okay, I get it. So if what you want is a simple explanation, that's it. Bourque never went back that night, which is what his wife says. So the only people there were Miner and Patterson. And the dog, of course. Mattie. Steve, I know one reason, which is—"

"The dog," he said. "Sorry. What were you going to say?"

"There's this story I heard, from Geri Driscoll. Patterson's practice was large animals, too, and what he did was deliberately send Miner out to some farm where there was a bull that kicked. So Miner went out there, and it kicked him, just as planned, I gather, and Miner ended up in a manure pile, which was exactly what Patterson knew would happen. Or maybe he didn't exactly know it, but he knew it was likely, and he sent Miner, with no warning or anything."

Steve sounded less sympathetic than I'd expected. He pointed out that bulls are going to kick some of the time, and where there's a bull, a manure pile shouldn't come as a big surprise.

"He could've been killed!" I said. "Besides, it must've been so embarrassing. He must've felt so humiliated and also furious, because Patterson set him up."

"Guys'll do that," Steve said. "Sounds like Patterson staged some kind of initiation."

"Yes, but Miner failed it."

"Not necessarily. It depends more on how he took it."

"Well, he took it badly, I think. I would, too."

Steve said nothing.

"Okay," I said. "You don't want to say it. It was one of those stupid male rites. It was a silly macho test, and he flunked. He took it like a girl."

"Half of the veterinary students in this country are women," he said. "Most of them would've passed."

"So he took it like an anorchid. Is that better? A mental anorchid."

Steve laughed. Do I need to translate? Well, you can't show a male dog in breed, in conformation, unless he's got both testicles where they belong. In a cryptorchid, one or both haven't dropped, a monorchid has only one, so an anorchid has . . . ? It happens in dogs, too.

"I still don't think Patterson should've done it," I said.

"Look, Holly. If Miner was afraid of animals and didn't want to get dirty and couldn't laugh at it, the last thing he should've done was become a veterinarian."

"I guess. Maybe that's why he's so . . . Do you know, when you were away, and Rowdy got that ear infection? Did

I tell you this? He muzzled Rowdy. It was the first thing he did." Rowdy and Kimi had been stretched out on the floor, but when Rowdy heard his name, he stirred, clambered to his feet, shook himself, and ambled over to me. "And," I continued, "Rowdy didn't mind very much, but I did."

"That's what he does with Willie," Steve said. "Since, uh . . . Without Jackie around, he keeps him muzzled."

Without Jackie around. Rather, with Jackie in a plastic body bag in the freezer, where there were no—I repeat—no worms. And later, with her body reduced to ashes in a mass cremation.

"Willie does bite," I said. According to Rita, talking about dogs is a defense, but what was I supposed to do? Sing that horrible song out loud? "Or at least he nips," I added. "But Rowdy loves vets, and he wouldn't bite anyone, anyway. Of course, he is big." I stopped. "Jesus. You don't think . . . Steve, Cliff Bourque brings in his bitch, Mattie, right? Suspected bloat. She's retching. Maybe she's going to vomit. What's the first thing you *don't* do?"

"Yeah. And there's a second thing. I didn't tell you about that. One part of Miner's story is real fishy. Patterson takes over. It looks like G.D.V. syndrome. This is a large dog. He's got a second veterinarian there. And the first thing Patterson does is send away the second veterinarian? And if there's a chance of vomiting, yeah, you never use a muzzle, because the dog could aspirate."

"I'm getting confused. Mostly now we know what didn't happen. So what did? Mattie got sick. Bourque called Miner, and they met there, at the hospital. Bourque went home."

"And Miner slapped a muzzle on her," Steve said. "He knew better, you know. He knows better. And he wouldn't have left it on."

"But he was afraid she'd bite," I said. "A large dog? And maybe she was terrified. That's so stupid. It's one of the things Chinooks are famous for, not biting. They're totally gentle, totally unaggressive. You'd think Miner . . .

Steve, wouldn't her record've said what she was? That she was a Chinook?"

"Sure. Of course it would."

"And a veterinarian wouldn't forget that. No veterinarian would. I mean, if someone brings you in a Karelian bear dog? A Lundehund? Whatever? That's unusual, right? It's interesting. You're not going to forget that."

He nodded.

"Well, Miner said he did! That's crazy. I mean, this is a fussy guy who spends half an hour picking over the details of Rowdy's entire medical history before he treats a plain old ear infection? Steve, this guy has such an eye for detail that he rearranged the ornaments on my tree. At the party, when you were away? Did I tell you about that? He rehung them in perfect little neat rows. It was weird."

"He gets lost in details."

"Yeah. Anyway, at the party, Jackie was talking about Oscar Patterson and telling everyone about what'd happened, and she mentioned that the dog that died was a sled dog. So, of course, I asked what kind, and she said she didn't know, but Lee would. Anyhow, later, when they were leaving, one of us asked him. She did or I did, I don't remember. And he said he didn't know. Or he couldn't remember. But what I do remember is that, first of all, he was kind of irritated at her for pressing him about it, and, second, he said something like, 'What does it matter?' And at the time, I didn't know him, really, and so what? But she must've thought that was pretty strange."

"Yeah. It's possible he could've forgotten, but if he had? Jesus, he would've spent an hour going over all the possibilities."

"And she must've known that better than anyone, that any detail *would* matter. So she'd've known something was wrong."

"So why didn't he tell you? He probably did remember."

"I think he just plain didn't want to talk about it. No,

there's another thing. Nobody was drinking all that much, but he must've had a fair amount of wine. I mean, he'd talked about it before, obviously, but I'll bet it was when he was cold sober. He'd had a few drinks, it was late, he was tired. He didn't trust himself. But Jackie must've caught it. And once she sank her teeth into something, she wouldn't let go, would she? And if she just worked it out and took him up on it?"

"I thought she seemed real devoted."

"I think she was. But what she wasn't was sneaky. And she talked all the time. Maybe she really was shocked, and she threatened to turn him in, but I don't think so. Maybe he just realized that even if she wanted to keep it a secret, sooner or later, she'd open her mouth and say something. Maybe it wouldn't even have been anything important, but he'd always have had to worry. He'd never have known for sure, not with her around."

"Back up," he said. "Bourque brings in the dog, Miner muzzles her, Bourque leaves."

"And Patterson shows up. He finds Mattie dead, and he rips into Miner. What Patterson walked in and found was that Miner had killed Mattie, or that's what it amounted to, anyway. She died because Miner was afraid of big dogs."

"Christ, if I walked in on that—"

"Plus Patterson and Miner already have this history, the bull and the manure pile and all that. And Patterson used to barge in and take over from people anyway. Also, what he did to Brenner? Anyway, Patterson would've been livid, and he did something: He hit Miner, threatened him, whatever. So what Miner saw coming was basically another bull and another manure pile, only worse this time, because what he'd done was real malpractice. What Miner must've really wanted was to get rid of the whole situation, only he couldn't, of course. He couldn't bring Mattie back to life. The closest he could come was to get rid of Patterson. I wonder what he did to him."

"In a veterinary hospital? You must be kidding. Take your pick."

"Yeah. Anyway—God damn. You know what? Cliff Bourque's been right all along. For a start, he knows that he wasn't there and that he didn't even see Patterson. The poor guy. No wonder he's half crazy. Anyway, so there's Miner with two bodies, Mattie's and Patterson's, and I guess that's when he discovered this business of imaginary dead dogs. Patterson wasn't all that big. Their records probably look like yours, only that time it was a Newfie or something. With Jackie, it was easy, I guess. He could say that his wife had left him. If a guy tells you his wife walked out on him, you focus on him and how he's *been* left."

"Yeah," Steve said. "You don't usually ask where she's gone."

21

A VOICE WITH THE TONE, timbre, resonance, and range of Rowdy's lifts itself above the ordinary canine woofs and arfs maybe once or twice a century. On the morning of the twenty-fourth of December, he melodiously burst forth in the definitive performance of the Malamute Variations. His theme began with one long, frigidly clear, weirdly male soprano note, descended to rich midrange, then plunged to a prolonged, all-stops-open basso profundo. I pulled a pillow over my head and swore. My eyes felt as if I'd been crying in my sleep. An unshaven human male cheek scratched the back of my neck. Steve's voice joined the howling in a verse of "Good King Wenceslas." Then he straddled me and yanked the pillow from my fists.

"Would you shut that dog up?" I said nastily.

"Holly, don't be mad," he said. "You have two Alaskan malamutes, and your veterinarian loves you."

"Could I ask you something? Why are you so *happy?*"

"I've been thinking about something."

"What?"

"If one of us'd said the wrong thing to him? Jesus, we're lucky to be here. And now I get to fire the little bastard and move back to Cambridge and run a one-man practice again. Besides, I'm in bed with a tough woman. But I don't mind because she has such beautiful breasts."

Sometime during the next hour, the dogs, who'd been let out and in and given their ample morning rations of nutritionally perfect, vet-recommended premium canine chow, nosed out a package under the tree that I'd assumed to contain a copy of my Aunt Cassie's husband's latest tedious academic book. Apparently, though, unless Uncle Arthur had for once managed to produce a colorful work, the present had been a large, flat, tomelike fruitcake, or so I inferred from the waxy-looking red and green bits and the brownish, doughy mass that Kimi regurgitated onto the kitchen floor.

One of the convenient things about breakfasting with your vet is total freedom from the expectation that you'll lose your appetite if a dog throws up or that you'll at least quit chewing your English muffin while you scrape up the vomit before the dog decides that, gee, now that it's already half digested, maybe it'll stay down *this* time.

"I hate to ruin your good mood," I said to Steve, "but you can't fire Lee Miner yet, not unless you've got some excuse besides the truth. If you tell him that? You were right, what you said before. He'll probably jab a needle in your arm, for God's sake. Though, actually, he probably won't do anything. Why should he? There's no evidence."

Steve was eyeing Kimi. "Probably soaked in brandy," he said. Then he looked up at me. "I'm going to have a talk with what's-his-name." He waved a thumb in the direction of the house next door to mine. As I've mentioned, my friend and neighbor Kevin Dennehy is a Cambridge cop of elevated rank.

"What's Kevin supposed to charge him with? Not knowing where his wife went when she walked out on him? Those bodies are gone. Patterson's is long gone. I mean, he disappeared about three weeks ago. And Jackie . . . Jesus, this makes me sick." I stopped and took a deep breath. "Groucho died this Tuesday, right? Just after you got back. And Jackie—" I had to stop again. I swallowed, waited, and continued. "Groucho's body was picked up on Wednesday, so that's when Jackie's was, too. And that John Kelly business isn't evidence. In other words, all we can prove is that nobody can find anybody. Yeah, right. Any. Body."

"Dennehy's smarter than he looks," Steve said.

"Yeah, he's probably smart enough to go find Cliff Bourque, who's probably hanging around somewhere semidrunk and sounding paranoid, and then Kevin will tell me how naive I am, and, at a minimum, Cliff Bourque will be hassled, and Cambridge might even have to send him back to New Hampshire. 'Merry Christmas, Cliff! Sorry about your dog, and, by the way, thanks for almost getting run over to save mine.' "

As I'd been talking, I'd been debating the pros and cons of telling Steve about that ridiculous and sinister business of the lilac bush. It now seemed less silly and more menacing than it had, but I felt no sense of personal threat. Cliff Bourque had followed Lee Miner that night; he'd tracked his prey. Maybe Bourque had even been surprised that the trail led to my party, the party he'd decided not to attend. It seemed clear to me that Cliff Bourque meant me no harm at all, but Steve might not agree. I decided not to mention the episode.

"Could be we're giving him too much credit," Steve said.

I was startled. "Cliff Bourque?"

"Miner. He wrapped everything up tight here, yeah, but we can't be positive there's nothing in those records, up there."

"So let's call and find out. Or at least let's try. We don't even know if they're open today."

Lorraine, who administers these kinds of things for Steve, had declared the day before Christmas a holiday.

Steve was on call, and Miner was due to take over later, in the early evening, when Steve and I were leaving for Owls Head, or that's what Lorraine had decided.

"No," I added. "Even if they are, call Geri Driscoll. It'll be quicker. Tell her in confidence that you found some odd transactions that started after Miner got here. Tell her that you don't know what's going on, but would she look at their records? Starting with when Oscar disappeared, three weeks ago, whenever. And Steve? Get her to look at everything, not just cash payments. Make sure she checks to see if anyone's supposed to have brought in an animal that had already died. Or if another animal died around that time."

"She won't—"

"Steve, take it from me. She'll do anything you ask her. If I call, she won't even remember who I am."

I watched and listened while he was on the phone. He got the story out okay. After that, she did most of the talking. He turned unbelievably red.

He hung up and said, "That woman is disgusting."

"Yeah. She's also kind of sad, but in sort of an evil way, if you ask me. She says that if Patterson doesn't show up soon, she's getting an abortion, just to spite him. It's so . . . it's so coldhearted. If I didn't . . ."

"What?"

"You know, Steve, Geri was practically there that night. Their house, hers and Patterson's, is right near the animal hospital. Also—"

"Yeah?"

"What makes her so sure that Patterson's alive?"

"Wishful thinking," Steve said.

"Maybe. Anyway, she'll look?"

He nodded. "She'll call back."

The phone rang a few minutes later, but the call was from Steve's answering service. After a few words of instruction to be relayed to an owner, he started to bolt out the door, came to a halt, and said, "Holly?"

"Yeah?"

"If Brenner shows up, don't open the door. Don't let him in."

"Steve, he doesn't even know my real name, never mind where I live."

"People know you," he said. "You're not hard to find. All he'd have to do would be to ask around."

"I'm not afraid of Brenner," I said defiantly.

"I know. That's what scares me. Don't open the door."

After Steve left, I felt at loose ends. Regardless of what happened, including whatever I did, it seemed unlikely that Steve would go to Maine with me for Christmas. He obviously couldn't leave Lee Miner in charge of his practice, and he'd never find someone else on a few hours' notice. In other circumstances, the dogs and I would have gone by ourselves, but how could we? Steve and I hadn't really reached any decision about what to do. We hadn't heard from Geri Driscoll. Lee Miner was probably eating a late breakfast in Steve's kitchen over the clinic or walking the muzzled Willie, with Cliff Bourque presumably still tracking him.

If you don't have a dog, what do you do when you don't know what to do? To avoid missing Geri Driscoll's call, I propped open the door to the side yard and went out there to work the dogs. With Kimi, I didn't do a run-through, but concentrated on getting her sits absolutely straight in front and at heel position, speeding up her drop, and keeping her prancing with me instead of lagging on her about-turns. Those details are where you lose points, of course. Before long, my hands were icy and raw. When I train with food, I want control over exactly when I pop it in the dog's mouth, and I avoid wearing gloves. A winter-long case of chapped hands is one of only two disadvantages of training with food. The other is the mess you find in your washer and dryer when you forget to empty your pockets.

By the time I began to work Rowdy, the sky had turned such a deep charcoal that I wouldn't have been surprised to see a flurry of cinders mixed with snow. I pulled some white work gloves from my pockets, put on a pair, and used three more for the directed retrieve. In the ring, you have the dog retrieve one of three gloves, whichever one the judge designates. Getting the correct glove is the kind of task that malamutes learn almost effortlessly. Where they fall to pieces is on such challenging exercises as walking by your side. Didn't Einstein flunk algebra? After Rowdy had joyfully brought back the gloves a few times, I had him retrieve a metal dumbbell from an old set of scent discrimination articles. Even golden retrievers aren't naturally wild about the taste and feel of metal. Rowdy had already learned to take and hold metal objects, but he certainly hadn't learned to like them. I had him bring back the metal dumbbell only once, and when I took it from him, I rubbed his shoulders, told him that he was the greatest obedience dog in the history of the Alaskan malamute, and gave him a hunk of Vermont cheddar.

Finally, the dogs did the group exercises, the long sit and the long down. Afterward, while Rowdy was slavering at the sight of Kimi's "I've still got mine, but you haven't" routine with her dog biscuit, I worked on my article about the Chinese crested, then finished wrapping my last two presents, a distinctive gray-and-white natural fiber scarf for my father and a very long box containing a set of PVC jumps and hurdles for Steve and India. As I was curling the last loose end of ribbon, Geri Driscoll finally called. When she asked to speak to my big boy, I thought she meant Rowdy, but once I realized that she'd never seen him, I convinced her that Steve was unavailable and persuaded her to leave a message. It was short.

"Tell him I didn't find a thing," she said. "Not a thing." She sounded disappointed, mostly, I suspected, because she'd had to settle for talking to a nonperson.

"So," I told the dogs when I'd hung up, "if you're so smart, tell me whose it was? Whose body?"

I said the same thing to Steve as soon as he called. "So which was it? It had to be Oscar's, right? Because that's the one he absolutely had to get rid of. Mattie's I guess he just dumped in the woods somewhere, because if some hiker comes across a body or a skeleton or whatever, and it turns out to be human? Jesus, every forensic pathologist in the state of New Hampshire probably comes running, and before long, your corpse gets identified. And then someone figures out that he didn't just die; he's been put to sleep. If that's how Miner did it. But if some hiker finds a dead dog?"

"Yeah. The average hiker's going to make a wide detour, and that's it. Except you'd think that while they were searching for Patterson . . . But maybe not."

"Steve, is Miner around? Upstairs? Have you seen him?"

"Not yet, but he's got to be around Cambridge somewhere. Willie's here."

"Upstairs?"

"Down here."

"Well, I hope he's behind wire mesh," I said.

Steve laughed. "The worst he does is nip. It isn't even a nip. It's a little pinch. I like him. He's a spunky little guy."

"Apparently Miner does, too. Most husbands whose wives have dogs like that would've . . . I mean, as long as he was at it anyway . . ." It's the part of the job that every good vet hates most. I changed the subject. "So how's your emergency?"

"False alarm," he said. "They thought something'd got stuck in the dog's throat, and it turned out they were right. Needle from the Christmas tree. Scotch pine."

"But you . . . ?"

"The dog's a real big mixed breed, and he's an easy ten pounds overweight. He's a real chow hound, and they're nice people, but they're not too careful. So when I heard he was retching . . . Like I told you, you always have to rule out G.D.V."

"Steve, at the Bourques'?" I said. "Jesus, there are pines all around the house. It's called Pine Tree Kennels, for God's sake, and their other businesses are all Pine Tree, too. Jesus, maybe that's all that was wrong with Mattie."

"That'll do it. Any small object, if it's in the back of the throat, if it's near the pharynx or the larynx. Then you'll get retching but no vomiting. But—"

"And Mattie wouldn't have looked all that sick." I was thinking out loud. "There wouldn't have been anything else wrong with her. Anneliese said that Cliff said that, that Mattie didn't look all that sick. And even Anneliese wasn't positive that her abdomen was swollen. And she *was* sure that Mattie hadn't got into a bag of food or anything. Jesus. So Cliff was right again, Steve."

"We don't know that. And that's a real dangerous assumption for an owner to make."

"But just in theory . . . Look, suppose that's what it was, okay? Mattie gets a pine needle stuck in her throat, she starts gagging, and Cliff takes her in so Lee can examine her. Cliff leaves. And Patterson walks in. He knows exactly what you've been saying, okay? You have to assume it's bloat. But even so, he walks in and finds Miner there in the middle of the night, and the big emergency turns out to be a pine needle?"

"Any veterinarian—"

"Yes, but the people who live around there aren't veterinarians. What do they know? You didn't laugh at that story about the manure pile—basically, you thought it was Miner's fault and sort of an occupational hazard—but *they* thought it was hilarious. Probably they wouldn't have thought this was quite that funny, but I'll bet they'd have found it sort of funny, especially if Patterson embellished the story a little."

"It's possible," Steve said. "But it's the scenario we already worked out."

"No, it isn't," I said. "Not really. It's still possible that Miner muzzled her. But there's one big difference."

"If her problem was a pine needle at the back of her throat," Steve said, "she didn't die of G.D.V. syndrome."

"And if she didn't," I said, "then Miner wasn't left with two bodies after all."

22

Obedience competition involves only two group exercises, the long sit and the long down. In the midafternoon of the day before Christmas, I introduced Rowdy and Kimi to a third: the long shot. Instead of tossing my duffel bags of clothes, kibble, water bowls, leashes, and presents into the back of the Bronco, I packed in nothing but an empty crate and my dogs, who were taking advance credit for the impending snow. How could I tell? By the white arctic glint in their warm brown eyes.

Just as I backed the Bronco out of the driveway and into Appleton Street, the first snowflakes began to fall. To avoid the worst of the early Christmas Eve traffic on 93, I intended to pick up Route 2 by Fresh Pond, but as I drove by the armory on Concord Avenue, I decided to make a short detour. I never meant to find Cliff Bourque and take him with me. He'd lost Mattie once. It would've been heartless to offer him the slight and probably false hope that she might still be alive. Even so, the impulse to tell him nagged at me. If I told Cliff Bourque everything? Regardless of

Mattie's fate, he might quit stalking his prey and get on to the kill. And if so? Well, Bourque might get caught. Rightly or wrongly, I didn't care what happened to Lee Miner. I wouldn't tell Cliff Bourque, then. I'd just take a few minutes to try to find out where he was. With luck, I'd discover him in a safe stupor beneath someone else's dormant shrubbery.

I cruised past Steve's clinic. Because of the holiday, the parking lot was empty except for Steve's van. Cliff Bourque wasn't crouched nearby, grenade in hand. I pulled the Bronco into a gas station, turned around, fought my way back into the traffic, and drove by again. This time, I scanned the wooded area opposite the clinic. In other words, I searched for Cliff Bourque in the place I'd first seen him. Stupid? I didn't know where else to look. At any rate, if he'd been perched sniper-fashion high in the leafless branches of a Norway maple while he prepared to pick off Lee Miner, or even if he'd just been leaning against a tree trunk, I might not have spotted him. The traffic was even thicker and moving even faster than it had been on the day Cliff Bourque dashed through it to save Kimi. I did my best to look for Cliff, though. I did. But I didn't see him.

After that, I followed my original plan, but almost as soon as we crossed into Arlington, I regretted the decision to take Route 2. A sand truck had prematurely dressed the highway with a layer of salty dirt that every speeding little foreign compact tossed in the face of my big, muscular Bronco. Each sweep of the wipers gave me only a moment's vision of the road and steadily ground the grit into the windshield. As the snow thickened, I cursed Ford for the absence of rear wipers and damned every car manufacturer on earth for failing to contrive some device to rid me of the mud on the side windows. I could hear and sense that there were cars on all sides, but except for an occasional blink at the road ahead, I couldn't see them. Driving the Bronco northwest along Route 2, then northeast on 495, I felt like a kindly, sightless Newfoundland forced to run with a pack of Yorkshire terriers, destined to crush one.

Although I'd topped up the Bronco's reservoir of window washer fluid before we left Cambridge, my steady pumping emptied it somewhere beyond Lowell. I was tempted to pull into the emergency lane and onto the verge of the highway to add fluid, but I was afraid of being clipped by a passing car. At the next exit, I pulled off 495 and stopped briefly in Tewksbury, where I got out to add wiper fluid and, while I was at it, to lock the hubs of the front wheels in case I hit an unplowed road and wanted to shift into four-wheel drive. As soon as I got back in, the snow that had accumulated on my hair during my two or three minutes in the storm began to melt in the good Ford heat. The car smelled of dogs and mud.

I got back on the highway, turned on the radio, and, over the noise of the defroster, listened to a couple of weather forecasts. Newcomers to this area typically pass through a stage of supposing that despite the presence of MIT and other local scientific institutions, Massachusetts has the world's most incompetent meteorologists. We don't, of course. What we have is unpredictable weather. Those of us who have been here a while treat weather forecasts the way an astrology skeptic treats horoscopes: When a prediction comes true, we're astounded at the coincidence. Most of the time, though, a good, accurate weather report in eastern Massachusetts is one that limits itself to describing what it's like out right now. According to the radio, the snow was coming down heavily, and we could expect between eight and twelve inches, possibly much more, unless, as could well happen, the snow turned to rain or the storm blew out to sea.

We made it to Haverhill, left 495, and turned north without running over any of the internal combustion Yorkies. Lights shining from the windows of the small stores and businesses along the road created the cheerful illusion of prosperity. In the parking lot of a plumbing supply place, dozens of unsold Christmas trees trucked down from Maine or New Brunswick rested under strings of multicolored lights against a maze of makeshift wooden supports. Sloppy letters slapped in white paint on a plywood sign advertised the trees at half price. I had a sense of time running out.

At the turn to Charity's, I shifted into four-wheel drive and followed the tire tracks through the snow along the unplowed road. Three or four cars passed in the opposite direction, and I had to pull far to the right to let them get by. A bright flood at Charity's back door showed the nearby outbuildings and lit up the dusting of white on the wreaths and bows. I left the Bronco at the side of the road. From one of the runs attached to the ex-garage, a golden dog yapped sharply at me, and my hope rose, but when I'd taken a few steps, I could see that the dog was a yellow Lab, and a male at that.

The barking of the Lab and the other dogs brought Charity to the door. The house was very hot and smelled of roasting lamb. The kitchen table and counters had been cleared of the stacks of artful little dog clothes. Charity was wearing a red wool dress. She'd brushed her hair and applied a thick layer of crimson lipstick.

"Holly Winter," I reminded her. "I picked up Groucho. I'm a friend of Hope's?"

"I'm, uh, expecting her," she said, "but with the snow . . ."

"I can only stay a second," I said. "I should've called. It's about a dog?"

She looked relieved. "I've got to warn you," she said. "I'm almost full up. There's one run empty, but there's no room in the house. I've got a cousin coming, and she doesn't like dogs. She's afraid of them really, but she won't say so, and if you do, she gets offended, so I have to keep them all outside when she's here. Did you want—?"

"No," I said. "It's about . . . When I was here before, you had a dog in one of those runs right near the back door?

A kind of yellow-gold female, something like a shepherd, shorthaired."

"Lady," Charity said. "Really, she should've been in here with me, but there was no room, which was why I was so glad when he finally came and got her. I was starting to think he was never going to show up."

"But he did?" God damn.

"You probably passed him on your way in."

"Just now?"

She nodded.

"When he brought her in," I said. "Was that, uh . . . This may sound kind of strange, but did it happen to be in the middle of the night?"

She laughed. "I guess you'd call it night if you don't have a lot of dogs that want their breakfast. I'd just got up." She paused and added happily, "I'm up at five."

"A kind of pale-looking guy," I said quickly. "Midtwenties maybe?"

"You know him?" she said.

"I've been trying to catch up with him," I said. "Thanks. I'd better get going."

Barrelling down the road, past the dark machine shops toward the main drag, I tried to remember the cars that had been leaving when I arrived, but I'd been concentrating so hard on getting the Bronco out of their way that I hadn't really noticed them. It seemed to me that if they'd been big 4 × 4's like mine, I wouldn't have yielded the road so courteously. In fact, I had the vague impression that they'd all been small cars like Lee Miner's. When I'd seen it in Steve's parking lot, I'd thought that Jackie, not Lee, must have picked it out. That bright red was her color and Willie's, too, not Lee's. Oh, yeah. The make and model. Well, look. Can you tell a Belgian Malinois from a Tervuren? A malamute from a Siberian husky? A Keeshond from a Norwegian elkhound? Well, can you? At a glance? If you show dogs, they probably don't even look alike to you, but if not? Well, I don't show cars. I could, you know—my home town, Owls

Head, Maine, happens to be the home of a famous museum of transportation—but I don't. The Miners' car was small and red, and it wasn't something distinctive like a Jaguar, a Corvette, a Saab, a Mercedes, or an old Morgan. Even so, I thought that I just might recognize it.

And I did. Only a few miles after I'd swung onto 495, I spotted a small red car ahead of me in the right-hand lane. On the way to a dog show, almost anyone could be driving a small red car with a bumper sticker asserting that happiness is a Scottish terrier, but on 495 on Christmas Eve? When Miner had just left Charity's? So that part was easy.

The traffic heading south was lighter than what we'd hit on the way north. The plows hadn't been by for a while, but the Bronco was built more for snow than for grit, and I was finding the driving easier than I'd expected. I was feeling so elated, especially after I'd caught up with Miner, that instead of listening to the news, Christmas carols, or a talk show on the radio, I popped in a Hank Williams, Jr., tape and turned up the volume. Repeated fast-forwarding and reversing to play your favorite song over and over wrecks the whole tape, but I just had to hear Hank sing that sad, beautiful song, "Living Proof."

Living proof.

23

I HATE TO FIND MYSELF STUCK behind a dawdler. It happens all the time in crowded obedience classes. You and your dog are striding along at a normal brisk pace, but the sluggish handler and lagging dog ahead slow you down to a dull creep. Don't let them! Once your dog gets the idea that a normal pace is very slow, he'll get bored, and a bored dog is a lagging dog. Speed up and pass!

But I wasn't training a dog. If I passed Miner, I'd simply lose sight of him. Even so, it irked me to poke along at a maximum speed of forty miles an hour, and when I'm behind the wheel, I don't irk easily. I'm so used to Boston drivers that it startles me to see someone stop at a red light. If the car in front of me signals for a right turn, I expect an abrupt left. Miner's driving, though, was not only slow, but, even judged against my Boston standards, really rotten. The small red car would speed up to forty, drop to twenty, then leap forward, and it moved erratically between the right-hand lane and the breakdown lane, sometimes straddling the two. Whatever the make of the small red car, it was no Bronco, and Miner probably lacked the confidence-boosting sound of Hank Williams, Jr., too, but I was not in a charitable mood. I wanted that dog, and I didn't like waiting.

As we left Lawrence and entered Andover, the storm changed. Instead of blowing, the snow fell evenly and heavily. In case Miner hit a car invisible to him in the thick snow, I dropped back. The little red car slowed to a steady twenty and began to hug the shoulder, then suddenly veered left and barely missed a car abandoned in the breakdown lane with no warning lights or flares. In spite of the near miss, Miner immediately pulled right again, and my confidence vanished.

"Jesus Christ," I said aloud. "This son of a bitch is looking for a place to stop."

What I'd mistaken for nervous driving made sense. He needed a place to pull off the highway for a few seconds—it wouldn't take him long to open a door and shove Mattie out—but, first, he wanted to shake that Bronco that had been on his tail since Haverhill. When I'd dropped back, maybe he'd lost patience or lost sight of me and started to scan the highway in earnest. Or was he simply watching for the intersection with 93 South?

In case the Bronco had been an unintended deterrent, I pulled ahead, and the red car resumed its weaving. At a minimum, I was making him nervous. But what if I made him so nervous that he crashed into another abandoned car? Or if I frightened him so badly that he pulled over and stopped? I could plow the Bronco right through his little car, but not without killing the dog. And if he let her loose? The traffic was lighter than it had been on the way north, but there were still plenty of cars and trucks on the highway, including, it suddenly seemed to me, a terrifying number of eighteen-wheelers, big rigs in the hands of tired truckers who wouldn't let snow like this drag out their long hauls.

Just before the junction with 93, a huge moving van

thundered by in the fast lane. My clammy hands gripped the wheel. Miner's turn signal warned me that he was taking the exit for 93 South, and I followed. The traffic on 93 was heavier than it had been on 495, and the blizzard was blowing again, throwing great sheets of snow at my windshield. I kept playing the song over and over, and I began to sing along with Hank about living proof. Living, yes, but for how long? And if he let her loose on this wide highway in this heavy snow, could I do for Cliff Bourque what he'd done for me? From the cab of a speeding eighteen-wheeler, Mattie and I would be equally invisible in the snow until only a second before the impact hurtled us momentarily in the air, and we'd be dead before we crashed onto the highway. Rowdy and Kimi? After the accident, the cars and trucks for a mile back would smash together in deadly pileup, and the Bronco wouldn't be spared. There were people in those cars and trucks. They barely crossed my mind. Is that a horrible admission? Maybe so.

I told the dogs that I loved them and then concentrated on harassing Lee Miner. I'd speed up and tailgate, drop back, then roar ahead until I almost hit him. I don't know whether the tactic persuaded him to keep going. It may have had no influence at all. I suspect that it is what prompted him to take the Medford exit from 93, but it's possible that he'd planned to follow the back route to Cambridge all along. In Medford Square, Miner punctiliously came to a stop at a red light. According the rules of the road in Greater Boston, a driver in my position is entitled to lean on the horn until the offender ahead gets the message that he's done something outlandish and either barges forward or moves aside. Alternatively, it would have been perfectly normal for me to assume that his car had gone dead and to pass him on either the left or the right. In flagrant violation of common law, though, I pulled up behind him, pressed my foot on the brake, took my hands off the wheel, stretched my arms, closed my eyes, and sighed heavily. Even at Miner's pace, we'd be in Cambridge in no time. So far as

Miner knew, he was on call and had the clinic to himself, and Steve was in Owls Head, Maine. I knew better, of course. I knew better.

On Alewife Brook Parkway, about halfway between Medford Square and the intersection with Mass. Ave. at the Cambridge-Arlington line, Rowdy woke up. Like most malamutes, mine had always been excellent travelers. If you have to choose between malamutes and children as your companions on a long car trip, don't hesitate. The dogs will sleep or look out the windows. They won't keep insisting that they have to go to the bathroom or make you stop for ice cream and then drip it all over the car. They'll never ask if you're almost there. If your destination is familiar, they won't have to ask; having taken an intelligent canine interest in the passing scenery, they'll know. Five or ten minutes before you arrive, when the children would be jumping and screaming, the malamutes will perk up their ears, wag their tails, and, if they like your destination, issue some happy whinnies and woo-woos. In fact, Alaskan malamutes don't just make the perfect traveling companions. They make the perfect . . . Well, never mind. Too much is made of that already.

As I was saying, about halfway between Medford Square and Mass. Ave., Rowdy woke up, and when he began to make noise, I initially assumed that he'd assessed where we were and was glad to be back home. But the sound was wrong, a loud, deep, insistent growl. I could hardly believe it. Rowdy always waited until we got to a rest area. Then I remembered the fruitcake. Kimi had returned her share. Rowdy had kept his. Until now. Ordinarily, I might have told him to wait. I wasn't sure he could. I'm not particularly car-proud, and, in any case, I've had plenty of practice in stain and odor removal, but it's really abusive to force a fastidious dog like Rowdy to soil his own quarters.

Where else could Miner be headed except to Steve's clinic? The Bronco was built for snow. After a brief stop, I'd catch up. Ahead on the right was what I remembered as a small baseball field with a parking lot. I pulled in. When I opened the door and stepped out, the snow in the air and underfoot felt heavy and wet. Much more carefully than I'd done that day at Steve's clinic, I eased open the tailgate and got both dogs safely out. With my hands locked on their leashes, I walked them to the field. Then . . . Look, I hate euphemism, but who wants the details? Rowdy was in a hurry, but he wasn't sick, okay?

And he wasn't the one who slowed us down. The sight of the open field of deep, even snow drove Kimi into a near frenzy. Some dogs are eternally half puppy. She wanted to bound around, dash in circles, plunge down, leap up, and race across that wide expanse of white. She nearly tore the leash from my hands. Rowdy, who still considered her only half civilized, watched her jump around and yank at the leash. Then he calmly and gently pounced on her and held her to the ground. I knew he'd do it. I counted on him. Obedience moralist, are you? Yes, she shouldn't have been out of control, and, yes, I probably shouldn't have let Rowdy do my work for me. He was fast and effective, though. And remember? I was pressed for time.

With the dogs back in the car, I moved as quickly as I could and reached the intersection with Route 2 in what felt like no time. In Cambridge, a plow gone astray may occasionally leave an accidental path down the middle of a side street, but the city does remove the snow from the major roads. Plows and traffic had cleared the Fresh Pond traffic circle, and cross-country skiers made dark, graceful shapes on the paths near the pond itself. The maintenance service run by a cousin of Lorraine's had already plowed out the parking lot of Steve's clinic. Miner had parked the small red car where Steve usually left his van. Lights were on downstairs in the clinic, but the upstairs apartment was dark.

I looked around for Steve's van. Maybe he'd moved it when the plow arrived. I hadn't planned to do this alone. The dark windows on the second story reminded me of Jackie Miner. She'd lived up there. Where had she died?

The gruesome playground dirge that had plagued me the night before suddenly began to run through my head again, but this time, instead of the endless replaying of the nasty little refrain, I heard the first verse. Remember? Or have you managed to forget?

> *Did you ever think when a hearse went by*
> *That you might be the next to die?*
> *They wrap you up in a big white sheet*
> *And . . .*

And I'd lost the next words. They didn't matter. Lee had bent Jackie's arms and legs, and he'd shrouded her in a thick garbage bag before he'd dumped her in the freezer like a dead dog. He hadn't even wrapped her in a big white sheet.

24

I PARKED BEHIND THE CLINIC, where the Bronco wouldn't be visible from inside. When I got out, I locked the door and checked to make sure I'd locked the tailgate, too. Then I moved quietly toward the building and under the windows. I don't know what I expected to see. The windows are high. The blinds were down. I saw what I'd seen from the Bronco: lights. Inside, a dog barked. Mattie? I took quick, silent steps to the red car and looked for dog tracks in the long streaks of packed snow left by the plow. I checked the wooden steps to the back entrance to the clinic, too, but they'd been carefully shoveled and showed nothing. When I moved back to one of the windows, it seemed to me that over the swish and spatter of cars passing on the street, I heard someone talking. A voice on the radio? It sounded maddeningly neutral, probably male. Steve's distinctive rumble should have been easy to recognize. I didn't know.

I wanted so badly to hear Steve's voice that I imagined the window opening and Steve leaning out. He'd grin, I'd grin back, and we'd have nothing more pressing to do than take our four beautiful dogs to Fresh Pond to play in the new-fallen snow. Steve and I would run, trip, and land in a fresh drift. Then we'd make angels in the snow while the dogs leaped over us and chased each other back and forth. Kimi would dance her great, joyful circles; Rowdy would roll and twist; India would yelp with excitement; and little Lady, Steve's pretty, timid pointer, would hide behind her master.

But the window remained shut. Was Steve there at all? If so, he'd certainly have identified Mattie as a Chinook the second he saw her. He'd seen Bear, and once you know what a Chinook is, you can't miss. If Steve were in there, he'd make sure that nothing happened to her. Of course, that was exactly what Oscar Patterson had tried to do, too, wasn't it? And Patterson had been a veterinarian. He'd been Miner's employer. They'd fought, presumably about a Chinook dog. Patterson had died.

For the first time ever, I wished I were one of those dangerous people who never so much as run out for groceries without making sure that their car guns are ready in case some fool drops a carton of eggs or spills the milk. I do own a handgun—why is another story—and I briefly considered tearing home for it, tearing back, and staging some kind of Annie Oakley act, but I was afraid that either Mattie or Steve would be dead by then. The only weapon I had was Lee Miner's fear of big dogs.

When I opened the tailgate and grabbed their leashes, Rowdy and Kimi leapt joyfully out, tails waving back and forth like beautiful white plumes. That's how the breed standard says a malamute's tail is supposed to look, you know, like a plume waving. It's a good standard. It says, among other things, that a malamute's eyes have a soft expression that indicates an affectionate disposition. Affectionate? If you ever want to take along a pair of dogs as defensive weapons, you're better off with almost any breed other than a malamute. But I knew that Lee Miner wouldn't gaze deeply into Rowdy and Kimi's big brown eyes. Malamutes look something like stocky, muscular, gentle, friendly wolves, but to anyone who's afraid of dogs, they just plain look like wolves.

You probably don't carry around the key to your veterinarian's living quarters, or maybe you do, but my key to Steve's old apartment was on the ring with my own house and car keys. I hoped that Lorraine hadn't had the lock changed. I inserted the key, and it turned. I eased open the door and listened for Willie. There was no sound, not even the voice I'd thought I'd heard from outside, but the apartment is carpeted to help with the soundproofing. I certainly didn't hear the growl and bark of a Scottie. I don't like muzzles, but if Willie were there, I fervently hoped he had one on. With Rowdy and Kimi hugged in tightly at my left side, I went softly up the stairs. At the top landing, I flipped on the lights and looked around. Then I headed for the door to the interior stairs that lead down to the clinic. Rowdy and Kimi looked at me as if to ask what I thought I was doing. Where were Steve, India, and Lady?

"Trust me," I whispered.

As soon as I pulled open the double door to the stairs, I heard Lee Miner, then a second man. Not Steve. I didn't want to go down there without the protection, however uncertain, of my dogs, but I didn't want the jingle of their tags to announce our arrival, either. I fished in the pockets of my parka. If you train dogs, you won't be surprised to hear that the contents of my pockets consisted of one key ring, a few miniature dog biscuits, many small hard lumps of really, really aged Vermont cheddar, the powdered residue of freeze-dried liver treats, three white cotton work gloves, a mass of empty gallon-size plastic bags—portable pooper-scoopers—and a tangle of nylon training collars. I wrapped my hand around the tags on Rowdy's rolled leather collar, unbuckled it, slipped on one of the training collars, and fastened his leash to it. Then I performed the same muffling operation on Kimi.

Like the apartment, the stairs are carpeted. The dogs and I descended slowly and silently to the landing that's halfway down, and I'm proud to report that, for once, Rowdy and Kimi behaved perfectly. The stairs, the landing, and the hallway below were dark, but, of course, I knew my way around. As I took my first step down the half-flight that leads from the landing to the broad, wide hallway that forms the center of the clinic, a dog suddenly barked, a big dog, maybe a shepherd. A couple of small dogs added high-pitched warning yaps, and I heard a growl that sounded like Willie's. I paused briefly, then kept moving until we reached the bottom landing at the foot of the stairs. When I stopped, both dogs sat. You don't train dogs? That's an auto sit, automatic sit. Although I'd kept them tightly hauled in at my left side, I hadn't told them to heel, and they weren't in their normal position for brace work. Rowdy was next to me, Kimi on the outside. Both dogs must have assumed that I'd forgotten to give the command and that I'd changed my mind about where they belonged. Regular collars off, training collars on, handler keyed up and nervous? What would any obedience dog think? No question about it. We were about to enter the ring at some new and peculiar kind of match or trial.

A rubber wedge held open the door to the exam room directly across the hall. Lee Miner, his pale face washed ashen by the surgical light, stood with his back to the counter that runs across the far wall. I tried to remember that in the blackness of the stairs, we were invisible to him.

I couldn't see the second man, but when he spoke, I finally recognized his voice. "The straight story, you runty little bastard," Cliff Bourque said.

Miner answered quickly and mechanically, as if emphasizing something he'd already said. "Gastric dilatation and volvulus. Gastric torsion. Bloat. And the wonderful Dr. Patterson didn't need my help, and he let her die." His voice was smug and gloating.

"Pain, you little fucker," Bourque said. "I'm asking you about pain."

Miner ignored him and said with a tone of tremendous superiority, "The great Dr. Patterson let your dog die. Emergency treatment was required. Mr. Bourque, if you say that you weren't there, you weren't there. I never said I saw you, you know. I never said that. Never. I heard you. That's all I ever said. And I can see it now. This other man arrived, and instead of caring for your lovely dog, your Dr. Patterson argued with him. And your beautiful dog died. And he'd know I'd know, of course. So he ran away."

Bourque said one word: "Mattie."

"Mr. Bourque, you're not listening to me." He actually sounded put out. "You loved your dog, but I loved my wife! And now he's come and taken her away. But we've got to have faith! They'll find him! All we need to do, you and I, is wait very, very patiently, and they'll catch up with him. You go back home to your wife, and you wait. And I'll tell everyone it was all a terrible mistake. I've talked to you, and now I know that it wasn't you I heard. It wasn't, was it? And now I know. No one will bother you ever again. You go home and finish grieving for your lovely dog."

"Her name was Mattie." He stepped toward Miner and into my range of vision. He looked larger than I remembered, and his face was cold and hard. "Everything. Every goddamned last detail. How long it took, how much it hurt. And call her by her name. Her name was Mattie." Then he spoke her name again with a terrible intensity, almost as if he were trying to call her: "Mattie."

The barker and the yappers were quiet now. In the silence, a dog whined loudly. My left hand rested on Rowdy's shoulders. His muscles tensed. In spite of the darkness, I looked down toward my dogs, then placed my palms in front of their faces to signal them to stay. When I looked up, I couldn't see Cliff Bourque, but the swinging door to the small room off the exam room was moving. Miner's back was to me now. He seemed to be fiddling with something on the counter.

Bourque suddenly stormed back through the door shouting, "You stinking son of a bitch!"

At his heels trotted a glorious, large-bellied Chinook, her body wagging, her eyes radiant with delight. She never took them off Cliff Bourque. Mattie. Living proof. I sighed. It's evidently what I do just as I enter the ring. Rowdy and Kimi shifted slightly in anticipation. I could hear them breathe. I kept watching the bright room. Bourque raised his arm. His hand held a heavy leather muzzle.

He spoke quietly. "You fucking *muzzled* her, didn't you? That's what you did. You poor bastard, you were afraid of a *dog*. And when you got rid of me, you slapped a muzzle on her. And then Patterson walked in, and before you could rip it off, he saw it."

Like a schoolboy being chastised by his teacher, Miner stood rigid, his narrow face frozen, his hands held submissively behind his back.

Although Miner looked terrified, Bourque sounded almost compassionate. "You poor little chicken shit son of a bitch. You were scared he'd tell on you again." His voice was low and gentle. "But mostly you were just scared. Not scared of anything. Just scared, weren't you? I know what that's about. I know all about that. So you killed him. You didn't even know what you were scared he'd do, did you? But you knew if you killed him, he couldn't do it. You poor bastard."

"I never hurt your dog," Miner said. "I love dogs. I never hurt your dog, Mr. Bourque."

"I wonder why. Yeah, I wonder. But you thought you'd got it all sewed up, didn't you? If Patterson's going to be Mattie, then she's got to be dead." He began to laugh. "Jesus Christ!" he said. "I just thought of something. Jesus Christ. Patterson would've loved it. He died like a goddamned dog, and he went out like one, too. I should know. Hell, I'm the guy who paid for his funeral. He'd never've believed it. Christ, it's a shame he never knew." He glanced down at Mattie and added, apparently to her, "And the damnedest thing is, he wouldn't've minded at all." Then he looked toward Miner again and asked in tone of neutral, friendly curiosity, "Hey, so what'd you do with your wife? Same thing?"

I heard no threat in his voice and saw none in his face. It seemed to me that he'd be content to take Mattie and go home and that he'd never tell the story to anyone, even his wife. Once in a while, maybe, when he was alone with his Chinooks, he might say a few words about it to them and marvel at how strange life is.

Miner pivoted slowly to face Cliff Bourque. His hands were still primly and dutifully fixed behind his back. Clasped between them was a large hypodermic syringe. In the near darkness, I managed to tie Kimi's leash tightly to the stair rail. At my side, Rowdy waited for the first command in this interesting new obedience event. I dug the fingers of my left hand into the thick guard hair at the back of his neck and down into the warm, wooly undercoat. My fingers found the training collar. Rowdy and I moved forward into the dim light of the hallway. I unhooked his leash, bent down a little, held my left forearm and hand parallel to his head, and pointed directly at the syringe. If Miner saw Rowdy coming? If Miner didn't panic after all? Or, in his panic, stabbed wildly? If Rowdy grasped that needle by the sharp, deadly point?

Suddenly, I moved my hand forward and said firmly, "Rowdy, take it!"

Rowdy was primed for the ring. He shot forward and bounded into the little room. His glossy dark back shining in the light, he made directly for Miner, who spun toward him and, with a sharp reflex jerk, pulled his hands protectively toward his face. When I'd pointed to the hypodermic and Rowdy'd sighted along my arm, had he understood? I suspect that when he forged forward, he meant only to retrieve whatever object he encountered first, whatever looked anything like a dumbbell or a glove. But when Miner raised his arms? And gripped that object tightly in his fist? Then Rowdy clearly got the object of this strange new game. He leaped and, as he did so, he must have opened his jaws, ready to grasp this peculiar dumbbell of strange design.

Ever seen the jaws of an Alaskan malamute? At the sight of Rowdy hurtling toward him, Miner must almost have felt those thick, sharp teeth digging into his face, ripping apart his hands and crushing them. I'll never know for sure whether Miner dropped the needle first or whether Rowdy grabbed it from his hand. But no more than seconds after I'd sent Rowdy on the directed retrieve, Miner, screaming and shaking, had his arms wrapped across his face, and Rowdy held that hypodermic in his gentle mouth. He'd probably never even touched Miner.

I ran to Rowdy, reached out and took the hypodermic by the safe, blunt end, and said, "Drop it!" He did. "Good boy," I said. "Good boy." Never forget to praise your dog. Never.

"Don't just stand there," I told Bourque. "Get him. Pin his arms, for Christ's sake. Where the hell is Steve? Jesus Christ, he's not—"

I started for the little room where Bourque had evidently found Mattie. By then, Kimi was woo-wooing with outrage at missing the fun, and the kenneled dogs had taken up her call. When I pushed in the swinging door to the small adjacent room, I expected to find Steve comatose on the floor. He wasn't there. Elsewhere in the clinic? Dead. In the kennels, maybe, his body in one of the cages. Just as I was heading there, I heard his voice rise above the arfing and wooing and yapping of the dogs.

I ran into the center hallway.

"Jesus Christ, Holly," Steve said. "What the hell is going on here?"

Next to him stood my next-door neighbor, Lieutenant Kevin Dennehy.

"That's what the cop's supposed to say," I told them. "That's Kevin's line, right? 'Now, now, what's all this about?' Or is that just in the movies?"

"Holly—" Kevin started to say.

"Miner's in there," I said, pointing to the exam room. It felt like a second directed retrieve. "Cliff's holding him. He could use some help."

Kevin evidently felt that he could, too. Before long, he'd summoned a squad car and, for all I know, some other help as well. I heard some noise, but I didn't pay much attention. I was busy piling together a lot of soft blankets and towels to make a cozy whelping area in a corner of Steve's kitchen. When he delivers puppies at the clinic, it's usually on the operating table, when he has to do a Caesarean because the bitch is in trouble. On that Christmas Eve, he became the first veterinarian in Cambridge, maybe the first anywhere, to provide an obstetrical patient with a comfy birthing room. The father was not present at the delivery, but I think that Mattie didn't miss him. Cliff was the only person she wanted in attendance.

In between his occasional checks on Mattie, Steve kept apologizing to me and to himself for having left the clinic. He kept reminding me—and himself—that he'd had his beeper with him and that when he'd left, he intended to be gone only long enough to find out why I wasn't answering my phone. When he'd found that the dogs and I weren't home, he knocked on Kevin Dennehy's door, and Kevin's mother had sent him out to drag Kevin away from some lodge of the Ancient Order of Hibernians, where Kevin had been helping Santa Claus, his cousin Mickey, to distribute the presents at a Christmas Eve party.

"Look, Steve," I said. "Lots of animal hospitals around here never have anyone on the premises at night, ever. And you didn't know where Miner was, and then you couldn't find me. . . . Anyway, this just shows that you were right to begin with. Or that Lorraine was. You do need a second veterinarian, or you at least need someone to live here."

"Jesus Christ," he said.

The first puppy, a male, arrived just after midnight, and seven more little Chinooks were born in the early hours of Christmas. Cliff let me name Mattie's firstborn. He probably expected me to pick something Christmasy, but I didn't. As I've said, these names are a bitch. I called him Living Proof.

25

CLIFF BOURQUE SPENT CHRISTMAS in Steve's apartment with Mattie, Bear, and the puppies. Steve offered him a key, but he said that if he needed to go out and get back in, he'd use the same credit card that had popped the lock the night before, when he'd wanted to wait there for Lee Miner. On the day after Christmas, the Vietnam buddy Cliff had been staying with drove him and his dogs home to New Hampshire. Anneliese had told me that Cliff had lost a lot of buddies in Vietnam. She never said that he'd lost them all. She'd trusted me a lot, of course, but not quite enough to tell me that one of the guys from his outfit lived in Cambridge; and not quite enough to confide that she and Cliff had talked by phone every few days since he'd left.

That's how Cliff Bourque decided that it was safe to come out in the open and confront Miner: He heard from Anneliese the rumor about Jackie and Patterson. Before Jackie's disappearance, it had been in Miner's interest to have Bourque suspected of having murdered Patterson. Afterward, though, as Bourque realized, it was to Miner's advantage to have Patterson presumed alive. The rumor that Miner's two victims had run off together explained both disappearances, but Miner couldn't accuse Bourque of doing away with Patterson and also claim that Jackie and Patterson had run off together.

Whenever Steve and I discuss why Lee Miner killed Jackie, Steve attaches great importance to the little red car, which turns out to have been a BMW. If Rita's there, she adds that those crystal lamps Jackie had in the living room were real Waterford. I don't show lamps, either. Steve and Rita agree, though, that the main reason Lee murdered Jackie was that the second she heard him say that a detail didn't matter, she knew for sure that he was lying.

But the question that interests me isn't why he murdered Jackie, but why he let the dogs live. Why didn't he kill Mattie and toss her body in the woods instead of driving her to Charity's? Of course, he knew that Charity wouldn't recognize him. Patterson was Charity's vet, but Patterson made house calls. Miner had heard about her—that's why he'd taken Mattie there—but neither of them had ever seen the other before the late night or early morning when he'd shown up with Mattie. Also, he must've felt confident that no one would identify Mattie as a Chinook.

But why take the risk? Why let her live at all? And why let Willie live? He did—and does—you know. He spent Christmas Eve safely, if tediously, kenneled at Steve's clinic. But why did Miner spare him? If Jackie and Willie had both vanished, nothing about Miner's story would have been suspect. Marriages break up all the time, and husbands don't necessarily know where their departing wives have gone. The bond between Jackie and Willie, though? That was a true union, till death us do part.

Steve's explanation is simple. He says that Miner didn't become a small-animal veterinarian to kill a healthy pregnant bitch of a rare breed and certainly not to kill his own dog. Steve says that when an owner insists, it's one thing, but that when Miner had to choose, he chose life.

Rita says that Miner's vocational choice represented a counterphobic defense, by which she means that his fear of big dogs was the reason he became a veterinarian in the first place. Big dogs had some great unconscious symbolic significance for him, and as a veterinarian, he repeatedly murdered and rescued the object of his fear. Rita adds that his superego allowed him to act on his impulses only within the confines of his profession. As a veterinarian, he could put dogs to sleep, but as a person, he couldn't kill them.

Is that true? Or did he intend to kill Mattie that Christmas Eve? When he left for Charity's, maybe so, but my hunch is that all the way back to Cambridge, he kept trying to make himself do it and kept putting it off. I think that's one reason he drove so erratically. I've come to believe that he'd have let her live. I'm not sure why, but I think it's true that Lee Miner found it easier to kill people than to kill dogs. I can understand that. While we're on the topic, I should tell you that *Dog's Life* rejected my article about Brenner. He's still getting away with murder. The only piece of news I have about Brenner is so freakish that I hesitate to pass it along. I'm doing so only on the condition that you don't ask me to explain it. I can't, except to tell you that Oscar Patterson left his entire estate to the baby that's due in June and to the baby's mother, Geri Driscoll, now Geri Driscoll Brenner. Oh, yeah. Brenner's collar and leash? The ones Kimi wore when we dashed out of there? Purloined goods? Not really. Souvenirs, I guess. Remember, I paid cash.

But I've leaped ahead of myself. A week after Christmas, UPS brought the urn containing Groucho's ashes. I intercepted the delivery woman and carried the parcel up to Rita myself. When she found out what I held in my hands and how it had arrived, she said, "UPS? Jesus." Then she started to cry. I put the unopened parcel on her kitchen table, and we sat there looking at it.

"Rita," I said, "there's this theory I read about. It's about souls."

"Please!"

"I mean it. The theory is that dogs have only a finite number of souls, okay? So they have to share them. I'm not making this up. Anyway, when a dog dies, a new dog gets his soul. So you see? It means that when you lose a dog, you've got a chance of getting him back again. That's how the theory originated. Daniel Pinkwater's malamute died, and then his wife found another malamute that was obviously the same dog."

She stopped crying. "Daniel Pinkwater?" She sounded incredulous. "From National Public Radio?"

"People with malamutes can be on public radio," I said. "And Daniel Pinkwater happens to be a dog writer, and it's his theory. Actually, it isn't a theory. All he did was observe it. So the point is that it's sort of like the old Woody Allen joke? Where he says that he was thrown out of NYU for cheating on a metaphysics exam. He looked into the soul of the boy sitting next to him."

She started crying even harder.

I tried to console her. "Rita, don't you get it? Metaphysics is about what underlies appearances, not just physical realities, but—"

"Holly, for God's sake, this is *Cambridge*. Pick up a cab in the Square, and there's a good chance that the driver knows what metaphysics is. It was probably his dissertation topic. So—"

"So I didn't know until I looked it up," I said. "Anyway, the point is that it's how you get your next dog. You cheat. You keep looking into the souls of the dogs sitting next to you. And one day, you'll find Groucho."

Then I started crying, too. I've sat next to a million dogs since Vinnie died, and I haven't found her yet. Probably the AKC has done a deal with God: Utility Dogs get to keep their souls for eternity. That's why Alaskan malamutes are such deliberately lousy obedience dogs. It's a guarantee of perpetual return to earth. They don't want to stay in heaven. They like it here.

So do Scottish terriers, thus the nickname. Diehard. In late January, the day after Steve, Rita, and I snuck Rowdy, Kimi, and the urn into the Mount Auburn Cemetery and scattered Groucho's ashes over the pond, Rita kept an appointment she'd made to consult Steve about a new dog. When she returned home, Rowdy announced her arrival by rushing to the kitchen door and growling ferociously. Kimi joined him. Over the din there arose snarls, yaps, and the rasp of canine nails raking the outside of my door, then the pitter-patter of Rita's high-heeled boots and little dog feet ascending the stairs.

I flew out of my apartment, reached her landing, and pounded on her door.

"Rita!" I yelled. "Open the door!"

When she did, Willie stuck out his head and barked loudly. Then he fell silent and fixed his gleaming black eyes on my ankles.

"Isn't he beautiful?" Rita said. "I never intended to get another dog so soon, but it was just like—"

"Rita, that dog has serious behavior problems."

"And I'm fully licensed," she said triumphantly.

"Among other things, he bites."

"Steve says that it's an assertive breed, and, of course, he's been through a lot. It isn't aggression, you know."

Willie snarled at me.

"Yes," I said.

Rita smiled proudly. "It's called real terrier character."

Epilogue

A FEW DAYS AFTER EASTER, the Bourques called me with some great news. The Chinook dog, once nearly extinct, had just been added to the list of 146—now 147—breeds and varieties recognized by the United Kennel Club, the largest working-dog registry and the second-largest all-breed registry in the United States. I said congratulations. I meant it.

The Chinook is a potentially great obedience breed. I could be wrong about the deal between God and the AKC, and, of course, the UKC is a separate organization. Do canine souls migrate from registry to registry? From breed to breed? Could an AKC golden retriever return as a UKC Chinook? Just in case, I plan to spend a lot of time hanging around UKC obedience rings. I'll sit next to a lot of Chinooks. I'll cheat.